Auldicia Rises

By

R. L. Sloan

Books by R. L. Sloan

Embellish

Justice Served:

A novel of the Embellish Saga

Auldicia Rises

By

R. L. Sloan

Copyright 2011

San Antonio, Texas

Auldicia Rises (The Embellish Saga, Book 3)
All Rights Reserved
Copyright © 2011 R. L. Sloan
v2.0
Edited by J. Alexander
Cover Art designed by J. Alexander, Genesis Productions©

Harrison House Publishing
www.theharrisonhousepublishing.com
info@theharrisonhousepublising.com
Paperback ISBN: 978-1-4507-5153-7
Library of Congress Control Number: 2011936664
Harrison House Publishing and the "HHP" logo are trademarks belonging to Harrison House Publishing.

PRINTED IN THE UNITED STATES OF AMERICA

For all of us who love life...keep living.

Acknowledgements

This book is dedicated to my family and all those who have loved me through its process. A very special Thank You to our Father and Savior. Thank You, Lord, for loving me. I would also like to give a special Thank You to all the folks that have now become fans of the Embellish Saga. Thank you so much. May God bless and keep you all. My loving husband Joseph and my sweet daughter Linda have stood behind me the entire way. I love you both dearly.

Glossary

The decedents:

Basira (Ba'seer'a) Caraway --- deceased vampire twin to Basrick Caraway; Basira was poisoned with Colloidal Silver by Justice Treemount

Mathis Bouvier (Boo'vee' ay) --- deceased detective of the San Antonio Police Department; hexed love interest of Childress Treemount.

Olvignia (Ol'veen'ia) Henderson --- deceased grandmother to Solis Burkes. Olvignia was killed in an explosion at her home, initiated by Childress, Klein, and Erland Treemount

Leonine Henderson --- deceased grandfather to Solis Burkes; husband to Olvignia Henderson

Lindsey Henderson --- deceased mother to Solis Burkes; death occurred for Lindsey at the age of 29 years old, with mysterious circumstances surrounding her death

Frances Treemount --- deceased mother to Childress, Klein, Justice, and Erland Treemount

Bureau (Bu'row) Treemount La Deaux (La'Doe) --- Mambo of Dogwater Swamp; Aunt to Childress, Klein, Justice, and Erland Treemount; Sister to Frances Treemount

Bose (Bosz pronounced with a long "O") Puente --- Vampire kinship brother to Nacio; caretaker of the Puente Mansion

The living:

Urgata (Ur' gata) --- daughter of Bureau

Solis (So' leesz) Burkes --- raped by Klein Treemount as a child; survivor; mortal enemy of the Treemount Clan

Nacio (Na' see' o) Puente aka Nacio Galvazio De Puente --- vampire, ex-slave from the Middle Passage, Canary Islander; Owner of Puente Masonry

Armando Caraway --- European vampire, friend to Nacio and Solis; lives within the Puente Mansion; husband to Patience Caraway, father to Basrick and Basira

Patience Caraway --- European vampire, friend to Nacio and Solis; wife to Armando Caraway; mother to Basrick and Basira

Basrick (Baz' rick) Caraway --- surviving vampire twin to Basira

Nayphous (Nay' fuss) Aljeneau (Al' jen' o) --- Fiancé to Urgata; eye candy to Childress Treemount

Chase Henderson --- uncle of Solis Burkes; victim of the Treemounts

Priestess Auldicia (All' dee' see' ah) --- Powerful African Voodoo Priestess Vampire; whereabouts Unknown; believed to be dead; ancestor to the Treemounts; demon possessed.

Tahiti --- Daughter of Bureau; tramp, gold digger

Nuke Henderson --- Owner of the Laurence Funeral Home and Sunset Services and other conglomerate assets

Hymn Platt (Him) --- Puente Masonry Foreman

1

Something wicked comes

East Central Hell

Vast in all its glory, the Texas-Louisiana Gulf Coast became a well for lost souls of those who died at sea; pirates, soldiers, and African slaves. Much blood and grief wash out to sea. Sacrificial blood used to seal a pact between the living and the voodoo gods travels in from the Gulf to satisfy their thirst.

Underneath the ocean floor surface is a footed path, known to many condemned souls as the gateway to East Central Hell. Brimstone fire comprises the gate pillars, burning a soul repeatedly upon entry. East Central Hell is also the home to Vulkus, the blood and lust demon that ripped Auldicia from the Realm of the Living, condemning her to Hell with him. Her failed attempts to get pure souls to the realm forfeited her reign on earth---a costly mistake for her and a willing recipient for Vulkus.

"You are mine Auldicia for all eternity. Never let that notion slip your mind. Only the blood sacrifice of a legacy from your bloodline completed on hallowed ground would free you from my clutches. And the chances of that happening, my dear, are a snowball's chances in East Central Hell."

"I shall return to the living realm and repay my debt to you Vulkus. When I do, I will exact my revenge on you by burning your sac with searing brimstone over and over for all eternity."

"Oh do keep speaking my dear. I like it hot, and I like it dirty." At the entry of her sex, Vulkus drew back and plunged his entire arm sized sex deep into the blood-slicked folds of Auldicia's body. Her screams caused him to piston faster, drawing his own body in and out with the force of a rock crushing sledgehammer.

"You will never leave here. I watched you try to conceive with that ingrate, Nacio, on earth. In fact, I watched you with many insolent peasants you took as lovers. None of them could satisfy you. Their blood was weak as well as their seed. You were unsuccessful then, as you will always be."

Vulkus continued with his savage, sexual play as Auldicia's eternal pain continued each second, each minute, each hour for a millennium, for all eternity. Time in East Central Hell moves slowly in the minds of the condemned, but centuries went by in the earth realm.

Once sated, Vulkus summoned for two bowlegged, rot-faced, humpbacked demons dropping brick shaped excrement from their backside wherever they walked, to come and return Auldicia to her cell. The broom closet sized cell yielded only enough room for her to walk in and about face to look out of the hell-fire bars roasting her each time she stood too close to them, which was always. As she stood, blood and black seed Vulkus left inside her, oozed down her thighs. She heard a mocking cackle from Vulkus echo throughout the chamber.

"You will never leave this realm Auldicia, and you will do well to remember…you are mine."

Standing in agony, she recalled her time in the realm of the living.

She once ruled in the realm of the living as an Obiyafo, an African witch vampire, and distant cousin to the mythical goddess Medusa. Although a powerful Voodoo Priestess in her own right, she needed blood and many souls to keep her reign on earth. While she was in her African village, she terrorized many. Beguiling to all men who looked upon her beauty, she lured potential betrothed grooms from their marriage beds. Once a groom became a victim to her, she would take his body in many lustful encounters robbing him of all of his seed and his blood.

In the midst of heated lust, she would take shape in her true form, as an 8-foot demon with horns, a head full of sea snakes, and talons. Finger long fangs would descend from her mouth to clench the neck of her unwilling partner. With the seed overflowing in her womb, instant conception would take place, filling her with a child to be born.

Within moments after conception, she would roar to the sky as her legs fell apart to give birth. Once she bore the child, she would bite her offspring, marking the child, placing a curse on its soul, making it a vampire for all eternity.

Bereaved brides would find their grooms lying in the jungle as food for savage beasts during the night. Centuries passed as she spawned more vampire children on earth. Copulating with a man who had a pure soul made her more powerful. Such a man existed in a little nearby village, who was destined to be a king. Nacio stood to inherit a kingdom.

Handsome and fierce, many village women, old and young, wanted Nacio. His kingdom held wealth untold, and his soul, the purest. She knew if she were to capture and take his body, she would satisfy Vulkus and keep her reign on earth forever, perpetuating evil generations for centuries.

On a hot night deep in the African jungle, she appeared to Nacio. Against his father's wishes, Nacio told his parents he was going to hunt food. Instead, he left the village with the intentions of hunting and killing Auldicia.

Rumors of the Obiyafo Auldicia had made way to his village long before this particular night. With the knowledge passed to him from his parents, Nacio knew the necessities for safety from her harm.

With preternatural reflexes, she thrashed Nacio on his back, and straddled him wide, taking him into her body. Slowly, with him deep inside her, she began to grind on his sex, the friction causing her to moan wantonly as she neared her first climax.

Without fear or struggle, Nacio remained motionless underneath his captor. Unbeknownst to her, he reached for his hunter's pouch. It held a capped seashell with blessed silver mineral water from the village priests. A silver hunting knife, blessed with the silver mineral water would be the weapon used to behead the vampire witch while in the throes of lust.

She threw her head back as her sex clenched, attempting to milk Nacio of his seed. Nacio reached up and dumped the silver mineral water down her throat, burning her. He quickly began to shout a binding protection chant to immobilize her giving him mere seconds to use his knife to behead her. A loud hiss from skin searing smoke and a choking gurgle came from her mouth as she dismounted, forcefully pulling him from her body.

"Hey owey oma bantonde," he declared. "You will die this night Auldicia, and you will never have my seed."

Being the nobleman, he left her in the jungle believing the silver mineral water would end her life, as he could not. This one moment sealed his fate, unleashing the worst curse upon himself that he could imagine. Later, slave traders along the African-Moroccan shoreline would come and capture Nacio and several children she had birthed. Because he chose not to surrender to her lust, she subsequently turned him into a vampire in the new world. Even after her last attempt to get his seed, it was unsuccessful, causing Vulkus to rip her from the realm of the living.

Another dared to defy her power. A voodoo mistress named Olinka fought her, binding her from the use of her powers. Placing a curse upon Olinka's family, she vowed life long suffering to Olinka's family which she would see to the end of their existence.

Even with her unsuccessful attempt, she vowed to have Nacio at all costs, no matter if it meant burning in East Central Hell for all eternity lying in bed next to Vulkus.

"I will have you Nacio. You will be my beloved, and you will give me your seed, and I will rule again."

†

Vulkus sat impatiently on his throne. The mere thought of Auldicia leaving this realm was unsettling. Having been sexually sated not long ago, his desires flared once more.

Menacingly, his sex unfurled with the head slithering from his lap into his right hand for attention. The size of a grapefruit was no match for the crowning head of his sex. Obliging happily, Vulkus let his shoulders fall back against the rusted, nail covered throne, as boils on his hand tore open pus flowed, wetting his shaft with each stroke.

In full length, Vulkus had a shaft that appeared as a sword with a grapefruit sized crown speared at the tip; excruciating pain for any creature to endure. Vulkus could wait no longer.

"Bring her to me," he shouted to the demons. He could hear the bricks of excrement falling from their worn-out backsides with each step they took to fulfill their master's request. Anticipation felt nearly as good as the entry. He could barely contain himself, as black seed surfaced from the rather large opening at the crown's tip.

"I said bring her to me, now!"

Above, on the surface of the ocean floor, remnants of human flesh and traces of sacrificial blood settled at the East Central Hell gateway. Consistency of the traces indicated, it belonged to only one known voodoo family, the Treemount Clan.

A great earthquake shook so violently, the movement affected the realm of the living and the realm of the condemned. If it were imaginable, more screams and chaos ensued amongst the condemned souls of East Central Hell. For those souls felt the pull of a portal tearing open between the two realms preparing to release some lucky chump back to the living, but not without a price.

Auldicia felt the tilt in the floor of the brimstone fire cell she stood in. A smile crept across her blood scabbed face, as she too knew what was to come. Her release back to the human world, spoken from the mouth of her demon captor Vulkus in jest had just allowed the fulfillment of the prophecy he spoke of. A victory chuckle left her throat as she watched the brimstone fires vanquish right before her eyes. Vulkus shouted to no avail.

"We're in hell, but what the hell is happening?" Confusion quickly set in, deflating his erection.

The two rot-faced, humpback demons rushed to their master's quarters as he stood still, shaft hanging flaccidly to the floor.

"We believe a portal has been opened sire, and Auldicia is being transported through to the other realm."

"No, stop this foolishness now. She cannot go."

"It appears the gateway has been satisfied with the flesh and blood remnants of Auldicia's family line. Treemount blood had vanquished the fires at the gate permitting her return, master."

With the need to release his seed and the anguish of Auldicia returning to the living realm, Vulkus shrieked louder than the condemned souls in East Central Hell. This only added to the already measurable earthquake in both realms.

"Damn you Auldicia. Damn you."

†

Opening her mouth to smile wide, Auldicia's fangs cut through the flesh in her mouth. The taste of Treemount blood summoned her closer to the East Central Hell gateway for her sacrificial pardon back into the realm of the living. Souls that drowned repeatedly in eternal hell fire surrounded the edge of the gateway.

Auldicia delivered an over exaggerated saunter up the fire bricked path to the gateway, as envy and jealousy blazed from the eyes of the lost souls. Flesh from her feet slowly incinerated with each step she took, but the joy of victory allowed her to ignore the pain. Once there, she calmly turned and bid farewell to the Realm of the Condemned.

"Goodbye you burning bitches…I'm going back."

†

A warning from the United States Geological Survey Agency to Louisiana and Texas Gulf Coast residents had only come a few hours prior to the first tremors. Aftershocks caused two oil tankers to collide a few miles off the Corpus Christi Shore. The scientists were to record all earthquake activity before it occurred. The difficulty with the situation is there has never been any seismic activity recorded off the Texas coastline, ever. The agency's greatest fear was the impact the aftershocks would cause to the spewing oil well off the coast of Louisiana. A natural disaster on top of a man made one never held good outcomes for anyone involved.

At 2 a.m., things took a turn for the worst as Corpus Christi Gulf coast residents were bracing to evacuate from the area. A possible tsunami threat was issued due to the earthquake after-shocks along with the off-shore tropical storm that was upgraded to a category five storm. The National Weather Center names storms according to alphabetical order, naming this first storm of the year Hurricane Auldicia.

The unrest on the ocean's floor between Texas and Loui-siana continued for several hours. Waves measuring 150 feet slammed into the seawall of those coastal towns flooding and washing away small beach communities.

A portal between the realm of the Living and the Realm of the Condemned unzipped, allowing Auldicia to pass through a membrane of earth. Ascension to the current realm was complete. She lay buried in a watery grave of murk and filth. Her grave dis-turbed the lair of unconcerned sea creatures at rest. The creatures had very little time to swim further out to sea to escape the salinity of the water and the air pressure caused by the storm. They would not be able to withstand the violent natural changes this storm brought. They too would suffer death at Hell's hand during Auldi-cia's ascension.

The earth below sea level continued to shift as her body drifted upward toward the surface. Nearby sea animals fled as glowing green eyes cast shadows on rocks and seaweed. Red hair tangled around her arms and neck veiling her face as her move steadied closer to the surface.

Soon, she found herself telepathically summoning the

voodoo gods Agwe and Guede, to bid her passage into the living world. All debts paid.

"Zembewee ogana, lotono Ogate, Ogate, Ogate Agwe Ogate Guede. Oh fathers of darkness, let me return to you, let me pass, let me pass, let me pass to you Agwe, let me pass Guede. Just beneath the water's edge, she heard the gods call her name.

"Come forth, child of ours. Come forth. Come forth reentered into this world with your debts to us paid. Power and reign, returned to you and your legacy lives on, but your bloodlust and desires will continue. Come forth child of ours…Auldicia.

Drawing her right arm back, she punched her fist through the water's surface feeling air pressure from the winds as the waves continued to bring her huge body forth. Lightning scrawled throughout the sky, sending one vein of its power to strike beneath the ocean surface, closing the portal and earth membrane she had just crossed. The lightning striking beneath the ocean surface caused the death of many sea creatures.

Auldicia's ancient body washed ashore with a towering 150-foot wave that slammed into downtown Corpus Christi, Texas. Its force caused a power outage that stretched for twenty miles. Area high-rise buildings sustained remarkable destruction, and other structures completely flattened, leaving only minor support beams as reminders they once stood.

As planned, the off-shore community of Corpus Christi, Texas had completed a mandatory evacuation. Still, some residents remained behind and those lives were lost at sea. Recordings of the hurricane and tsunami registered through satellite Intel.

Auldicia's ascension was astounding. To humans, evidence showed a major natural catastrophe had occurred, but to those from the world of voodoo and black magic evil forces were at work. Death and destruction lay over all the land.

Atop several high-rise buildings, dorsal fins of sea creatures hung over the rooftops. Several Squids and other Octopus tentacles hung smeared to remaining shattered glass windows. The head of a Sperm Whale peeked out through the front of a small shoreline Hotel. Its tail completely severed lying in a nearby intersection.

High winds continued raging as Auldicia's body lie on the beach. Taking note of the earth around her, she stood covered in sludge. Small blue crabs hung from her tendons and ligaments, nibbling away at her remaining centuries' old flesh.

Raising her arms, she looked down at her outward form in disgust. In disbelief, she knew what she needed to return her once beguiling beauty.

"I must feed, or I will suffer."

Hunger and desire hit her at once. Her fangs, porous and brittle, elongated as she threw her head back sniffing the air, looking for fresh human plasma. Only a male would satisfy both needs. Her desire for human flesh was uncontrollable. With the smell of death all around her, Auldicia fell to the sand pulling her bony knees to her rib cage.

Dragging her sex across the wet sands, she began to moan and writhe in pleasure bringing on the first enjoyable climax in centuries, yet it was not enough to sate her. A hiss escaped her lips as she climaxed once, twice, three times.

"More… I need more."

Soon, Auldicia recalled the mocking words of Vulkus just after he brutalized her body before her pardoned escape.

"None of them could satisfy you…you were unsuccessful then…you always will be…you are mine…you will do well to remember…"

Auldicia blocked out those mocking words from her memory with a renewed vow.

"I will be successful Vulkus, and I will erase your existence from both realms…as soon as I bear a child with my only object of desire, Nacio.   He will have me and we shall rule together."

Just then, the eye of the storm came ashore, and she picked up the scent of a human male nearby. Tracking the scent of his sweet plasma, her hunger increased. Auldicia walked hurriedly to the location as the aroma grew nearer.

Plasma had its own distinct aroma, and she followed it to the inside of a severely weather-beaten hotel hacienda. Although weak from the need to feed, she had a remarkable strength left to lift a shattered glass door from its hinges, throwing it across the parking lot filled with overturned cars and three yachts with broken masts lying sideways.

The starving predator she was, nothing would keep her from her feeding, nothing. Once inside the hacienda, Auldicia headed down a long hallway. Thick, sweet plasma filled her nostrils, inebriating her brain. Room 222 was quiet, but she could hear the short panting breaths of the male in possession of what she needed.

Placing her hands on the door, one quick shove brought the barrier down. Wafting from the area nearest the window, a closet stood next to it. The panting quickened as the man called out for help.

"Who's there? Help me? Is it safe to come out? I thought I heard more wind and glass breaking?"

"I am here. Look upon me."

Auldicia pulled the accordion door to the closet open to find a tow headed male with ice-blue eyes. Startled, at her filth and nakedness, the man let out small shout.

"Jeez, lady, what happened to you? You need help worse than I do. I only got a cut that I know will heal soon. You look like you need a few transplants."

Ignoring his insolence, she noticed blood trickled from a cut across his inner right thigh near his groin. Still starving and fully aroused, she slowly neared the man, allowing her eyes to follow the trail of blood away from his thigh and over to the impression of his shaft underneath his jeans. Auldicia ran her tongue over her fangs, allowing her hips to gyrate, offering her affections to the confused male who stood before her.

Sensing his doom, without any sudden movements the male tried to ease past Auldicia. His fear heightened, as he glanced at her talons curling in response to his attempt to flee her presence. Snapping her jaws shut, her fangs clicked as saliva slid from the corners of her twisted mouth.

"And where might you be going little prey? I have needs and hungers and desires…for human flesh." A pain-filled shriek echoed through the demolished hacienda as the man's eye bulged from his head while he watched from a broken mirror across the room as Auldicia sank her fangs into his neck.

Screams turned from pain to moans of misery and pleasure at first as she slowly sucked the life-giving plasma from the dazed man, bringing him to an agonizing arousal.

In a flash, Auldicia ripped the man's pants from his waist and straddled him wide. Knowing his arousal would lose stiffness as she continued to take his plasma, she ground her hips to a rhythm that increased with each draw of blood.

Feeling shudders beneath her, she knew her prey was about to give her his seed. Reaching her own release first, she roared as her sex clenched and teased his crown milking him dry. Now, she had what she needed and wanted, Auldicia continued to draw deeply, draining all the life from the man, blood and seed. His shriveled testicles and wilted crown were comparable to a newly shed snakeskin.

After she dismounted from her pleasure, remnants of blood slid to her chin while she watched her skin and flesh regenerate to its majestic form. Red, and blond locks of hair regained color as she smiled at the transformation. Thanking the gods for her return, she called for protection.

"Avac, Avac, Avac. Elemamae. Fodo atae. Thanks be to you, thanks be to you, let no harm befall me. Bear my fruit."

Full of seed, by magic her womb began to swell, stretching her newly regenerated skin across her abdomen, as her curse perpetuated itself.

Lightning struck above the hacienda, illuminating Auldicia as the fetus took its rightful place, the conception complete. She squatted as the child passed through the birth canal. Pulling the child by its foot, Auldicia pulled her first newborn from her womb, with few comforting words.

"You will serve me all the days of your life." She sank her sharp fangs into the newborn, marking it and cursing it for all eternity. Once she was sated, Auldicia dropped the child onto a mattress lying adjacent to the mummified man on the floor.

A blue comforter hung from the dangling ceiling fan blade. With skilled hands, she tore the comforter, twisted and tied it into a toga, to cover the returning voluptuous spread to her hips. She turned and walked out the door, leaving the hacienda and her newborn behind.

Victory claimed her emotions as she set out to uphold her vow.

"I will find Nacio, the object of my desire. We will bind to each other, and he will give me his seed. I then will destroy Vulkus and the family of my archenemy, Olinka. All those who do not pledge allegiance to me shall be destroyed."

Looking towards the sky, she summoned her forces with a thrumming telepathic chant her children would heed. After all, the continents were full of many of her children waiting for their mother's return. Raising her hands sent a clap of thunder and lightning across the darkened sky with this message, as the eye of the storm passed over and the hurricane winds blew once more.

"Come forth children, come forth. Your mother is here. Mother first has returned... mother first is here."

†

Agility returned to Auldicia. Flesh and muscle covered her centuries' old bones, cooling the brimstone heat they roasted under while in East Central Hell. The rain and earth underneath her feet brought a soothing relief with each step she took. Sensitive nerve endings revitalized from the plasma she took from her first feeding in centuries.

"My throat is no longer parched, but my heart is empty. Desire for the lover who owns my soul overwhelms me. I must find Nacio and finish what we started."

She turned her nose up to the drizzling Corpus Christi skyline, searching out his scent. She smirked at all the destruction she caused. Her eyes rolled to the back of her head once her satisfied nose caught his scent just north of where she stood.

"Ah yes. I remember the place where my love is. It is the place where I turned him into a blood drinker and predator. It is the place where I planned to take and store all of his seed...until that damned Vulkus ripped my soul from this realm. I plan to call San Antonio home once more."

Like a cheetah in pursuit, Auldicia broke into a sprint up IH 37, bound for San Antonio. Confident with her senses restored, one mile outside of Corpus Christi, she teleported the rest of the way to San Antonio and arrived in Bexar County seconds later in Garden Ridge, Texas, home of Natural Bridge Caverns. She stood just outside the mouth of what used to be her lair and sacrificial torture chamber.

"Home, Sweet home. It won't be long now before my children come to me, as well as my lover."

A clueless groundskeeper stood just on the inside of the cavern. Befuddled, he looked at Auldicia through the glass like an exhibit on display. The black haired, blue-eyed groundskeeper looked to be in his mid thirties. Blessed with muscular legs and wall thick pectorals, he resembled a male fitness model.

Plexiglas covered the opening to the cavern, sealing off its entry. Obviously, humans now dwelled close by. This proved useful to her. Her feedings are intense, and as the humans wander into her lair, she will have sustenance as needed. Such as this one who happens to be available to her now.

She returned the glare, while the man's eyes fell on her breasts. The transformation back to human form proved successful. It allowed her to tantalize her prey as the seductress history had labeled her. Pushing in the Plexiglas with the new strength she possessed, the male quickly stepped back, but remained enchanted.

Still eye balling her breasts, the man licked his lips while Auldicia walked into his personal space.

"Do you want to touch me, my pet?"

"Yes, I want to touch and squeeze you."

The enchanted man stepped toward Auldicia with hands stretched out in front of him, cupping her pert breasts, torching her desire and her appetite. Sight of the man, made her fangs itch to sink them into his warm artery. He dipped to take a mouthful of her bosoms, giving her the perfect opportunity to strike.

Her electric green eyes illuminated the opening of the cavern, as her fangs pierced the man's flesh. Yanking the man's waistband to his shorts, she grasped the man's firm erection in her hand, taking them both down to the ground of the cavern. His mouth quickly released her bosom, as he went limp in her embrace. In one motion, she guided his rock hard flesh into her womb. First, he moaned in pain, then whimpered in ecstasy, then exhaled his last breath as she sucked the life-giving plasma from his neck.

Her ravenous appetite didn't stop with satisfying her thirst. Auldicia continued to sate her need by whittling the fat flesh from the man's body as well. So pleasurable to her palate, her fangs drew bone marrow from his strong healthy thighbone. Each lap she took caused the marrow to spread around the corners of her mouth and side of her face. Mummified and hollow, the man's remaining skin looked as if it had been freshly shed from a reptile.

Sated and thoroughly disgusted with the remnants of tethered skin, she quickly rid herself of the man's remains by throwing his carcass in the branches of some nearby trees outside the cavern, supplying a future snack for a family of buzzards sure to fly overhead.

Reentering her old lair for the first time in centuries brought back memories of long ago. Looking up into the vault of the cavern, she noted stalactites hanging like chandeliers.

The humans that entered this cavern would flee in horror if they knew these stalactites held the bones of victims sacrificed to the voodoo gods and Vulkus in order to keep her reign. Formations in the stalagmites from the floor of the cavern held the wasted flesh of those sacrificed. Oddly, some of the formations resembled screaming faces that belonged to humans that once lived.

Looking up into the vault of the cavern, thousands of beaming eyes looked back at her twinkling like stars. The eyes of bats that only she could see, looked on at her curiously.

One creature took a chance and swooped down to bite a chunk of cheek from her face. The bat didn't stand a chance as Auldicia turned, and ripped out the bony structure that held the bat's wings in place. It fell from her grip to the floor of the cavern, and she stomped the remains of the creature into the cavern's basin.

Impatience building in her, with telekinetic power, she cleared the area so as not to indicate danger to her anticipated human food as they wandered near. Again, she called out to her children, anticipating Nacio is among those to heed her call. Agonizingly so, the thought of him caused the desire to burn within her.

"I'm home children. Mother First is home."

Her trembling hands cupped her breasts, rubbing them over her toga. Nacio's name left her lips with a moan.

"Nacio I'm home."

2

Evil rain down

Deafening sounds of chaos shook the Personal Hygiene isle inside the Wal-mart. This proved to be a slight disadvantage in locating Believa, but not impossible. Crouching for an offensive attack, my grip tightened on a Dieth dart. I was ready to strike as soon as she came into view. Luckily, I had reloaded my supply of the double strength darts in my purse before I left, carrying them at all times. Believa Beaushanks is about to transform to a vampire, or it won't be long before she does. Justice must have bitten her before his hideous death outside the Puente mansion.

Making matters worse, it appears Believa has conceived a child. It is highly likely, that Believa was his consort, and he is the father. Running into her at this Wal-mart is pure fate, a destiny I intend to fulfill by stopping the conception and birth of more Treemounts, or battling the recently expired Justice Treemount's consort to the death.

"My leg, please help me, please don't leave me here." Ear-splitting shrieks filled the ransacked store, as one woman fell in the midst of a charging crowd whose only intention was to flee the coming storm. Several customers ran, snatching as many store items as possible. San Antonio is about to face one of the worst storms in history; an immeasurable hurricane on the Enhanced Fujita scale, the first of its kind.

Weather experts announced the storm name as Auldicia, which only spiked my already out of control adrenaline. Just hearing the name Auldicia, makes me cringe, reminding me of the family history my grandmother passed down to me. Auldicia is our family's ultimate enemy. I'm hoping the name is only a co-incidence and not the harsh reality that appears more clearly each breath I take standing here ready for battle.

Earlier in the day, a soot black layer of cloud cover cloaked the Alamo City's eastern horizon. Ominous gray darkened the sky, and I recognized it as a veil of black magic, informing every-one who looked upon it of its intentions of unthinkable destruction. Bexar County's southeastern tip is bracing for cyclonic rain bands that will surely flood the city. So much has happened in the last few weeks that would surely lead up to this catastrophic storm.

Childress had given birth to a female child. Justice had literally brought her to our doorstep, begging us not to let her become like her mother. Whole-heartedly, I knew the peace I had so longed for would be short lived, and we would be punished for keeping the child whom Patience named Blessing in our midst.

Childress has no idea I have access to her child. However, from the looks of the sky, it won't be long before she does. Jus-tice brought Blessing to us shortly before Basrick finally came to grips with his grief and beheaded Justice on the front lawn. Justice killed Basrick's twin Basira with Colloidal Silver, which of course is unforgivable. It seems the woman pregnant with his child is willing to risk both lives in a senseless battle. She's made it clear she recognizes me as I do her, and now I must stop her.

"Believa, I know you're in here. Show yourself so we can figure out what to do about the situation you've gotten yourself into. I know you're scared, but I can't help you if you fight me." The plea went unanswered.

Standing ready to destroy anyone who looked like the living dead, I eased up the aisle. Expecting her to jump out at me, I was careful not to hurt any of the fleeing customers. So many humans struggled to get their hands on items in preparation of being in the house for several days as the storm took out its vehemence on the city.

I needed eyes overhead to assist me in locating Believa in the middle of all the incessant shouting and shuffling. I steadied myself and closed my eyes, telepathically calling out for help, summoning any nearby fowl within range. A small mocking bird whose nest sat high in the store rafters, flew to a shelf just overhead.

"Find Believa, and lead me to her." The agile mocking bird took to the air, as I shared mental images of Believa with the bird now in flight. Visions of the flight seen through the bird's point of view were stunningly accurate, allowing me to see images in high definition so sharp, that I could see the plaque accumulated at her gum line, as she took short openmouthed breaths. She lay tucked away between two shelves on the Home Accessories isle, scared and defenseless.

Prowling at this point, I moved one aisle over at the end

opposite the one Believa occupied. Sweat, streamed down my cleavage causing an itch I didn't have time to scratch. Any sudden moves would alert her to my presence. In my line of sight, here exposed left shoulder made a prime target for the dart in my hand. Kneeling slowly, I raised my arm to take aim. A swift click sent the dart jetting through the air, alerting Believa to my presence. Her instincts kicked in, and she executed a defensive maneuver, rolling onto her side to dodge the dart. Landing on her feet as our eyes met, she sprinted up the aisle.

"Damn it Believa, stop. You can't out run me." The inherited strength from tasting Nacio's blood allowed me to make a few stealthy moves of my own. Several shelves were loaded with glass wall accessories, and all it took was one effortless push. Glass wall fixtures came crashing down as the shelves fell like dominoes, toppling onto her as she lay under a pile of what looked to be rubble.

Glass, wires, screws and hooks from the metal shelves lay scattered and piled high in the middle of the floor with dangerous sharp angles. Approaching cautiously, there was no movement as I closed in hoping a knock to the floor from the falling shelves would make Believa rational. Dismayed, I had no such luck. Clearing a path in the destruction, I looked for signs of movement.

"Believa, let's talk about this to figure out what to do. I know we can work this out. You're all alone now. Justice is dead, and you're going to need help with what's happening to you. Please let me help you." Still, there was no response from underneath the rubble.

"Let's work this out, because Justice is dead."

Metal scraped the floor as customers fled screaming, while glass crunched underfoot. Rumbling from the debris confirmed Believa to be alive. Amazingly strong and graceful, a shape arose from the pile fierce and crimson eyed. Her transformation had given her agility beyond reasoning.

"Sorry to trap you like this, but" I tried to finish but was just able to duck as a store shelf came hurdling through the air aimed straight for my head. Believa picked up two hooks and flung them in my direction. She found her way from underneath the mess and began tossing more metal, hoping to flatten me. Battered and bloody, she stood to full height and let out a barely coherent hiss while extending her fangs. Her transition to vampire was complete. Impatiently, I fired another dart, and she blocked it with her hand.

"Did you kill Justice? Why would you do that? You had no right to take his life. He loved me…he loved me. You will pay for what you have done."

"Uh, Believa I did not kill Justice, so get that straight. Secondly, I highly doubt he loved you. He loved no one. Couldn't you see that? Let's try to get you some help Believa. You've now turned into what Justice was; a vampire. When did you first find out you were pregnant?"

"No more questions, you tramp. You killed him, and you will pay." Believa took a flying leap, giving me a chance to release another Dieth Dart in her direction. Hitting her in the right jugular vein, we toppled to the floor as the hand-to-hand combat began. The dart seemed to have no effect, and she continued to charge forward.

When women fight in hand-to hand combat, the intention of the battle is to harm the physical beauty of the other woman in an attempt to make the other female unattractive to males. Bloody and vicious, women fight to deface their opponent. Believa's technique of fighting proved this theory true. Forcefully, she grabbed a handful of my black shoulder length locks, tearing the follicles from the roots. Grinning, she was all too happy with herself standing with her hand full.

The psychological impact of hearing each strand of hair ripped from my scalp was devastating. The echo sent me back to the moment Klein Treemount penetrated me. His brother Justice held me down as he waited to enter my little battered six-year-old body. Reserves of strength brought me from a victimized past by slamming my curled right fist into Believa's smiling face. She lost her smirk while I gained one. She gagged on her left incisor, falling over on her back. Bug-eyed and dazed, she stood quickly as her missing tooth stung the back of her throat, cutting down the length of her esophagus.

"Be damned, you snaggle-toothed bitch. I've already paid. You gave yourself to a monster Believa. Now you're carrying the child of a monster. You have no idea what lies ahead of you. You carry within your body the worst kind of evil, Believa, and now you are a vampire. Justice and his family have killed people for years for little or nothing. Now you are a permanent part of their evil."

"Stop talking to me." She leapt to her feet and lunged as we locked arms. Her grip on my throat took my breath away, yet I stood strong. A third dart sat in my shirt pocket. Reaching for it,

I stabbed the other side of her neck. Quickly, I pressed the plunger for the chemical and hormone concoction to enter her blood stream. Still, there was no effect.

"You can't stop me. Killing Justice is the last thing you will do. Bose was right. You do deserve to die, because you are weak." Believa just indicated she was aware of the plans Bose had to kill me, and probably Nacio as well.

"I told you I didn't kill Justice." Letting a few moments of silence pass as we both grunted to defend ourselves, I finally gave a confession that surely taunted Believa as we tussled.

"No, I didn't kill him…but I sure as hell enjoyed watching him die."

With my last word spoken, Believa swung a punch that landed in my gut, taking the wind out of me. Her strength was exponential due to the fact that she had just completed her transformation, and she was gaining preternatural strength by the moment. Bulging muscles covered her otherwise waif like frame, making her lithe and giving her the speed of a cheetah. Although her appearance was gaunt, no doubt due to the lack of prenatal care, I only imagined her being a force to reckon with once she has her first taste of plasma. Blood will make her stronger than steel.

Inhaling deeply to fill my lungs then catapulting to my feet, I turned and completed a round-off back handspring tuck combination to land behind my fanged opponent. Bewildered, she realized I stood behind her. She turned to find my left hand cutting through the air like an ax. Chopping her in the throat and making her gag once more, the impact of the blow sent her reeling ten feet across the floor, skidding to a stop in front of a Weed and Feed display.

"Get off your ass Believa, and come make me pay." I was taking no prisoners this round, and she knew it. Before I could reach her, Believa got to her feet and ran. Hot on her heels, I tackled her to the floor in a headlock, attempting to snap her neck from her shoulders. Slipping from my grip, she grabbed my shirt and flipped me over. I landed on my back with a thud.

Believa walked over to me, and raised her foot to stomp me with her boot. Not giving her the chance, I punched her right in the crotch. The force of the blow echoed off the tin cover of the Garden department as her pelvic bone shattered into small fragments. I'm hoping Believa is as dumb as she looks, but I know it won't be long before she learns that her existence depends on blood. Once she learns this fact, she will be aware that injuries like the one she just sustained to her pelvic bone will heal almost instantaneously. Her injury would temporarily slow her down, since she won't be able to walk very well, which will put me at an advantage.

I grabbed Believa's head and slammed it into the concrete floor. Instead of wincing in pain, she laughed as blood spurted out her nose. The battle had become deadly, and I needed to move her out of sight from any other employees or bystanders. I dragged her skinny ass, and I put her out like the Flintstone's cat behind the building by the trash dumpster. It seemed most appropriate for someone affiliated with the Treemounts. Totally immobilized in my vice grip, I quickly reached for my small handbag strapped around my waist. Along with a vile of Dieth was a small vile of Colloidal Silver. This liquid form of silver had proven to be deadly to vampires. I'm hoping this proves to be true in my case.

"I said you can't stop me. There is nothing you can do to hurt me or my baby, and I do plan to have this baby Solis. So you can just go to hell."

"You need to pay for being so damn dumb to get yourself in this situation, Believa."

Working quickly and holding her tightly, I drew the plunger back on the syringe and loaded it with the Colloidal Silver. Believa was laughing hysterically as my grip remained locked around her neck. Emptying the rest of the Dieth into the syringe, I injected the entire solution into her carotid artery.

Finally, her laughter began to taper off as she began to convulse, which is a sure sign the active catalyst in Dieth is beginning to work. Dieth is short for DES Dieththystilbestrol, a drug given in the 1940s-1970s to pregnant women to prevent miscarriages. Some women who took this drug gave birth to generations of female children who had breast cancer and transsexual male children. The other drugs in the dart mixture are Mifepristone that blocks progesterone which sustains a pregnancy and Misoprostol which induces cramps to cause miscarriage. Together this mixture is what Bose engineered to stop the mass reproduction of more Treemounts. Now that I've kicked it up with the Colloidal Silver, this will surely be a poisonous mix for Believa, hopefully ending her miserable existence.

"What did you do to me? I feel as though I'm slipping… slipping into darkness."

"Yes…and darkness is where you will stay forever."

Punching her with the speed of a Cobra strike, I put her lights out… for good I hoped.

Sheets of horizontal rain layered the air, cutting visibility to less than fifteen percent. Flashes of lightning scrawled across the sky, striking a transformer in the distance, blowing a power transformer.

Heavy raindrops pelted the asphalt of the parking lot as shopping carts began to swirl while the wind gust picked up. The last of the shoppers cleared the Wal-mart in an attempt to take cover. Sprinting to the car as hail peppered the roof of the Lexus LS, the black sky made mid afternoon look like midnight. Cranking up, I hit the gas, tearing ass out of the parking lot, hitting highway 281 heading back to the mansion. A sharp realization hit me.

"Damn, I didn't even get a chance to pick up anything for Blessing."

Horizontal rain and hail poured relentlessly as other drivers fought for frontend control of their vehicles on Highway 281. Crosswinds from the storm caused them to sway. A quick glance in the rearview mirror caused fear to twist my spine. A funnel cloud swirled in the rear distance where I had just been only moments ago. Watching the destruction from behind encouraged more speed, nearly causing me to miss the Cesar Chavez exit from 281.

I pray for strength as Nacio and I face whatever comes our way next.

Believa

What the hell is wrong with me? Believa thought to herself. I can't seem to feel my legs. I can't believe that bitch Solis just left me here to die in this storm.

Pain washed over her limbs as her hip muscles began to shrivel. Dieth and Colloidal Silver worked their chemical miracle through her veins. Her once plentiful breasts crumbled in, wrinkling as hormonal dehydration sat in. Free form testosterone ravaged her skin, making her face and backside an oozing oil slick. Pus filled zits erupted from every two to three inches across her back and shoulders.

Once known throughout the city for her figure, admirers claimed her butt and hips resembled large tricked out car tires, earning her the nickname Fifteens. The brutal Dieth cocktail deactivated the hip spreading estrogen in her body robbing her of the glorified assets she once donned. A barrel shaped torso was all that remained of the once coke bottle shaped vixen. Clumps of hair began to wilt from her scalp as she lay stunned. Convulsions set in.

A thunderclap shook the ground beneath her. Rain pricked and stung her face as she looked up at the sky behind the frail Wal-mart. The fierce wind began to carry shopping carts to the edge of the property line. A trash dumpster started rolling her way. With the little flexibility she had remaining, Believa dragged her rigid body out of the path as the dumpster scraped the asphalt slamming into a nearby lamppost.

Is that a train? Why is a train coming? There is no train nearby. Why is it so loud?

Unbeknownst to the gestating new fledgling vampire, fate would have the last laugh. Wind whipped her hair over her face, making her more vulnerable as the seconds passed. A few feet in the distance, a black tornado made its way toward her, sweeping away all in its path.

The lamppost and dumpster - gone, gobbled up, as well as portions of the store roof. The last of the few stray cars remaining in the parking lot took flight, as cyclonic suction swallowed them into the belly of the beastly cloud. Roaring with life to bring death, Believa felt the magnetic pull of the storm reeling her into her imminent doom.

"Help me! Help me, somebody, please!"

Her screams went unheard; unnoticed as the Wal-mart came crashing down. Rooftop beams bent like straws under the force of the wind. The tendons in her leg muscles stretched thin, as her legs ascended above her head. A flying beam knocked her unconscious, tearing her head from her shoulders, nearly beheading her. Her frail body swirled, as it pulled toward the vortex of the funnel. Effortlessly carried away like a boat downstream, her limp body violently blew beyond the fringe of the storm.

Raging across the city for ten miles destroying all in its wake, the vortex dissipated over an abandoned field in Northeast San Antonio. Strung high in a mature Oak Tree, Believa's partially decapitated head dangled over the edge of a branch while her naked body lay cradled in mangled limbs below. Hardiplanks, hubcaps, a flat-screen television, and the body of a Caucasian male each dangled from the many branches of the tree also. A loud pop followed by several snaps indicated the weight of the torrential rain soaked within the branches caused the tree to collapse. Believa's body tumbled with a splash to the tree's base.

Dead fixated eyes and a frozen expression made Believa's tethered head a mannequin to her detached body. Although she had just completed her transformation, Believa still experienced the pain process of human death. The fall brought about a quick jolt back to consciousness.

I just want to die. Am I dead? Please let me die.

Her heartbeat slowed, beating one last time then…silence.

I can't believe I've died and become this thing. I wish Justice were here with me. Oh my gosh…my baby. What about our baby? I guess it wasn't meant to be. I'll die all alone. Whatever it was Solis shot me with is killing my baby. I feel it. I want my baby, but now we both will die.

Believa lay still as breath left her body for the last time. Closing her eyes, she felt the vibration of a low thrumming that appeared to get louder each moment that past. The thrumming echoed deep within her body. The strongest motion rocked between her legs, deep in her womb, shaking her body. Louder and louder, closer and closer, the thrumming shook the base of the tree.

Believa opened her eyes.

3

Hell broke loose

Nacio

Many shadows danced on the walls of the Egyptian themed room in the Puente mansion. It provided sanctuary for Nacio in the days following Bose's death and Blessing's arrival. Gloom and angst set the mood at the residence. Nacio cherished his keeper whom he loved like a brother, yet his anger would not allow him to mourn his ended existence.

Nacio's six foot seven inch frame lay reclined in the chaise in the middle of the room. Effortlessly, his rippling biceps curled two 50 lb dumb bells. Black waves of shoulder length locks lay relaxed down his back, draping the edge of the chaise.

Bulging muscular thighs sat sheathed in a pair of black Jockeys. The sleek peek- a-boo opening revealed his semi-erect shaft pressing through. Passion lingered from the love he and Solis made earlier. He sat quietly as he pondered the recent events.

Fear I never thought I would have is evolving. The one person I called my brother and my keeper betrayed me; Bose. All I have left of any memories of him in this mansion, and in my heart is rage.

Bose attempted to kill Solis and he nearly succeeded. Had she not ingested my blood, she would have perished in my arms. I punished him with my bare hands, pulverizing his bones beneath my grip.

He raved on and on about his mother Auldicia's return. Auldicia turned me into the vampire predator I am. Only she would be foolish enough to attempt to return to this realm.

She never accepted the fact I refused to surrender to her lust, and give her my seed. Hell no…my fate was written long ago. The seed I carry within me shall only be given to the Mistress I am bound to…Solis. Before his demise, Bose spoke of the possibility of Solis conceiving. It is a possibility, but she is unaware of that fact.

Of all of Auldicia's unwilling consorts, she could never entice me to succumb to her charms. Only I see her in her true form. A woven mane of serpents nest on top of her head, with a womb filled with rotting flesh not even scavengers would consider for food.

She is a bitch dog, dropping offspring here and there, leaving them to fend for themselves or die. No female of such filth will ever mother a child of mine. Auldicia is lower to the earth than the dirt beneath my foot. I will crush her if she attempts to come after me.

Her rage will be unyielding…especially once she realizes I am already bound to Solis. Oh father, Solis will be in eminent danger and the target of Auldicia's rage. I will protect my mate and uphold my vows at all costs.

I feel our destiny is heading down an uncertain path. Everyone here has fallen helplessly head over heels for Blessing. Her deceased uncle, Justice, brought her to us swaddled and bubbling with joy. We knew she would be the only good Childress would ever give this world. Patience felt that caring for Blessing is the restitution for Justice killing Basira.

At first, their son Basrick resented Blessing, but by gosh, the little blond green-eyed bombshell stole his heart as well. One evening I sat watching Solis as she slept, and then slipped out down the hall. I peeked in on Basrick in the library when he thought only he was in the room, and Blessing lay in her bassinet. Eavesdropping, I caught the blooming of a beautiful new sibling bond between the two.

Blessing lay smiling at Basrick standing over her. He snatched the baby up, holding her at arm's length, fangs extended, predatory instinct taking over.

"I should throw you out the window…I could do it, you know. I could kill you, like I killed your uncle. There's nothing you could do about it. You shouldn't be here. There is nothing you can do for our family other than bring more trouble to our door step."

The beautiful baby girl held Basrick in her green gaze, cooing as she giggled, softening the wrinkle between his eyes. Misty tears came next as he held her close.

"My mother smiles again because of you…damn you little Ms. B."

Blessing donned a surname from her new sibling, and it was then, I knew, he too would be a prisoner to her every want and need.

Armando and Patience Caraway, Basrick's parents and our dearest friends, entered the library as Basrick held Blessing. The proud parents held each other as they watched Basrick and Blessing. So much had changed in their lives since their initial visit some time ago.

What started out for Armando and his family as just a visit between two old friends soon turned into an absolute disaster. Their daughter Basira ingested Colloidal Silver given to her by Justice Treemount on an evening she went to see him. It ended her existence. He and his siblings are enemies to Solis. Auldicia is the great ancestor to the Treemounts. In the midst of the mayhem, we found an unlikely ally, Detective Menlo Kildare, maternal first cousin to the Treemount clan. She discovered Justice had become a vampire, piecing together Basira had turned him.

Menlo had become Bose's consort, but things went awry when she took a gunshot to the head during a routine call while on the trail of a serial killer. Turns out, Justice had become the new serial killer in town and was involved in her shooting. Currently hospitalized in intensive care, Menlo remains comatose, with Basrick at her side day and night.

Basrick avenged his twin Basira's death by decapitating Justice out in front of the mansion. It was a nasty mess. Basrick proved he was a killing machine that takes his fight to the streets. He took Justice out as he spoke, in mid sentence, plowing him down and dismembering him simultaneously...a cold-blooded killer.

Armando and Patience taught him well, but his instinct to survive came naturally. Basrick is a Rippler, someone with the ability to slow or replay a moment in time. Basira also possessed this ability. It's because of this dexterity that Basrick took his twin's death so hard. He wasn't able to save her from her fated doom.

The Caraways originated as vampires in the 19th century from a corridor in Europe known today as the Rhineland. A beautiful country, but deadly. Many ancient vampire predators dwelled around Luxembourg, preying on beautiful, full-bosomed maidens. Lured away from their homes deep into the forest, the maidens fell into an ambush and were seduced. The attackers took plasma from them in the most savage way; biting the victims multiple times and turning them into vampire predators.

Living on a sprawling countryside estate, Armando and his family tended farm animals and crops for a living. Patience, having the beauty of a goddess and happily expecting their third child, unknowingly capturing the eye of the fierce countryside attackers. One autumn evening, Patience and Basira were out milking the herd and came under attack.

At the foot of a nearby hill, Armando and Basrick chopped wood for the night campfire. Hearing the screams of his wife and daughter, Armando ran to their aid with Basrick following.

Two naked, waif thin, black-eyed beings lay across the bodies of Patience and Basira, biting their necks and wrists with finger-length fangs. Their precious blood spurted from the multiple wounds received.

With an ax in hand and no time to spare, Armando swung at the creature draining Patience, landing the ax dead center in the creature's skull with a dull thud. This got the attention of the attacker, and the draining stopped.

Terrified, yet courageous, Basrick held a pitchfork in both hands and lunged forward jabbing his sister's attacker in the spine. Still lapping at his sister's neck, Basrick yanked the pitchfork from the creature's spine, and jabbed it into his hamstring. Shrieks of pain gurgled from the creature as he stopped draining Basira.

Armando and Basrick both attempted to get Patience and Basira away from their captors, but both men fell flat as if under a spell. Armando watched as the vampire who had drained Patience turned to him, and the ax embedded in its head fell to the ground as if some unknown force removed it. With speed beyond reason, the vampire sprang on top of Armando, ripping a chunk of his neck from his body.

Cold black eyes from Basira's attacker fell on Basrick. Soon, Basrick found himself hyperventilating as he began moving in reverse motion. He replaying the last few moments over again, and removing the pitchfork from the vampire's hamstring. Confused and completely immobile, Basrick realized he had just gone through a time warp of some kind. Fleetly, he also had his neck ripped open by the fangs of the vampire.

On that night, the entire Caraway family lay slaughtered in the fields of their estate. As a world traveler, I would travel to Europe from the African-Moroccan coast. On this particular excursion, I happened to be crossing the countryside that evening and caught the smell of death lingering in the night air.

I located the family finding sheep covered in human blood, and a trail of the blood leading to the forest. I took the bodies of the family back inside their home, placing them in the basement, knowing they would arise as predators themselves. Making certain no humans came to the home while the transformation took place; I waited for the family to rise.

Armando was the first to complete the transformation. He arose with an appetite for blood and revenge. Patience rose next after her husband. Although blood thirsty, her vengeance was fueled by the loss of the child she carried. Basrick and Basira awoke vengeful as their parents.

Explaining to the family what occurred, our friendship was forged, and we set out to hunt down their killers. From that moment, we have come to be as close as any family. Protecting our own at all cost, there is no way the Caraways would ever leave either of us to fight against any enemy alone.

They stood by Solis and I as Bose became our enemy. Bose's elimination allowed Basrick to step in and oversee the Puente Masonry. Luckily, he briefly apprenticed with Bose to continue manufacturing the Dieth formula to eliminate the Treemounts.

Basrick has done well stepping in as a replacement for Bose. He's identified a new foreman at the masonry, named Hymn Platt, who has the knack for keeping the shifts moving. Many generations of the Platt family have known the Caraways and the fact they are vampires, becoming loyal allies to us all. We were happy to have Hymn join us.

It is possible that I could run the masonry, but I choose

to spend as much time as possible with Solis. I've waited for an eternity to find my bride, and then I had to wait until she grew into an adult before I revealed myself to her. I refuse to let anything or anyone keep me from her any longer.

Solis continues to deal with her own appetite for vengeance. She intends to put all the Treemounts in a deep, parasite-filled grave. She plans to punish Klein for her rape, Childress for torturing her uncle Chase, all of them for killing her grandparents, and Erland for just being stupid altogether. I'm in love with her beyond my soul's existence; so no matter how stubborn she is, and I realize she always will be, she's my baby and no one will take her place.

Nacio dropped the dumbbells to the floor, and picked up a single strand of her curly black hair, stretching it long underneath his nose to inhale her scent. Drowning his senses, he licked his lips, running his tongue over his fangs. Plank hard, the crown of his full erection sprang through the peek-a-boo opening of his Jockeys, anticipating entry into her body.

Pacing anxiously, he awaited her return as the blustering winds howled outside. A quick pivot sent him to the window to see the sinister veil of clouds covering the glamour spell cast over the mansion.

Dread washed over him as he heard Solis telepathically speak to him, her presence drawing closer to the mansion.

Nacio, I'm almost home but I can barely see...the wind...

Her message trailed off without any more response.

Scantily clad and barefoot, Nacio found himself teleporting in the direction of where her scent emanated the strongest. Overcome with emotion, his instinct to protect Solis at all costs sent him into frenzy. He located their vehicle near the 281 and Cesar Chavez exit, about to career over the guardrail right into oncoming northbound freeway traffic.

Nacio completed his teleportation landing in the front seat next to Solis, just as wind gusts lifted the front of the LS making them airborne.

"Baby are you alright? You scared the hell outta me when you trailed off, and now I see why."

"Nacio we're gonna crash."

"The hell we are! Hold on to me." With no time to spare, he kicked open his door.

Solis reached over as Nacio grabbed her, pulling her into his grip as they jumped out of the now flying Lexus aimed to land across the 281 entry ramp. Holding tightly to his chest while they flew home, she watched over his shoulder as the car landed in the middle of the Institute of Texan Cultures Museum loading dock.

Soon, she found they were in the safety of the foyer at the mansion. Relieved and still out of breath, Solis slipped off her shoes, trying to gather her wits.

"I pray no one was hurt at the museum when the car landed. Damn, I'm gonna miss that car. You knew exactly where to find me."

"Yes ma'am, and don't you ever forget it. I will always

find you. We are one, or have you forgotten, Mistress? Oh, and don't worry about the car. Hell, I'll and have another one brought to us tomorrow, storm or no storm."

"No I haven't forgotten you can get to me from anywhere, Sweetheart. Thanks for reminding me."

They held each other's gaze, then shared a smoldering kiss. One kiss started the chain reaction, and once again, Nacio felt that familiar fire only Solis could ignite. Her lips nipped and teased his mouth open, coaxing his tongue out to slather hers. Caressing her made him want to retreat to their room. Solis grabbed a handful of his shaft, as he ground in her palm.

"Watch out now. You are starting something, and we aren't even in our room yet."

"So… Armando and Patience are probably doing the same thing if Blessing is asleep. I've been rock hard all day waiting for you, and then you go out shopping and nearly get yourself off'ed. I can't let you do anything."

Just then, Armando and Patience appeared at the top of the grand staircase, looking disheveled and quite sated. Armando stood looking bewildered as Patience tied her robe standing behind him.

"Nacio what's up? I sensed you leaving moments ago and feared there was trouble. Is everything alright?"

"Yeah, for now. Our mistress here nearly got herself dusted in what looks to be a tornado coming on."

Patience looked as if the wind had already had its fair shot at her long curly brown ringlets. Uncombed and all over the place, her wind-blown look proved Nacio's earlier sentiments true. The couple seemed to keep each other physically satisfied quite well. Concerned, she went down the stairs to make certain Solis was safe.

"Solis, were you hurt?"

"No. Thanks for asking, but we do have another problem on our hands."

"Let me run back up and get Blessing and I'll be right down."

"Yes we all need to sit down for this. It's not pretty."

Sure enough, Patience took two steps up the staircase, and then became a blur as she raced to get Blessing before the meeting in the living area. Nacio took Solis by her hand and led her to the room.

Patience had Blessing in her arms; both mother and daughter were radiant and inseparable. No one would ever guess that Blessing was not her natural child. The baby was all too happy, swaddled in her mother's arms. Yes, Patience had stepped in as her mother, the only one Blessing knew at this point. Patience and Armando planned to keep it this way. No one dared to question them about their decision.

Everyone gathered in the living room, and Solis explained what started out as a simple shopping spree turned into a death match.

"I've been gone so long, because I ran into Believa

Beaushanks; or someone who was Believa Beaushanks. She had completed the transition to a vampire. Evidently, she and Justice hooked up and got busy. We battled and I wiped the floor with her ass, but it gets worse."

Nacio stood and started pacing, dread slowly changing his expression.

"So you took her out, right?" Pacing faster, it dawned on him about the 'gets worse part'. "Wait, what 'gets worse?"

"I was looking for some little outfits for Blessing in the baby isle, and that's when I bumped into her shopping for a pregnancy test. I guess to confirm what she already knew. When she realized who I was, she hissed and her fangs erupted from her gums, and she kept holding her abdomen as if to protect her unborn child."

Nacio came unglued, as if gutted with a hacksaw. "Damn, damn, damn, damn it! These fools just won't quit will they?"

Armando's expression changed, ready for battle on Nacio's command.

"Nacio, we sort of expected this. We worried there might be others he could have turned while he was running amuck in the city. He wasted no time finding a consort. It appears our fears were validated."

"Pregnant? What are we going to do?" Patience chimed. "We hadn't even anticipated that notion, even with all the hunting we've been doing to eradicate them. We totally underestimated Justice."

Pacing faster, with black locks billowing behind him, Nacio looked like a panther ready to kill prey. "Yes. He's proven he was next in line for intelligence after Childress. Let's hope Believa was the only one."

Solis swallowed hard, and the tension thickened in the room.

"Sweetheart, there's more."

Nacio's eyes went black. He froze, and all the air left the room.

"While we battled in the store, the warning alarm issued a tornado watch as a spin off storm from…Hurricane Auldicia."

With that said, Patience jumped to her feet, Nacio bared his fangs, and Armando began pacing. The shift of the mood in the room caused Solis to take a step back to fall on the couch as tremors and chills started up and down her spine. Armando broke the silence.

"Seriously, Nacio, you don't believe Auldicia would be foolish enough to return to this realm after all this time do you? I mean she couldn't…could she?"

"No one has known of her whereabouts on this continent or abroad as far as I know. For centuries, she's been gone. Once she turned me, she tortured me and then…just vanished."

At the mention of Auldicia's name, Blessing began to fret, putting Patience on guard. "There there, little one, be comforted."

Just as a mother acts to protect her young in the presence of danger, Patience excused herself to their suite.

"It's alright little one. Don't cry. Please excuse us. Solis, you and I will talk later after she's asleep. Okay?"

"Yes, no problem, Sweetie. Go and tend to Blessing."

Patience kissed Solis on her cheek, and she took the baby upstairs. Nacio continued piecing his thoughts together.

"Once I turned, she vanished, and I never heard from her again."

Solis threw a worried glance at Nacio as she wrapped up explaining the big battle.

"I had to load her up with several Dieth darts in hopes of stopping her. The vampire strength made it nearly impossible to take her down, not to mention the pregnancy. She obviously hadn't had any nourishment or vitamins. Her skin was horrible, and the mark he left on her neck looked infected. She was so thin, yet strong as an ox. The thing that finally took her out was a kicked up syringe of Dieth mixed with Colloidal Silver."

Nacio considered everything discussed, and then quickly thought of a plan.

"We'll need to keep extra Dieth and Colloidal Silver on hand when we hunt for females who are transitioning from human to vampire and who are pregnant. We'll also need to kick up pro-duction of the chemicals. Damn, this goes from bad to worse."

"Yeah, that's what I pretty much said," Solis agreed. "My grandmother reminded me about our ancestor, Olinka, and the battle she won over Auldicia. She always said that Auldicia owed a huge debt to a demon named Vulkus. Also, she mentioned that if any Treemount blood was spilled on hallowed ground, along with the birth of a legacy, a priestess induction ceremony would cause any priestess to become all powerful. The afterbirth waste plays into that factor as well, because it is the first blood of the legacy and the mother combined."

Everyone in the room looked on intensely as Solis continued her wisdom. Not one eye blinked, nor a breath taken.

"Wait. You don't think Auldicia actually returned, do you? I mean, Basrick killed Justice here. Could this ground be hallowed ground? My mother and grandmother warned that Auldicia has a power over the elements as well. The storm brewing outside looks hellacious. San Antonio has never seen a storm like this one. Do you think she is causing it?"

"Let's not jump to conclusions just yet." Armando ran his hands through his wavy blond locks hoping to rationalize everything. "I guess the answers lie with the Treemounts. We need to find them Nacio, and the sooner the better."

"Yes we do. A lot is riding on where Childress gave birth. If she gave birth on hallowed ground, it is a possibility. This area of the King William District and the ground this mansion stands on was once farmland, but it might have been home to start up church parishes for the first German settlement, which was before I came here."

Armando stood posted up against one of the ceiling-high columns in the corner looking out the window, tapping his foot to calm his senses to no avail, trying to comprehend what risks are at hand.

"Our mistress is right, Nacio. Look there in the east. The clouds have swollen with black magic. This storm is something we too should prepare to survive."

"Then let's increase the magic in the glamour spell that protects and keeps the mansion hidden. One thing for sure, if Blessing's birth and Justice's death brought Auldicia back to this realm, she is drunken with vengeance, as is Childress. Auldicia will stop at nothing to have her vengeance, and Childress is on the hunt for Justice because she believes he has her child. Once they find out Justice is dead and we have Blessing, all Hell will break loose if it hasn't already. We can't afford to take a chance. No matter what scenario we play out, we have to move. Let's reinforce that spell Armando."

Solis stood dumbfounded and demanded an answer.

"Wait, wait, wait. What vengeance are you talking about Nacio? Just what exactly does this bitch want? Just what are you saying?"

Nacio knew the woman he loved stood before him with as much vengeance of her own equivalent to the same amount of passion she demonstrated for him in their bed. Proceeding cautiously, he chose his words carefully. One wrong gesture, one wrong word would send Solis out into the streets in search of her enemy, and possibly to her death. Although he knew Auldicia still held lust for him, there was no way he could tell Solis this fact. Not if he loved her.

"Auldicia wants…" he paused and looked away. "She wants to rule this world, Solis. Everything your grandmother conveyed to you is true. I would bet my existence on it. So that means that Auldicia is coming back to take her revenge on Olinka's lineage as well…meaning, I must protect you at all costs."

"Ahh, hell naw…I will not hide from this, Nacio. I am so damn sick of Childress and those damn brothers of hers. And now her bitch ancestor is after me too?"

Nacio and Armando stood looking at her. Armando stunned at her explosion, Nacio not so shocked.

"Then let both of their asses come for me…I plan to whoop the hell out of Childress worse than I did last time. In fact, my hands are itching for it. As far as Auldicia is concerned, let her bring her ancient ass forward as well. If she wants a battle, I'll give it to her." Posturing with her hands on her hips, her tone was absolute and final, leaving them with few words.

"Ahh, Okaaay. Armando, you want to help me with the glamour spell please?"

"Right behind you, friend."

†

Nacio and Armando went outside, starting in the backyard court. The wind continued its fury, now sending tree limbs across the sky. With Protection Powder in hand, both made certain they were in unison when they began the chant to protect their loved ones.

"Olamde, Olamde, junto olom. Protect us, protect us. Keep safety near." They threw the Protection Powder in the air, as magic took hold of it, sending it swirling into the blustery wind around the mansion. The powder went from white to multiple colors before turning into a beautiful golden mesh, rising high above the mansion and then disappeared.

Satisfied with the color of the gold and strength of the spell, Nacio and Armando retreated into the home. There was much to do as the storm passed over. Armando's worry shifted to his son, Basrick, who was currently at the hospital with Menlo.

"I need to make contact with Basrick. He'll need to know what's happening and be on the lookout for anything strange, and for the Treemounts."

"How's Menlo's progress? Any change?"

"Not much. She's still comatose, taking a feeding tube, and getting physical therapy to avoid muscle atrophy. Basrick refuses to leave her side."

"I realize that. I just hate Bose had his way with her, and then left her for dead. But that's why he is no longer here amongst us."

"I'll get him on the phone. Looks like you have a long night ahead of you with Solis."

"I know. She's riled up good, and I have to deal with it. Our written destinies are starting to take shape. Her grandmother knew it when we met, and now I have to see to it that Solis can endure what's before her. Our future depends on it."

"You know you have our loyalty and strength at anytime you need it, my friend. Just say the word."

"Thank you Armando. Loyalty is everything to me. I appreciate all you do. Well let me not keep our mistress waiting."

Armando laughed, because he knew there would be many words of reassurance given to Solis, so that she would not go off into battle too soon without preparation.

†

Brushing her curly black locks, Solis stood in front of the mirror in a red satin thong-teddy. Still blazing at the possibility Auldicia might have returned to destroy everyone she loved, she waited for Nacio to finish reinforcing the glamour spell on the mansion. He walked in just as she turned to walk to their bed, flashing her thong and cheeks. In overdrive, he knew it would be tricky making love to her when she was this angry.

"So you mad at me now?"

"Of course I'm mad…but not at you. I'm pissed at the damn Treemounts, Nacio. I'm sick of only half enjoying life, fearing it's going to end in tragedy because of them. I just want to live my life. That's what I told my mother and grandmother the night they both came to me in my dream."

"Darling, we will enjoy our lives together, but you have to face your destiny first. That means kicking the hell out of Childress and her bunch."

"But when will we enjoy our lives? Hmm? I'm tired of

always living on the edge. I just want you and our families to live in peace."

Nacio slowly pulled her to him in a tender embrace. His hazel eyes looking directly into hers as their noses touched. He inhaled the air she exhaled. The length of his hands slid down her back to the fullness of her split cheeks, as the thong she wore peeked out. He hated seeing her distressed. It made him want to go and scour the state of Louisiana looking for the Treemount idiots.

"One thing you should never doubt is the fact you've got me, baby. Nothing's going to change that."

"I wanted to enjoy you for as long as I could before I started growing old and you stayed the same. You won't turn me into a vampire so, I feel I have to get as much time in with you as possible, but I can't if we're always fighting these damn fools. I wanted children, but it doesn't seem I'll be able to even enjoy that either. So knowing that, I want all of you to myself for as long as possible."

"I am so proud to finally have you as my own. You are an amazing woman Solis. You've survived a horrific childhood, escaped death, and you continue to stand strong. Sexy doesn't even begin to describe you, and words can't describe how happy you've made me."

Her warm breath on his lips sent his swollen shaft jutting through his Jockeys to press against her abdomen. She enjoyed every bit of arousing him, even when she was angry.

"Sssh, say no more. I repeat, you and only you have all of

me. Right now you have me…and I stand before you as your mate in need of you in the worst way. Won't you ease my ache Sweetheart?" Holding his hand out, he lured her to their bed.

He backed away from her to sprawl his towering frame over the California King with his shaft unyielding and stiff as a sail mast, waiting for her to guide him inside her moisture.

No longer angry, Solis climbed in bed and stood straddled over his face. Feeling naughty as any harlot on the street, she slowly bent over, peeling her thong from between her cheeks, revealing a trail of her own creamy arousal as it slid down the insides of her thighs.

"Woman you are making me crazy." Nacio licked his lips to keep from drooling. As the need to taste her grew stronger, his fangs extended.

"I'd better be, and don't you forget it."

Agonizingly slow, she continued her seductive teasing to lower her body over his shaft. The predator in him let loose, and he caught her hips in his grip and brought them to his face, tasting her as if for the first time. The laps of his tongue sent shudders through her as she cried out.

"Nacio, please don't stop. I couldn't stand it if you stopped. Don't stop."

"I won't. You are mine."

He turned her over on her back, while careful not to smash his heavy sac as it hung between his massive thighs. It was his turn to tease her. Taking his time, he guided himself into her inch by inch, making her more impatient.

"Give it to me. Give me what's mine." Moaning he continued to play tit for tat until Solis flipped the script and grabbed his cheeks from behind, plunging him so deeply into her that he cried out in ecstasy.

"I will never let you go…ever! As long as I walk this earth, you will never be free of me."

Words Solis waited for a lifetime to hear. Words that awakened her own instincts as she pulled him to her and forcefully bit his neck, causing his moans to shake the walls, releasing his seed he so willingly gave her. His release pulsated until his seed filled her womb full.

To her, his plasma never tasted so sweet, as she lapped. It was because she had tasted his plasma, the desire to have it was growing stronger as their love for each other grew.

"Take it, Sweetheart it's yours. Whatever you want is yours. I'm yours. All that I am is yours," he vowed as the pressure of another release sent shock waves through his body; the ecstasies making him declare his love in Spanish.

"Te quiero mucho, mi esposa. Te quiero por toda mi vida…siempre." He translated to her through misty tears.

"I love you so much, my wife. I'll love you all my life… always."

One last stroke brought her to a slippery climax that spilled out of her, washing over the sides of his sac to settle in the center of their bed.

Content, they lie tangled in the wet sheets as Solis drifted off to sleep in Nacio's arms. Holding a handful of hair, he softly repeated his vow.

"Te quiero, toda mi vida…siempre…always…always…I'll love you all my life…always."

✝

Thunder clapped as the rain peppered the rooftop. Eyes half lidded, Nacio lay under his mistress, listening to the rain hypnotically thrumming. He'd never paid much attention to the sound it made on the rooftop in the past, but tonight it was so soothing, so familiar. He listened closer as the thrumming grew louder and louder. A voice called out, commanding him.

"Come all children…your mother is here…Mother First is here. Come to me, come forth."

Completely enthralled, he fell under siege to an unseen force that summoned him, separating him from the comfort of his bed, from the arousing touch of his mistress, from the protection of the glamour spell around his home.

"Come ye forth…Mother First is here."

✝

Solis awoke with her teddy hanging off her shoulder, and her thong twisted around her ankle…and to an empty bed.

"Umm, I guess Nacio's downstairs."

Longing for another round of hot and sexy mischief, she put her desire on hold to go find him. She sprang out of bed and slipped into the red satin robe on the coat hanger.

Downstairs, she found Patience in the kitchen warming some plasma in a goblet. When she met eyes with Solis, she couldn't help masking a sneaky little smirk.

"I take it things are back to honeymoon business as usual with you two? The walls never lie you know," Patience alluded to the indiscreet screams of passion the couple shared, confirming their reconciliation.

"Yes, Nosy Mosy! We took care of business."

"You know he is insanely in love with you. You know that right?"

"I know, and I love him the same."

"He would do all within his power and kill anyone who stands in his way to protect you."

"I know. I just want to be able to protect him as well. By the way, has he come downstairs? I fell asleep, and when I woke up, he was gone. I thought he might have come down to have some plasma."

"He doesn't need protecting honey. He just needs to be loved, and you do that wonderfully. But no, I haven't seen him." Both women giggled as the cell phone Patience had in her robe rang. Basrick shouted in the phone.

"Mom, she's awake! Menlo just opened her eyes...she's

come out of the coma!"

"Darling, that's wonderful! Have they assessed her yet?"

"No, but I'll call you back afterwards."

"Basrick, please be careful. The storm is brewing, and I want you safe. Keep an eye out for the Treemounts. Solis explained that there is a Tornado Watch with a spin off storm…from the hurricane named Auldicia. Nacio and your father have reinforced the protection spell on the mansion."

"Mom, you don't believe the name of the storm has any merit, do you?"

"We don't know sweetie, but we hope not. You just be careful, okay?"

"I will. I love you."

"I love you too."

†

Menlo's eyes flicked open with a start. She glared at the lights over her bed without blinking. Basrick camped out at the hospital each day since Menlo took a bullet to the head. Instinct confirmed Bose and Justice caused her near-death experience. Kissing her face, he whispered in her ear, as he sounded the call light for the intensive care nurse to come to make her assessment.

"I knew you'd wake up, sweetie. I'm so glad you let me see those beautiful blues of yours once more. Thank you for coming back to me. As long as I'm here, this will never happen to you again…I swear my blood on it."

Menlo's eyes were wide open, fixed on the lights above her bed. In slow motion, she turned to look at Basrick, tears streaming down her face and unable to communicate verbally with the breathing apparatus down her throat. Grabbing her ears, she shook her head in agony.

The intensive care nurse rushed in to calm the now combative Menlo as she gripped her head, writhing beneath the sheets. Basrick stood near as the nurse gave Menlo a sedative. Anxiety eased as she calmed herself, allowing the nurse to slip the breathing apparatus out of her mouth. Her voice was hoarse and scratchy as the agitation left her body.

"Make it…make it stop…please. Please I don't want to go. I don't want to go."

Basrick looked on in bewilderment. He couldn't understand what she meant.

"Menlo, sweetheart what is it? What do you want to stop?"

"Don't you hear it? Listen… do you hear it?"

"No, honey I don't. What do you hear?"

"I hear it. It's calling me to come and go to her." After her last syllable spoken, she drifted off into a slumber.

Basrick was at a loss. He tried to get Menlo to speak, but she coasted off to sleep.

"Who, Menlo? Who's calling you?"

†

Menlo lay in twilight slumber as the thrumming in her head became louder and louder. The sound made rest impossible.

"Come forth children…come forth…Mother First is here."

"Don't they hear that sound; that message? Please, you all must make it stop!"

The thrumming vibrated throughout the corridors of her mind, enthralling her.

"Please make it stop."

†

"Basrick says that Menlo is awake," Patience told Solis. "The nurse is with her now."

"Wow, she has finally come out of her coma! He sure has been loyal to her."

"Yes, it's good to see he is beginning to heal and grieve the death of Basira less each day as we all are."

Just then, Armando shouted from upstairs, his voice shaken with despair.

"Patience, come quickly." Before another word left his lips, Patience blurred past Solis, and up the stairs to their suite."

In the crib, Blessing's eyes lit up like green emeralds; something had come to life within her; the cause unknown. Her eyes cast rays of light across the walls and ceiling.

"Good Gosh, Armando, what's happened to her?"

"I don't know, my love. She was asleep when suddenly the rays of light threw shadows across the room. I immediately became unnerved due to the sinister presence I felt, and then I called for you."

Solis swallowed hard as her stomach tied itself in knots. She backed away towards the door. The dread she felt grew stronger with each second.

"I'll get Nacio. He needs to see this. This isn't right. Something is wrong."

The French doors to the balcony outside their room swung wide open, wildly blowing the sheer curtains. She stood in the room alone. Fear eating away at any courage she possessed, she took a chance on telepathically calling out to him.

Nacio where are you? Baby please, tell me where you are? No answer; her question, unanswered. Sweetheart, please answer me.

Her worst fear is now a reality…Nacio was gone.

Childress Treemount

4

The Hunt is on

Childress mocked the Loas Agwe and Guede when she savagely killed her Aunt Bureau, thus placing more evil upon her family. Killing a blood related mambo was punishable with eternal flesh burning in Hell. Arrogance and conceit was enough for her to take her chances with her soul.

Urgata agonized over her mother's death, stunned at the fact that Childress would kill her mother without any regard. Urgata knew that there was no way Childress could have possibly known the fate that was to come her way for doing such a thing. Nayphous ran to comfort Urgata. He threw a hateful glance at Childress. This proved to be a bad move on his part.

"Childress, how could you kill your aunt like this? You have damned yourself."

"What the hell are you looking at, Nayphous? I'm going to find my child. Then I'm coming back here for you."

"I won't be here, so don't waste your time."

"Either you are with me or against me. Make the right choice."

"Like I said…don't waste your time."

Clearing pasty mucous from her throat, Childress spit in his face, and then stormed off. With power rolling through her veins, she barked out orders to assemble her brothers.

"Klein and Erland, let's go."

Urgata finally found her tongue to speak to the cousin she hated fiercely.

"Childress the gods are going to come for you soon, and I'll be there to see to it that you suffer for what you've done. I promise you."

Reveling in her new power, Childress allowed the hatred she had for Solis, Justice, and now for Urgata to drive her motives. Raising her hands to the sky, she whispered a hex that made all the on-lookers fall to their knees in fear.

"I am the Queen Mother. As the wind blows and rain washes the earth, I will destroy my enemies—starting with my brother Justice. He will be punished to death."

Childress turned and looked at Urgata and allowed her lips to turn in a wicked smile as she hexed her cousin.

"You have spoken your last words, my dear cousin. I hope you enjoyed them. You will speak no more."

Nayphous looked at Urgata as she stood before him terror stricken with no sound coming from her mouth. Childress muted her voice, rendering her unable to speak.

Childress laughed as Mother Nature threw a lightning bolt across the sky to hit a tree, causing it to slam into the gothic looking house as it stood by the swamp. A fierce wind split the sky, peeling the clouds back that formed in the night horizon, pouring torrential rains over the land. Black magic was the source of this storm, and all who stood in it were in grave danger.

Knowing that she wanted her brother Justice and Solis dead and to reunite with her daughter, she set out on her new mission.

"Let's go fools. I want my baby back."

Klein and Justice fell in line behind their new Priestess sister. Erland's hex that Bureau placed on him earlier dissipated, and he found his words once again.

"Ha ha, you got the damn hex now Urgata. See how it feels not to speak, you silly trick."

Erland's cruel taunt caused Urgata to fall to the ground near her mother Bureau's lifeless body. Bureau lay in a pool of her own blood. The last few drops curdled down her neck as Urgata held her mother in her arms one last time. Dilated and fixed eyes stared up at Urgata from her mother's face. With no words to speak, she couldn't even bid her mother farewell as she crossed over into the realm of the dead.

Holding her mother and rocking her slowly, Urgata jumped as her mother's hand grabbed her arm. Bureau's mouth moved as she attempted to deliver a silent warning to her daughter while holding her hand. Petrified, Urgata tried to free herself from her dead mother's grip but could only sit and watch her mother struggle to inform her of the message she had from beyond.

Bureau's cold fixed eyes focused on Childress, Klein, and Erland as they hurried to the Cadillac she once owned, to make their getaway. Unable to verbalize, Bureau communicated with her daughter telepathically, delivering a message from the voodoo gods Agwe and Guede to mark Childress and her brothers.

She comes, child…she comes. Auldicia has come from the depths of Hell. No one is safe. When you hear her call out to you, don't give in to her. She'll make you a condemned slave. Do not heed her call. She's calling all those in her bloodline now. Childress must pay for what she has done. Punishment is inevitable for her.

Mama what will you have me do? I don't know what to do…she's taken my voice.

That is only temporary my child…but you must stop Childress. You can't do it alone. Find her enemy, Solis Burkes. In order for Solis to fulfill her destiny, she must defeat Auldicia and Childress…you will be of great help in doing this. Do not let Childress find the baby… for if they do, our family, along with mankind, will perish. Childress will have to pay the debt she owes to the gods. They will hold her soul accountable for the debt, and she will suffer the rest of her days on earth until her debt is paid to them.

Urgata sat breathless as her mother instructed her on how to stop her deadly cousins.

Chant with me to put the Hex of Shadows in her eyesight. Each time she closes her eyes she will be haunted by demons.

Both women began the chant sent to Bureau from the angry

voodoo gods Childress duped when she spilled Bureau's blood instead of sacrificing the child to whom she gave birth.

Ahane, mumfundo santo imbende olango, ilalga. Let your eyes close once, twice during the night, and the shadows of the night will bring you fright…to suffer all your life.

Urgata watched as her cousins left in the storm. There was no way Childress knew what lie ahead of her, but she would soon find out.

Never forget I love you Urgata and always will. I've been blessed to be your mother in this world. Know that we will never be apart, and I will always be near you. I bequeath to you my knowledge and my power to become the new mambo of the south. You must help Solis defeat your Hell bound cousins.

I know mama. I love you too.

Urgata's eyes were burning hot as coals, as she looked in the direction her cousins had just fled. She pulled the sewing scissors from her mother's neck, and sliced a wound in her right hand. Placing her bleeding hand over her mother's now open flesh, Urgata mingled their blood together. In doing so, she escorted her mother's soul to the realm of the dead. Urgata closed her eyes as she watched her mother cross over, feeling her mother's soul slip away.

"Goodbye mama, until our souls meet again."

Among the crowd of onlookers, Nayphous stood silently behind Urgata, touching her shoulder. He knew his atonement must be sincere in order to correct the damage he'd done screwing around with Childress.

"Come on Urgata. Let's cover her, while we go in here and call the police. Childress and those dumb asses won't get far, but we have to get prepared for what's to come."

Urgata opened her eyes as she looked over her shoulder at Nayphous, touching her hand to his.

"No they won't get far. I will see to it that Childress's ass pays for what she's done. My mother just told me that she has released an ancient evil from Hell upon us. We have to find her enemy, Solis Burkes, and unite with her to stop Childress, and my ancestor Auldicia."

"Ahh, damn. She's really done it this time. It's going to take all we have to stop her."

"We?"

"Yes, we. You are not doing this alone Urgata. I love you, and I beg your forgiveness."

"It wasn't your fault Nayphous. She influenced you in the worst way."

"I love you, and I won't let you go."

Nayphous took Urgata in his arms, promising to love her from henceforth. His sentiments were admirable, but the fact remained he could still smell the scent Childress left on his upper lip from their sinful foreplay in his bed. He held Urgata close, as he looked over her shoulder in the direction of the Cadillac taillights in the distance.

Urgata gathered her strength to run arm in arm with Nay-phous heading toward the house. Inside, she raced to her mother's room to find the address book she kept in her drawer. Nayphous kept true to his intentions and sicced the police on Childress and her brothers. He quickly dialed 911 and reported Bureau's murder, to a bored operator.

"9-1-1…what is your emergency?"

"I'm calling to report a murder. The murderer is Childress Treemount and her brothers, Klein and Erland Treemount. Our location is…"

"Sir, I have your location, police and ambulance are on the way."

"Uh, ma'am, you need to send the Coroner…I said there's been a murder."

Alphabetized in her mother's neat handwriting, she dialed her sister Tahiti's number first.

"We're sorry, but you have reached a number that is discon-nected, or is no longer in service. If you feel you've reached this number in error, please hang up and try your call again," a disap-pointing all-too-happy recording suggested. Tahiti had run off several months ago after the birth of her son, Moffitt, the two year old with the man-sized head.

"Oh dammit, Tahiti! Where are you? Your mother is dead

and we can't even contact you," she uttered.

Nervous, she starts to dial her sister Menlo's number. A family rift had split her sibling off from the rest of the family. Menlo blamed their mother for her father abandoning them early on in childhood. She hadn't spoken to their mother in over 20 years. This phone call was not one she favored placing. She dialed the number, and the phone began to ring. Nayphous entered the room.

"We got her covered up. I called the coroner, but because of the storm it will be awhile before someone gets here."

"Thank you Nayphous." Just then, a man's voice picked up the phone.

"Hello?" Basrick's voice echoed clear and strong.

"Yes, I'm looking to speak with Detective, Menlo Kildare, please."

"She's unable to come to the phone at the moment. Who am I speaking with?"

Urgata's heart pounded beneath her wet blouse, still wet from rain and her mother's splattered blood. Giving the man her identity, she began to explain the tragic news.

"I'm Urgata, her sister."

"Hello, I'm Basrick Caraway, her...uh...friend. She's been hospitalized for a gunshot wound. Today has been a good day, and she is on her way to recovering just fine." He remained guarded on how much information to share with Urgata. He knew, from what Menlo told him and his family, they had not spoken in several years.

Urgata knew very little of her sister's life in the last 20 years, so she had no reason to question Basrick's relation to Menlo. Basrick certainly wished he were more to Menlo---far more.

"Will she be okay?"

"Yes. Her prognosis has changed and she should be discharged soon. Is there something I can help you with?"

"Well, sir, I called to let her know that our mother has passed away. Actually she was murdered."

"Murdered? You have my condolences." Basrick held Menlo's hand as he held her cell phone.

"Do you know how it happened?"

"Yes…my cousin Childress stabbed her to death on the night she gave birth to a baby girl."

Basrick stood silent on the other end of the line. Defensive strategies running through his mind, he formed his next words very slowly. He knew that baby girl he now considered his sibling; Blessing.

"Where is Childress now? She needs to be stopped."

"We've notified the authorities. My cousins took my mother's car. They won't get far. Childress explained that she was going to get her baby back, and she wants to kill her brother Justice."

Basrick smirked at the last statement. He had already disposed of Mr. Justice Treemount, making the world a better place. Again, not to give away too much he remained guarded.

"Once Menlo awakens, I will give her your message."

"I'll settle things here with the police. She and my mother haven't spoken in many years. I wanted to let her know about the arrangements once they are made, but I'm not sure if she will come to the funeral. I do miss my sister and would like to visit with her."

"You are free to come to the hospital, but she's in no condition to travel. It would be best for you to proceed with the arrangements for your mother. Please take photos so when Menlo is ready and able to process what has happened she can see the photos of her mother's funeral service."

Urgata agreed to Basrick's recommendations, given the circumstances of the relationship.

"I agree. I never got between mama and Menlo's differences, but I never stopped loving my sister."

Basrick expressed his concern for the situation at hand, "My worst fear is for Childress and that she might attempt to get back at you if she ever finds out you called the authorities on her."

"I'm not worried about her. She will get hers soon enough. After I'm done with the funeral I will be coming to see Menlo.

"She is hospitalized at Metropolitan Methodist." Basrick felt Urgata's concern for her sibling showed her sincerity in keeping their bond strong. With no deception detected in her tone, he felt confident to ask what her intentions were for Childress.

"Urgata, what do you plan to do?"

"I plan to avenge my mother's death."

Without hesitation, Basrick confirmed her upcoming visit to San Antonio.

"I'll see you in a few days."

†

It appeared the tables were turning quickly, with many variables changing, making the situation with the Treemount family worse.

Basrick remained with Menlo. Listless, even under the influence of a strong sedative, she winced as she slept. He called the mansion to notify Nacio and his parents of what's happened. The phone rang, and the sound of chaos coming from his mother's voice put him on edge.

"Basrick, Nacio's missing! He's gone!"

"Gone? What do mean, mom?"

Patience responded quickly as things continued to unravel at the Puente mansion. "He was here awhile ago, and now he's vanished. Solis is a wreck, Blessing's eyes are glowing green, and we don't know what's causing it all! Basrick, please be careful. We think maybe somehow it is all linked to Auldicia."

"Mom I just got off the phone with Urgata Treemount

LaDeaux, Menlo's sister. She called to tell her their mother was dead. Childress stabbed her to death on the night Blessing was born. Childress is on her way back to San Antonio, on the hunt for Justice and for Blessing."

Maternal instincts kicking in, while vampiric power rolled throughout her body. Patience readied herself for battle.

"Like I said son, let the bitch come and try to take this baby. She will receive a punishment she won't soon forget."

"Urgata is coming to visit with Menlo. She plans to stop Childress. Do you think we should align with her to stop them? If Nacio has gone missing, we are going to need all the help we can get."

"You said she is coming to see Menlo, correct?"

"Yes ma'am."

"Then make certain, this is not a trap. We don't know how she will feel if she found out we have been exterminating her people. Check her out to make sure her intentions are true. If that's the case, we can meet her somewhere in town until things are sorted out."

"How's Solis holding up?"

"Not good. She keeps trying to leave the safety of the glamour Nacio and your father put in place. Auldicia is out there somewhere, and we can't take a chance on our home being revealed."

"What do we do now, mom?"

"Wait for the best, son. It's all we can do at this point."

5

What I need

Gravel flew from underneath the carriage of the Cadillac DTS as Childress covered her now size 10 foot over the accelerator. Her dry ashy feet had grown during the pregnancy, now her foot planked over the gas pedal. Swollen, leaky breasts oozed milk each time her bra brushed against her nipples. At the first gas station they came to, she would have to change her maxi-pad. Drainage from the birth continued to trickle down, lessening each day. Klein commented on the wet breast milk stains visibly noticeable on her chest as she drove.

"Damn, girl. You oozing breast milk. Here, put some in this here cup, so when we stop I can get me some Frosted Flakes."

Not in a playful mood, Childress backhanded her brother, splitting his upper lip with a nasty cut.

"I bet you won't say nothing else, you moose faced bastard."

Erland let out one big cackle before her eyes fell on him in the mirror. His laugh quickly tapered off as he looked out the window.

An unfamiliar feeling of longing made Childress press

forward. The feeling of loss had only visited her when her mother died. This time the loss overwhelmed her. Believing the longing for her baby girl caused her feelings, she heard the first hallucination hit her.

You will never see your baby again you sorry wench. Believe that! The baby is gone, gone, gone, heeheeeheeheehee!

Childress shook her head as she hollered, thinking it had been Klein or Erland irritating her already anxious state of mind. Little did she know, Bureau's curse began the promised torment the dead mambo set in motion for her.

"Ya'll shut up you hear? Don't say that mess to me or I'll put your asses out on the side of the road, you hear?"

Confused, Klein turned and exchanged glances with his brother sitting in the back seat. Mental illness was no stranger to the family, but Childress had never experienced hallucinations…at least, not until now. Klein's impression of keeping order in the 100 mile an hour moving car proved no good.

"Quit driving so fast Childress! You gonna get us busted, hell. I told you, I can't go back to jail."

Childress paid her brother no mind, as she stomped her foot down on the accelerator pushing 120 miles per hour. The speedometer needle quivered, as did her hands while a visual hallucination visited her in the rearview mirror. A smoky, silver and black, formless shadow spoke to her with venom in its tone.

Yes, you wench, why are you driving so fast? I told you the baby is gone. Soon you will be too.

She slammed on the breaks, sending the car skidding into the side of a guardrail, causing sparks and catching the attention of a Louisiana State Trooper. His siren blared while he gained speed in his pursuit.

Sparks continued to fly with metal grinding away at the door. Coasting, the DTS finally came to a halt. Sirens continued the ear-splitting squeal until the door of the trooper's squad car swung open. A mean shaped, knock-kneed, thighs-rub-together, pigeon-toed, sweaty arm pit, country bumpkin Deputy approached the car and stopped 25 feet from Childress. With his gun drawn, he gave a command and expected it carried out. Wise, he had already called for backup.

"Get out of the car, and put yo' hands up, nah!"

Mere seconds passed, giving her little time to throw together a good lie in hopes of maintaining her freedom. Still a little shaky, she dared to look at the deputy in her rearview mirror… shaky, because she didn't want to look upon another silver/black shadow taunting her reflection.

She opened her car door. Preparing for her best damsel in distress, role she tore a split up past her thigh to her hip in hopes of enticing him. Audacious, she knew one look from her would coax an erection from him without her lifting a finger to touch him. His accent let her know, he grew up deep in the Jefferson Parrish area around Dogwater Swamp. She let loose in her native tongue, getting his attention.

Childress batted her eyelashes that hooded her jade green peepers. The lie she told came easily. She explained to him she tried to go to the corner store last Saturday to get a new battery for her car, but the store had closed, and now she was tired from the drive.

"Hey there, Cher. I was headed to the cawna sto' las Sad day fo' a new battry but they'd closed. I was tryin' to git my battry befo' this Sad day passed, and I'm tied, yea."

The Deputy's sweaty pits widened each step he took closer to Childress. Her two fools sat silently in the car as they watched the scene unfold.

White knuckles gripped the gun chamber as the Deputy smiled at her, uninfluenced by her mystic charm.

"Why I know you. You Frances dawhter, Childress. Boy, they afta' you an' these two fools. Ya'll goin' to jail, Cher."

"The hell I am." Childress raised her hands to the sky just as the Deputy pulled out a Ju Ju charm to block her spell. No stranger to certain parts of southern Louisiana life, the Deputy practiced a bit of voodoo and knew when a spell took place. Just then, she blinked while a silver/black shadow grinned over the deputy's shoulder, mocking her.

Like he said, you going to jail, wench. How ya' like me now?

The shadow lunged at Childress, knocking her to the ground. Her scream drowned in the pitch of more sirens when a fleet of Louisiana State Troopers arrived surrounding the wrecked Cadillac.

"This is the Louisiana State Police. You are surrounded,

get down on the ground and put yo' hands behind yo' head."

Neither of the brothers surrendered willingly. Klein attempted an escape.

"Be damned. Nuh uh! I owe child support, back pay, I sued a few, and I owe taxes. I ain't goin' back, I tell you. I ain't!" He leaped from the passenger's side and tried to make a run for it. He discovered his only escape meant taking a risk treading the waters with the inhabitants of the Sabine River, gators, moccasins, frogs and all. Screwed, he surrendered cursing and hollering about civil rights.

Overwhelmed at the unfolding events, Erland simply became catatonic and checked out. He held up his arms, standing frozen in place like a track athlete sprinting for the finish line. After hallucinating for weeks about dragonflies, a real one flew by and nested comfortably in the center of his scalp as his brother and sister surrendered.

In one of the state police cars was none other than Dr. Kross Malveaux, head Psychiatrist at the Huntsville State Penitentiary in Texas. Childress is a patient of Dr. Malveaux, and has been for the last several years. His eyes met those of his delusional patient. Hers glistened in the distance, as several female police worked swiftly to apprehend her into custody.

Dr. Malveaux felt exhaustion wash over him. He knew the kind of work that lay ahead of him. He needed to put Childress back in her right state of mind, if she ever had a right state of mind. A nearby state trooper voiced his opinion into his shoulder radio.

"10-4, we have suspects in custody. Repeat, we have suspects in custody, over. Indeed, we caught the hellions as they were trying to cross the border back into Texas."

The first responding deputy approached Childress reading her Miranda Law and stating the charges. Hot and agitated, a few curse words sat on the tip of his tongue, but he bit them back…for now.

"Childress Roarquel Treemount, you are under arrest for the following charges: The murder of Bureau Equel Treemount LaDeaux, aggravated assault with bodily harm, the murder of Detective Mathis Bouvier, resisting arrest, obstruction of justice, vehicular theft, fraud, larceny, kidnapping , and parole violation. If you give me a minute I could probably dig up about forty more charges between here and the Texas border."

For once, she stood silent then she laughed hysterically. Soon she found herself shuffled and corralled into a Paddy wagon.

A loud, child-like giggle slipped from the Deputy's throat as he walked over to Klein, and read his rights, then his charges.

"Mr. Klein Treemount, you are under arrest. The following charges are yours: the murder of Detective Mathis Bouvier, kidnapping, parole violation, three counts of murder in Texas, fraud, tax evasion, child support arrearage, aggravated assault with bodily injury, aggravated sexual assault, theft, grand larceny, possession of a controlled substance with the intent to distribute, grand theft auto, and finally unlawful possession of a firearm."

Klein spit a large wad of phlegm in the Deputy's direction, landing with a pasty thud in the back of his closely cropped nape. The man stopped dead in his tracks, as the hot spit slid down his neck. He turned and let his southern expletives verbally assault Klein.

"Why you glove compartment sized nose ass Sumbitch! They gon' tho' you ass underneath the jail, and dare somebody to come claim you."

It was all Klein could do to keep from sniveling as the Deputy walked away. They packed him away in a filthy-from-the-inside-out squad car as he hollered for Childress who was also under siege.

Making his rounds, the happy deputy heel-toed over to Erland. He shook his head regretfully as he stood before the catatonic young man. He read his rights, but choked in more giggles as he attempted to read the charges.

"Somebody come git 'dis damn fool outta here. Call down to the State Hospiddle and let 'dem know we got a live one here."

Two hefty law enforcement agents picked Erland up by his arms, stiff as a board. Rigidity had set in, and they found that his muscles allowed no flexibility. They shackled him standing straight up in the back of his own separate Paddy wagon. Literally, this vehicle came with padding for Erland's safety, due to his mental fits that seemed to come over him at the strangest of times, like now. The community knew of the Treemount family history, and the arrests today were no different.

All of the Louisiana State Police roared, high-fived and clapped each other on the back for the big bust they just completed. The Treemounts had made national news for months and now they were in custody. It appeared to be a time to celebrate, but Dr.

Malveaux knew otherwise as he stood in the distance watching his patient.

"Ya'll have no idea what you've done, but I'm sure we will find out soon enough."

✝

"Stop driving this damn truck so rough! Oooh…you just wait 'til I get outta here. I'm going to put a hex on you so tough you are going to scratch the skin off you own ass for relief. I mean it. Let me loose, I tell ya. Let me loose!"

Childress whooped and hollered all the way to the New Orleans Police Department. Trouble for her had just begun, but she had no plan to escape it just yet. Spooked, she had been afraid to use her abilities, for fear of another shadow vision taunting her.

Upon arrival, her entourage consisted of two female guards walking 9 feet ahead of her, flanked by six guards on either side of her, and two walking behind her. Shackles on her ankles only allowed short quick steps, which she needed to keep up with the fast moving guards. Nearly falling twice, one female guard named L. Duchamp caught her by her blond-red curls before she hit the floor, tearing the follicles from her scalp. The guard shook the hair free from her fingers. Rage set in, and the threats came once more.

"Let's go Treemount, and quit clowning."

"Listen here, Cher. I promise when I get loose, I'm gon' tear yo' ass up…just so we're clear and there are no hard feelings about the ass whoopin'. Got it?"

"Yeah, yeah, yeah. But you forget, you are back in *The Clink* where you belong, hussie! And guess what? You will be here for a very, very, long time."

All of the guards escorting Childress, front, side, and behind, heckled in laughter as they arrived inside. Metal cage locks slammed shut after the other guards buzzed them into different cellblocks to get her processed in. Her extended fingers needed dipping through black smudgy ink to confirm her fingerprints. She was to serve her time in jailbird orange scrubs with tan flip flops for her feet.

An escort took her by the arm and held the door open to an isolated cell monitored by closed circuit television from across the hall. The cell door slammed shut, engaging the locks. Reality finally hit Childress.

"Damn, I'm in *The Clink*...again."

Looking to grasp the severity of her situation, Childress sat still on the bench, while four crickets jumped across the floor, chirping in unison. Soon, she heard the low audible pitch. At first, the sound appeared garbled, then it steadied. That sound, that low humming sound that seemed to grow in strength.

"Where is that noise coming from? Why does it sound so familiar? I know that sound and I'm going to follow it."

The thrumming she heard called to her. She jumped from the bench and clenched the bars, in hopes of finding someone to set her free. Vacancy filled the halls.

"Hey, where is everybody? Help me. Let me out!"

"Pipe down Treemount, or else you won't like what's going to happen to you." Female guard L. Duchamp played dangerously close to the edge of her patience.

"Keep on threatening me, hear? I will make good on my promise I made earlier."

The guard shot the finger at Childress, as she gave a wheeze like snicker. The thrumming continued to grow. She knew she had to bide her time.

"It won't be long now."

†

Dr. Malveaux followed Klein and Erland to the New Orleans Police Department. Starting his work with Childress once more wasn't exactly what he wanted at this point in his life. His recovery from his last encounter with Childress still lingered over him from time to time. His wife nearly left him twice after hearing him moan her name while he slept. She formulated the notion he had been involved with her, and it was the cause of his transient erectile dysfunction.

He knew he couldn't go back to working with her if he wanted to save his relationship, yet a small part of him couldn't shake her enchantment. Childress represented a danger to his nuptials, so the good doctor decided to take a different approach and work with the next worst sibling in custody, Klein Treemount.

Klein and Erland had each gone their separate ways during the process into custody. Both men had a weak psyche, penetrable and easily manipulated with little stimulus. Oh, Dr. Malveaux had never spoken with either of the brothers, but surely for them to act as accessories to murder led him to believe them as simple-minded. When he arrived at Klein's cellblock, Dr. Malveaux remembered a scene from his favorite movie---the part where Clarice Starling met the notorious Dr. Lechter for the first time.

The surroundings in the cellblock presented several similarities. Acts of perversion took place openly for anyone to see. One inmate displayed a poster of a bikini clad blond on the wall. In the poster where the blonde's thighs met, the inmate sat licking the paper, making wet pasty slurping sounds as he enjoyed himself.

In the next cell, the inmate sat on a bucket-sized toilet with a clothespin attached to one nipple. During his elimination session, the inmate moaned in pleasure while the sewage smell wafted through the corridor. Dr. Malveaux quickly fetched his sweat-drenched handkerchief from his coat pocket to cover his nose and mouth until his arrival at Klein's cell.

Mr. Treemount sat with over three quarters of his body naked. He had taken off his scrubs, and tied the pants into a diaper with the shirt draped over his back like a cape. Startled, his eyes assessed Dr. Malveaux with suspicion.

"Who dat? And what 'da hell you want?"

Clearing his throat for clean smelling air, Dr. Malveaux took his first uncovered breath to introduce himself to Klein.

"Pardon me, Mr. Treemount. We haven't met yet. I'm Dr. Kross Malveaux, Psychiatrist. I've been assigned to help you during your stay here."

Confused, Klein let his 9 months of being back in the swamp linger in his dialect, and quickly responded to Dr. Malveaux, ending his question in "man."

"You said you here to 'hep me? How 'da hell you gon' hep me, man?"

Again, clearing his throat for clean air, Dr. Malveaux responded cautiously. He hadn't determined if Klein knew he had already worked with Childress. The police had sent him in with a wire attached to his chest to obtain a confession, hopefully one that would send the family to prison forever…although the death penalty would serve just fine.

"You say yo' name is Malveaux?"

"Yes sir."

"Uh huh. Well uh, whatcha want?"

"I'd like to know what happened to get you locked up… again. I'd like to see what we can do to get you in a position to help yourself."

"Whatcha mean like a plea or what?"

"Exactly, son. Do you think you could tell me what happened?"

"Yeah, I can do that. You ready?"

"Alright, son. That's a good idea. Let's start with your brother Erland."

"You mean, why don't we start with my sister Childress?"

Dr. Malveaux looked up from his iPad, as dread cloaked him. With his cover blown, his intentions had been clear all along. Evidently, Klein knew of Dr. Malveaux's relation to Childress, and suspected the police were setting him up for a confession. He wasn't buying it.

"I knew who 'da hell you is when you first come, and I ain't sayin' a damn thing. So take dat der clipboard or whateva da hell it is and git gone, ya bastard."

Stunned, Dr. Malveaux watched as Klein threw his make shift cape over his shoulders. Dressed like Superman, he stuck his left leg out and did the Stanky Leg, while he threw the finger at Dr. Malveaux signaling the interview had ended.

After Dr. Malveaux left, Klein sat himself on the corner of the bench. He caught his breath, and then the low thrumming sound settled between his ears, shaking his brain. Paranoid, he slapped his ears, thinking a cricket had somehow crawled inside.

"What the hell is dat? Dat damn humming sound?"

He hollered for the guards, but no one came.

"Hey, some bugs done crawled down in my ears. Bring me a flyswatter."

†

The opposite side of the jail proved to be a bit cleaner, but no less bizarre. Psychiatry is the study of the mind. It is the definition that defined Dr. Malveaux for the last 30 years. Every so often, the behavior of a delusional patient conjured a raised eyebrow from him.

Erland Treemount remained confined in a padded room with a small piss stained mat on the floor. Although a chair sat in the corner of the room, he continued his statuesque stance, frozen in place like a track runner, running some unknown race. Dr. Malveaux deducted Erland's catatonic physical immobility presented itself due to his drug abuse and withdrawals.

Dr. Malveaux indulged in the opportunity to glance at only the top of the stacks and stacks of Erland's mental health history. Schizophrenia labeled his DSM-IV-TR Axis I diagnosis. Knowing his efforts would be a lost cause, Dr. Malveaux tried to communicate with Erland.

"Hello, Mr. Treemount. My name is Dr. Kross Malveaux. I'm here to help you."

No response came from Erland. He simply refused to acknowledge verbal stimulus. Dr. Malveaux made certain to snap his fingers in front of Erland's face, and he noted the lack of response in his assessment.

"This is a sad waste of time here." He turned and left the cellblock.

After Dr. Malveaux left, the inaudible thrumming only the two older siblings seemed to hear finally seemed to get a physical response from Erland. The vibration lured him to a state of lucidity, bringing one arm down, then the other as his lips curled in a smile. The thrumming grew louder in his head, and he began to laugh hysterically.

†

A week passed since Childress and her siblings went to jail. Too dangerous to let out, all court hearings took place via video conference. The authorities had decided it was best to keep all three separated in case of an escape attempt. Her shadow hallucinations seemed to have stopped, but trouble started the first day of her lock up, and each day thereafter.

While incarcerated, Childress encountered a balding, hulking female inmate named Dozer, short for Bulldozer. A ripped torso and cannon sized biceps sat atop a V shaped waist making it clear Dozer was the cellblock bully. Mean-shaped from what looked to be a lack of estrogen, Dozer had no hips, no breasts, and buttocks behind her. With her long legs and short torso, they gave the appearance her crack started in the middle of her back, ending between her knees.

Dozer loved to humiliate others by inflicting pain and watching them bleed. Insecure, lonely, and threatened, she traveled with a little pack of bitch dogs who owned similar personalities.

A short female, round as she was tall named Presser, followed Dozer everywhere she went. The imp-like female's dwarfed limbs and fingers dangled at her sides as she walked with heavy fluid-filled feet. Jealous, envious, and resentful of Dozer and those around her, she used a low tone when speaking, except when she used her voice to instigate fights, spread rumors, and cause discord among the inmates.

Dozer's other Hench-wench, named Burla, looked just as hideous as her counterparts. She'd spent the last 20 years in and out of jail. Her face looked like it had melted off her bones, with skin settling under her neck. The skin flapped and slapped against itself during each conversation she held. Always smelling like Liniment, a person's eyes watered in her presence.

A habitual liar, Burla's claim to fame showed in her ability to swindle common folk and businesses alike. The entire gang looked to start trouble with the "fresh meat" on the cellblock.

Watching the three women enter the mess hall for meals, truly gave meaning to the phrase "misery loves company." Zeroing in on Childress sitting at a table alone, the Hench-wench pack surrounded her as her eyes focused on her food. Dozer tapped Childress on her shoulder, damn near dislocating it.

"You think you cute don't cha'? You'sa yellow-bone Creole who thinks she's cute don'tcha? Hey everybody, look at this trick here. She thinks she's cute. Oh and what's this? You leaking too girl? You pregnant or did you just have a baby? You got a mess there on your scrubs."

Childress said nothing, kept eating, and never looked up at Dozer. Still longing for her baby, she had no way to stop the leaking breast milk. Her not answering aggravated the bully, causing her to slap the tray from under Childress to crash on the floor.

"You hear me talking to you girl?"

Laughter exploded in the mess hall, as the androgynous

female inmates found humor in humiliating Childress.

Mere seconds passed before she looked up from the table. Certain the hallucinations had gone, she found the courage to fight back. Eyes in high definition green, Childress worked a scathing spell that redefined humility. The mess hall fell silent when her eyes landed on Dozer.

"Van coodo, ilampa, menhedo, altonde. You will not be able to sit or stand without protection."

Everyone standing in the mess hall heard the rumbling in Dozer's gut, then the squirting sounds began cutting through the air. A beaded sheen settled above her lip. Gastrointestinal cramps slammed into her torso. Clenching her buttocks together, Dozer quickly ran sideways toward the latrine as her bowels gave way. Presser and Burla backed away from the table, running to clear a path for Dozer and to flee from Childress.

Childress hooted and hollered her cackling laugh, signifying her victory over the Hench Wenches and their roid-raging leader. A face-slapping smell twisted the expressions of the nearby inmates, accompanied by a brown gooey trail of spots where Dozer dotted her way to the latrine. Satisfied her point had been made and well taken, she declared herself the new sheriff in town.

One guard passed the mess hall, shook his head, and kept to his leisurely stroll to the next cellblock.

"Alright you freaks, its time you get the message. The next one in here to make a move will find out what it's like to have your ass on fire."

No one blinked, breathed, or moved. Fear settled in with a new purpose.

"Have I made myself clear, Cher? If I'm not clear, I will make it crystal clear for you when the guard comes and scrapes the remainder of your ass off the side of this here building. Now, who's with me?"

The shift of allegiance in the room kicked up dust as the rubber from the inmates flip flops skidded to stand behind Childress.

"Damn right…that's what I'm talking about. You dirty twits work for me now, and that includes loose-ass, Depend Diaper wearing Dozer. Y'all got any questions?"

Everyone shook their heads quickly, terrified to even take a breath.

"I thought not. Now gather your asses 'round. We got work to do, Cher."

†

Once big and bad, now belittled and wearing an adult diaper, Dozer sat closely to the right of Childress and the latrine; stomach still bubbly and taking labored breaths. The rest of the Hench Wenches sat with their ears tuned in like antennas listening to Childress plot a jailbreak for tonight.

"I've found a way out this bastard, and y'all are gonna help me and my brothers make a move you hear?"

All heads nodded in unison. Childress thought she heard a whimper of protest from Dozer as she turned and looked in her direction. She grinned sheepishly, as she realized Dozer's stomach still bubbled and echoed through the silence in the mess hall.

"Take your stomach in there and crown the throne, Dozer. Hell, I can't hear myself think."

Dozer excused herself, taking slow cautious steps at first, and then broke into a jog to the toilet slamming the door behind her.

"Now what was I saying? Oh yeah, we are leaving to-night. There's a commissary truck coming through tonight, and me, Klein, and Erland will be in it. We need a distraction to make a move, and then we are gone. Anybody not with me on this, I will consider against me, and you see what I do to those against me and those who stand in my way. Do any of you really want to take a chance on what happened to Dozer happening to you? 'Cause, trust me, it's going to be ten times worse."

Burla spoke up on behalf of her and Presser, "We're in. What time is this going down?"

"Tonight is a full moon, so midnight. I'm going to distract that guard Duchamp, and then you need to come up with your own diversion. Once that truck rolls through at midnight, my brothers and me are gone. Got it?"

"Yeah we got it."

Just then, the door to the latrine swung open, and all that stood by gasped in disgust. Dozer slowly walked through the path made for her.   She eased her sore butt down on a bench at the table. Her face twisted in pain as those around her snickered. Childress grinned and paid her a compliment.

"Girl, you look cute, now sit your sore ass down and don't move 'til I say move."

†

Thirty minutes before midnight came quick and fast. Everyone made roll call, and sat in their cells. The same held for the male side of the jail. Klein and Erland shared the same cellblock but on opposite ends. Word had gotten to Klein and he received the drop on what was going down, and his anxiety took over. He finally untied the shirt to his scrubs he had been using as a cape, and unfolded his scrub pants he had worn as a diaper and loincloth.

On the women's cellblock, Childress was cool as a cucumber, looking out through her cell bars. Her eyes shifted back and forth, while guard L. Duchamp rattled her baton over the rusty metal. The clank made chips of rust fall to the floor, covering the toe of the guard's boot. Duchamp stopped and visited a minute.

"Well, look here. Are you comfortable Ms. Treemount? Heard you had a baby. Sure hope she doesn't wind up in here someday."

That comment alone, broke her concentration and Childress prowled close to the edge of the bars, holding Duchamp's gaze.

"You know I told you, when I got out of here, I was gonna tear your ass up. I meant what I said."

"Well, you won't see the light of day from the other side for a long time now will you Treemount?"

"Don't count on it tramp." Childress reached through the bars and snatched a piece of hair from the root in Duchamp's hairline. She mumbled a chant, hexing the female guard into a drunken trance. Soon, Duchamp unlocked the cell, while Childress stood in front of her.

"I told your ass once I was loose, I was gonna let you have it." Childress balled up her fist, drew back her arm, and sent a right upper cut across the guard's chin. Duchamp dropped to the floor like a fifty-pound bag of russet potatoes. Grabbing the keys attached to Duchamp's belt, she ran down the hall at the end of the cellblock and opened the storage closet. She found a cord and douche bag sealed in plastic.

Childress took the cord from the douche bag, and tied Duchamp's wrists behind her back. Before she left, she couldn't resist one last jab, at the now unconscious Duchamp. Childress kicked the apprehended guard in her stomach.

"Told you! You just got your ass handed to you, the Treemount way."

Childress worked a spell to cut the alarms, and then she unlocked the cell and freed the Hench Wenches. She gave instructions to them to meet her at the truck, ready to go.

"Beat the hell out of anybody that returns to that truck, and hold it until me and my brothers' get there you hear?"

"Yeah, we'll be there," Dozer said.

With the alarms disabled, she made her way over to the male cellblock. Uncertain of how long the spell would last, she acted quickly. A hunky brown skinned male guard with bulging biceps and a bulge below the waist accented by tight polyester uniform pants patrolled the cellblock. Childress stood in his path and slipped her shirt over her head, just as he reached for the whistle around his neck to sound an alarm.

She stood like bait before him, with her nougat colored breasts perky and at attention. Once his eyes fell on her assets, she ran and straddled her legs around his waist kissing him into distraction. The guard held her around his waist, while she reached for the keys on his belt. He cupped her breast in hand, and she caught his gaze.

"Rape, rape," She hollered. Soon the guard dropped her and ran. Childress pulled her shirt back overhead. She found Klein and freed him.

"Hey, where's Erland?"

"Down there in the Psych Ward."

"We need to get going now."

As Klein said, their baby brother sat locked up at the end of the cellblock in a padded cell. Relieved he no longer stood catatonic, they found him swatting at imaginary who knows what when they peeked at him through the observation window. With the stolen keys she took from the easily enticed guard, she set their baby brother free. Erland was glad to see his sibling, but anxiety had set in as well.

"Hey man, can you hear that? It's been in my head for the last week. That humming won't stop."

Klein agreed with his brother. "Yeah man, I hear it too. Where is it coming from Childress?"

"I believe it might be her. Auldicia. If she's here then we are getting ready to do some real damage around here."

"Auldicia? You mean *The* Auldicia? The one you said mama talked about in that book or whatever?"

"Yeah, that one. We have to find her."

"I think this noise is getting louder."

"Yeah, well, we'll follow the noise 'til we find her. Right now, we need to get the hell out of here. I don't' know how long this spell is going to last."

"Alright, well let's sky-up outta here, and head home. Then we will have to get another car, because we can't roll around in a damn jail commissary truck back to SA."

"Yeah, Yeah, one step at a time. Let's go."

✝

The three fools made their way behind the mess hall. Childress saw two legs sticking out from behind the dumpster. They belonged to the driver of the commissary truck. The Hench Wenches did their work as told, and sat crouched in the shadows waiting for their arrival.

Dozer had on the driver's uniform down to the baseball cap. Her manly shape proved negligible to the driver's, so as they left the campus of the jail, the gate guards would not find anything suspicious while they drove through the gates.

The marauders loaded themselves in the truck and started for the gates. At the checkpoint, the guards simply waved Dozer through giving them the okay to pass. Once on the other side of the gate, they all slapped and high-fived each other while Childress crawled in the passenger's seat. She looked in the side view mirror as the New Orleans jail became distant in the view. She chunked the duce to the jail in her view.

"Kiss my ass. I'm gone!"

Dozer looked over at Childress and asked a wondering question, as she drove.

"Where we headed?"

"Get me back to San Antonio, ASAP."

6

Choice Made

"Where is he? He's gone, Armando. My husband is gone! I know she's behind this, I know she is. Auldicia is the cause of all of this!"

Solis couldn't keep it together anymore. The love of her life had literally walked out the door, with no good-bye or farewell. Armando, always the voice of reason, stood by to provide comfort while things came crashing down.

"Patience, please stay with her while I go outside to check to see Nacio is outside on the grounds."

"Be careful, Sweetheart," Patience cautioned, as she held onto Blessing, whose eyes still glowed laser beam green. "We can't afford to have anymore mishaps."

"I will, Honey," Armando's voice whispered. "Just stay with her. We've got to find Nacio or things go from bad to worse."

Outside, Armando searched the garage building behind the mansion. Only the cars stood in the building. He teleported to the attic, only to find it filled with old paintings and artifacts. Next stop, the basement that was the entire size of the mansion itself, was Armando's final stop. He walked through the entire basement floor, and found nothing.

Just before he began his teleport back upstairs to the emotional chaos, Armando found a copy of a photo of Nacio and Solis lying on a bookshelf with some old textbooks that belonged to Solis. Nacio held Solis close in the photo taken at the Texas Taste Tease when the two first met. Another copy of the photo stands in a platinum frame on Nacio's desk in the library.

Back upstairs, Solis stood over by the window looking out into the night sky. Armando walked slowly to his bride with the photo of Nacio and Solis. Patience knew the search turned up empty.

Solis turned from the window, eyes full of tears. She looked upon Armando's face. She feared the worst, as reality set in. Armando handed her the picture of her and Nacio, and shook his head as misty tears seeped from his eyes. Solis lost it.

"No! No! He's not coming back is he?"

Armando stood silent, and wept with Patience by his side. The little family hugged each other and stood by while Solis let go.

"Nacio!"

†

Basrick sat in his usual place at Menlo's bedside. With her steady progress, she was transferred to a regular room. The hospital offered a state of the art physical therapy system for recovering neurological patients. Three times a day the physical therapy team came in and massaged her muscles and flaccid limbs, so that being bedridden wouldn't rob her of more muscle mass than necessary.

Looking at her for the last few hours made him feel things he couldn't explain; like how her small whimper in her sleep would make him want to kiss her lips softly, reassuring nothing would harm her again. Admittedly, he had stolen a few kisses while she lay comatose. The urge to bite his wrist and feed her his blood tormented him daily. He knew he could quicken her recovery, but felt unsure how Menlo would react to him since the betrayal she experienced with Bose.

Desire often seemed to take him at the most inopportune moments. Some nights as she lie asleep he would watch the rise and fall of her breasts under the thin sheet. Impulsivity and the natural predator within him struggled not to cause this innocent woman any more troubles than the ones that already plagued her. Although she had awakened off and on to eat and to respond to the nurse and attending physician's assessment, he and she had not spoken much. He wrote it off as emotional and physical shock.

Breathing steady and gently, the cord of her vein pulsated under the skin of her delicate neck. He wondered what her blood tasted like. Oh sure, he smelled it the night she was shot and brought to the hospital, but he wanted a taste. Two things happened simultaneously. His fangs erupted from his gum line, and his shaft stiffened just as the night nurse made her rounds.

Caught off guard, he put his hands in his lap in hopes of hiding his straining erection, but the crown surged over the top of the button on his jeans, settling just under his shirt. It looked as if he housed a ball peen hammer in his jeans. Thoughts of her heavy brown hair free falling over her breasts while sprawled out in his bed made him ache. The nurse breezed in, completed her assessment, and left. Menlo lie very still in bed. Her eyes fell on him and they never left.

"Why have you stayed here day after day with me? You don't have to do that you know?"

"I know I'm under no obligation, but I'm afraid my heart says differently."

Menlo tilted her head to look at him directly. Sensing she had no fear of him, Basrick moved in closer to her. Their lips inches apart.

"Thank you for being here with me. I don't want to see Bose ever again. He and Justice did this to me."

"I know Sweetheart, but you don't have to fear. Nacio killed Bose."

Her expression changed as she held her breath. Tears slid from the corners of her eyes as she looked up at the lights over the bed.

"And Justice? What of Justice?"

"Uh, well uh, Justice won't hurt you again either."

"Nacio killed him too?"

"No...I did."

Menlo held his gaze. Reaching out, she touched his face. No longer able to hold back, Basrick conveyed his desire with a kiss that melted away any insecurity or uncertainty she held.

"I've waited to do that for a while now."

"How long have you waited?"

"Since the night you walked into the mansion, and left with Bose."

Prior to her involvement with Bose, Menlo enjoyed pleasure since her first sexual experience as a teenager. Being a female police officer, she had to establish her bravery quickly. Carrying a gun, and having one pointed at you is serious business. There is no room for shyness or hesitation in the line of duty when your life or the life of someone else depends on it.

Fear no longer existed in her character, giving her a liberation to experience things openly, aggressively, and completely uninhibited. Her liberation allowed her to enjoy her sexuality without regret. If she found herself attracted to someone, she let her attraction to them be known. Although she had enjoyed being with Bose, she did indeed regret how things turned out with him, yet here she is...attracted to another vampire. It puzzled her as to why her feelings had her in the same situation again with Basrick.

Hearing him speak those words caused Menlo to pull him closer for another kiss laced with passion, causing him to ripple time. This would insure no more nurses would interrupt them while Menlo allowed her hands to linger underneath his shirt. Movement stopped all around them. The minute hand of the clock on the wall sat suspended, and Basrick's ability remained in full play.

The heel of her palm grazed the tip of his shaft, still straining and now stretching out from the top of his jeans. She licked her lips at the sight of his crown. He shuddered with anticipation.

"I won't do anything unless you ask me to."

"I'm asking you to do everything."

"Everything?"

"Everything."

"I've wanted to taste you. I've had to teleport down to the lab and pilferage a few bags of plasma to ward off my thirst for you."

"Bose bit me. You might not want my blood."

"I desperately want you, but I'm afraid if I bite you once more, you will be turned."

"I see. Well in that case, there are other ways to taste me."

With an acknowledging glint in Basrick's sky blue eyes, Menlo let her knees fall open under the sheet. Basrick knowingly obliged her request by folding back the sheet and settling between her thighs. A smile curled the corners of his lips as he dipped to taste her. Menlo arched her back as she grabbed hold of his head in response.

Feeling her hips jerk in pleasure as he suckled her flesh, Basrick felt all the guilt of feeling like a failure leave him. The redemption of protecting Menlo chased away the guilt of Basira's death. Intimacy with a lover is a privilege, one he hadn't experienced often. He knew her scent would linger on his skin for hours, intoxicating him and causing him to yearn for more.

Her moans for the pleasure only he could provide gave him a new purpose.

"Please don't stop. That feels amazing." One more dip of his textured tongue sent her through three squirting climaxes that left her in a pool of sweat.

"I want to hold you in my hand Basrick."

Without hesitation, he stood at the side of her bed and allowed her to free his shaft. Amused at her reaction, his smile soon turned to a moan and she began stroking him with both hands.

"I can't wait to have this."

"I can't wait to give it to you." His hips bucked in a fury, and her hands tugged and released faster and faster. Holding back was no longer an option.

"Menlo, I'm about to explode!"

A soft spilling sound pushed through the air, as his milky white seed gushed across her sheets by the cupfuls.

Their lips met once more, as she melted into his arms. He curled up beside her in the bed. He sniffed her hair, while she drifted off in a slumber. Basrick's emotional connection appeared stronger than ever.

"My purpose has returned, and I am restored."

†

After her nap, Basrick knew he would take his time bringing Menlo up to speed on what occurred since her hospitalization. He started the conversation off gradually, working up to Bureau's death and Urgata's expected visit soon.

"Menlo, there are some things I have to explain to you. I've been trying to wait until the right moment. But it appears time is working against us."

Tension in her shoulders indicated to him she braced for the news. No matter the severity, no matter how tragic, she waited for what he had to say.

"Your sister Urgata called your cell phone. She explained your mother was killed."

"What? When?" Menlo gasped, closing her eyes to comprehend what Basrick just said.

"She said a few weeks ago. You hadn't been as lucid as you have the last few days. So she and I have been in contact, but there's more Menlo," Basrick paused.

"It was Childress who killed your mother. Urgata explained Childress killed her in a voodoo sacrifice to the Loas just after your mother helped her give birth to a baby girl. Childress was supposed to sacrifice the baby to the Loas, but killed your mother to sacrifice to them instead of the baby. Justice brought the baby to us the night I killed him. She lives in the mansion with my parents. They named her Blessing. We assumed Justice went to Dogwater Swamp to get the baby and brought her back to San Antonio to give to my parents. I guess he was trying to atone for killing my sister Basira. I extend my condolences to you for all your pain."

Menlo cried hot tears in front of angry red eyes. Guilt found a new home in her conscience. She lay silent, as the reminders of her 20-year feud with her family flooded the corners of her mind. Her sorrow lasted only moments before the contempt she held for her cousin set in.

"Where the hell is Childress now? Nothing will be right until I have her ass in the ground. Where is she?"

"No one knows for sure, but there have been a string of events my parents seem to think is leading up to a much worse situation."

"What do you mean?"

"Nacio has gone missing. Solis said he left in the middle of the night, and no one seems to know where he is. Blessing's eyes have mysteriously started glowing green, and the storm that we have had for the last few days, including the tornado that touched down over on the North side earlier this week, we believe is tied to Auldicia."

"Wait what did you say? Auldicia? My great ancestor?"

"Yes. Urgata explained the gods weren't all satisfied with the offering Childress made. They expected the blood of a legacy child. Somehow in the middle of everything, Auldicia has returned."

"Then it's her I've been hearing in my head. It caused me to awaken."

"What do you mean?"

"I keep hearing this thrumming in my head. It's gotten louder just recently."

"What does it sound like Menlo? Is it a voice, a tone, or what?"

"It's like a voice and a tone at the same time, but more like a vibrating hum, but within the pattern, the message is...Mother First is here."

"Well this confirms our suspicions. Indeed, she has returned."

"So what do we do now?"

"We need to wait for Urgata to come for her visit with you. We'll start from there and once I know what Urgata knows, I'll let my parents know. Right now, Solis is going to need all the help she can get."

"That bitch Childress and those idiots have a lot to pay for. I'll make sure their payback is as painful as any they have caused."

"We need to get you ready to see you sister. I want to be here when she comes...if you want me to be, that is."

"Why would you go someplace else now? You've been with me all this time. I don't think I could stand it if I lost your support now."

"I'm worried about this 'summons' you are getting from Auldicia. I don't want to lose you either."

"I'll speak with my sister when she comes. Perhaps we can come up with a spell to help us and to help," Menlo paused. "Did you say Childress had a baby?"

"Yes."

"So I have a second cousin, named Blessing?"

"Yes."

"If her eyes are glowing green, it probably means she is hearing the summons as well. We will need to come up with a spell of some sort to keep her from heeding to its draw."

"I followed up on the research Bose was supposed to inform us of. It's how I learned what he was up to. I figured out he was involved in your shooting."

Menlo sat stunned, listening intently as Basrick clarified the details of Bose's betrayal.

"I read the manifests of the slave ship that Bose arrived on, during his enslavement. The slave that cared for him put a binding curse on him during his life. That binding spell must have kept him from showing his true colors all these centuries. The slave manifest identified Bose as a direct descendant of Auldicia."

Embarrassed at Basrick's revelation, he confirmed what she already knew, "Yes, Bose offered an ultimatum to join him on his quest with his 'mother' on her return to earth."

Disgust smeared her face as her mind flooded with memories of Bose Puente. She knew without a doubt she would punish Childress, and do everything within her power to keep Blessing from falling into the hands of her mother. Havoc would surely befall all of them if Blessing returned to her mother's custody.

"You said Urgata is coming here to see me?"

"She should arrive here first thing tomorrow morning. After the visit, I'm headed home to check in on things, and help come up with a strategy to get Nacio back. I need to check in on things over at the Puente Masonry as well. Mr. Hymn Platt, the new Foreman can run things for a while during my absence. We're going to need his help, because I don't believe this situation will end anytime soon."

"I'll need to check in with the department soon enough, now that I'm well on the road to recovery," Menlo voiced, as she nodded to the room full of flowers and cards from the Well Wishers at the San Antonio Police Department.

"Many officers have come by for visits. I had to glamour a few to keep them down the hall at the end of the floor, instead of right outside the door. They still feel the killers of the dead John Does and your shooter are at large, and they won't rest until they have a suspect in custody."

"What are we going to do about that?"

"Well, let's deal with one problem at a time. If necessary, I can glamour the entire department if need be. We can't alert humans to our presence. That would cause even bigger problems."

"True. You're right, one thing at a time. So does this mean you'll stay while I fall asleep?"

"You couldn't budge me from this room if you tried."

He pulled her to him, while she snuggled in close. Sleep didn't come easy with the thrumming vibrating louder and louder in her head.

†

Visiting hours at the Metropolitan Methodist Hospital began at 9 am sharp. Urgata hadn't seen her sister in 20 years. Anticipation and ambivalence plagued her every step she took. So many loose ends and distance placed tension on her sibling relationship. Menlo blamed their mother for so much. She hated all of the voodoo and black magic Bureau indulged in. Urgata only wanted to reconnect with her sibling.

"I wonder if she'll let me hug her." Urgata murmured under her breath.

The answer to her question remained just on the other side of the door where she stood. Anxiety clenched the walls of her stomach. Her trembling hand reached for the door handle.

Sensing a presence near, Basrick leaped from the bed and posted at the foot of the bed. Menlo sat up with a start. She looked at Basrick. He nodded letting her know not to worry.

"You sister has just arrived, and she appears apprehensive. She's standing at the door."

Menlo took a deep swallow, and returned the nod as he walked to the door. He went to the door and opened it, and actually had to gasp at what he saw. A replica of Childress stood before him. Urgata looked very much like her first cousin---nearly the same height, same hair color, same green eyes. Menlo's feature held opposite to her sisters. Urgata's jade green eyes met the aqua blue of Menlo's and tears clouded them both. Urgata rushed to her sister's arms.

"Menlo!"

"Gotti!" Menlo's rush of emotion caused Basrick to step aside as the siblings hugged and kissed each other.

"You still look the same. I've missed you so much. Why did we ever let this happen? Why?"

"I don't know, but I've missed you too."

"Has Basrick told you about mama?"

"Yes. I'm very sorry about that."

"I brought pictures of the service for you to look at when you are ready."

"Let me see them now. I want to get this over with."

Urgata searched the room for an approving look from Basrick, and she found her answer in a quick nod he gave her. He stood silently, as the two siblings held hands. Urgata handed her sister a high-resolution photo of their mother Bureau lying in a solid copper casket accented with bronze handles.

Menlo ran her hand slowly over her mother's face, as her plaited waist long hair lay beside her in a neat braid that nearly extended the length of the casket itself. A tear fell on the photo as she murmured.

"Mama, I'm so sorry." Her tear-filled eyes fell on her sister.

"Gotti, look what Childress has done to our mother and to me. This has to stop. It has to stop. I stayed away so long because I knew that someday things would end tragically. I never stopped loving you."

"I know Menny. I know. Time is against us. Auldicia has returned. I can hear her calling all of her descendants to join her in world destruction. Mama told me to ignore the summons, but I fear those that are weaker will not be able to fight the gravity of her call. Childress unleashed her when she killed our mother, and refused the gods the sacrifice of the baby. Justice took her baby, and now she wants the child back. He showed up with fangs in his mouth and speed like something I've only read about but never seen. Childress said a vampire had bitten him."

Basrick spoke slowly when he stood up. "Yes, it is what I am."

Urgata swallowed hard, but appeared unafraid and confident. "I've vowed to kill Childress."

"That makes two of us. I hear Auldicia calling to me as well. Her summons is the strongest in my dreams. You should know that Justice is dead. Basrick killed him the night he brought Blessing to us. That's the baby's name."

"Her name is Blessing?"

"Yes. Basrick's mother named her Blessing."

Just then, Basrick interjected by clearing his throat. Walking slowly over to the bed, he sat near Menlo and gave his input.

"Do you swear to join us in this quest? We need to know because time is running out. If Auldicia has returned for world destruction, we need to move quickly."

Urgata stood up and looked him square in the eye and vowed.

"I give all of who I am to stop Childress and Auldicia. I will not rest until I avenge the death of my mother, and the pain Childress has inflicted on my sister, and me."

"You?"

"She slept with Nayphous when she knew we were engaged to be married."

"That dirty snatch tramp."

Even though the thought of Childress slow screwing her man, Nayphous, hurt, with a face full of tears, Urgata let out a gut busting laugh at the dirty vagina word, 'snatch'. To call someone a snatch was one thing, but a dirty one was referring to someone in the lowest of terms.

"You are just as crazy as your mother calling her a 'dirty snatch tramp'."

"Who else would be so low to do something so evil? That

someone is Childress. Wow, Nayphous? I remember him as little boy. I've heard his music, and he's pretty tough."

"Yes, I thought we could be happy, but I just don't know where we stand now all this has happened."

As the two women continued to console each other, Basrick stood and gave Menlo a gentle kiss goodbye. He needed to get to the mansion, and fast. The countdown had begun and no one could fathom just what was to come.

"Visit with your sister. I'm going to the mansion to check on things. I'll be back later."

As he pulled away, Menlo grabbed his shirt, and pulled his lips back to hers in a sizzling kiss that had Urgata clearing her throat.

"Gracious, it's all of a sudden hot as an oven in here!" She fanned her face as she turned and walked to the window while Menlo finished slurping on Basrick's lips. "Hurry back."

"I most certainly will Detective Kildare. I most certainly will."

Basrick slowly let go of her hand, took two steps backward, and teleported out of the room right before the two women could even find words to be startled. Urgata grabbed her chest.

"Did you see that?"

"Indeed I did."

"That's just was happened the night Justice came and got

Blessing. He took off so fast, Childress blinked, and he was gone. So Basrick is a vampire too?"

"Yeah, and I have known about the vampires here in town just recently. By the way, who is babysitting your kids?"

"Nayphous has them now, but he will be leaving them with his mother for a few days, then he'll be joining me here."

"How's Tahiti?"

"Fine, I guess. Mama hadn't heard from her in over six months. We don't know where she is."

Tahiti was the youngest of the Treemount-La Deaux sisters, and the wildest. She had left home and led a life of prostitution at an early age. The Bayou 'ho was her nickname at 12 years old, and she had her first child at 13 years old. The only time the family saw her was either before or after the birth of a child.

"Menlo, how are we going to fight Auldicia? I mean, mama transferred her powers to me, but I can't do it alone."

Menlo had always hated her voodoo roots, but now she feared she would have to call upon them to help set things right.

"Listen, Basrick is staying with a family that has a voodoo Mistress. Her name is Solis. She and Childress have been school-yard enemies from day one. Basrick left to go and check on her. Evidently, her mate Nacio has fallen under Auldicia's spell. She turned him into a vampire, and now all Hell has broken loose."

"Solis? Yes! Mama said to find Solis and join with her to help stop them both. As mama lay dying, she put a curse on Childress's ass. It's the Curse of Shadows, so it won't be long before that hussy is hallucinating and shadows are chasing her. It was the only thing mama could do as she passed on. I mingled my blood with hers, and was able to see her cross over into the realm of the dead. She is at peace."

More tears slid from Menlo's eyes. Reaching for her service pistol in the nightstand, Menlo picked it up and looked at the silver plated Glock, and uttered a warning aloud to her absent first cousin Childress.

"When I find you, Childress, I'm going to empty this gun in your ass."

7

A long time

Untangling his arms from Solis's arms, Nacio hypnotically stood up from their bed. Naked, his brawny 6'7 frame cast shadows on the walls making him look like a giant fallen to earth. With an inebriated pace, he staggered over to the lanai just outside of their bedroom. The voice increased in volume.

"Mother First is here. Come children, come to me now."

Somberly, Nacio turned to Solis as she lay sleeping. He stretched his hand in her direction, but no connection made. Uttering her name aloud did not reach her slumbering ears.

"Solis, I love you."

Nacio turned to the voice that thrummed with evil power.

"Children, come to me now!"

No words left his lips to say goodbye to his mate. Enslavement had taken hold of his mind and body once more. His maker called to him, and he had to obey. Putting one foot in front of the other, he started his jog at a slow pace, and then teleported in the direction of the thrumming.

During the entire journey to only the gods knew where, the voice continued to increase in volume, nearly shattering his eardrums.

"Mother First is here."

Upon arrival, he landed feet first into pea gravel and clay. The impact was so hard; his immortality saved his leg bones from shattering instantly. Auldicia had indeed returned. The power she possessed emanated from the opening of the cavern. Futilely, he turned in an attempt to teleport away, but his legs and feet felt like cement shoes.

Just over his left shoulder, he heard footsteps shuffling through the gravel headed in his direction. In the dark, a figure of a woman shimmered into view. Infected bite marks, with veins branching around them sat etched on the side of her broken dislocated neck. Her dangling head shimmied with each step she took. A prominent baby bump in her abdomen, resembling an anvil weighted her down, keeping her steps slow and heavy. The unborn child in her womb actively kicked and elbowed in response to Auldicia's summons. Believa Beaushanks dutifully answered the call. Nacio stood in disbelief.

Believa still lives, the Dieth didn't kill her, and now her baby is responding to the summons. If there are others out there that Justice has impregnated there will be more of Auldicia's bloodline throughout the world. I must get free. I must try to reach Solis and let her know where I am.

Sending out his own telepathic energy, he tried to connect

with Solis. Auldicia's power rendered him helpless.

Solis sweetheart, can you feel me? Please, sweetheart, can you find me? His plea went unanswered.

Female laughter echoed from the cavern, ricocheting off the walls causing bats to flee, dropping bat guano as they few by. Globs of Guano splattered Believa's head, barely missing her mouth. Without her first feeding as a new vampire, her body has not regenerated from whatever wounds she sustained. A hideous sight, her expression of terror made it obvious her unborn child ordered her steps to the unknown doom that awaited her in the cavern.

"Help me. Please, help me!" With her larynx crushed, her windpipe grated against it making her voice chirp like a cricket as she stretched her hand out in Nacio's direction.

Unwillingly, his feet continued to move forward to the unknown. Not ready for the evil to come, he knew time had run out. Auldicia needed to reclaim him. Refusal would be his only offer. The pull from her energy overwhelmed him so much, so he felt his fangs respond to her nearness.

Attempting to teleport once more, he strained with no success. He tried to shift into mist, but found only brief invisibility and still no success. His slow trudge continued toward the vault of the cavern. Others who responded to the summons arrived. Nacio recognized a Bishop from a well-known local church trudging up behind Believa. A ghastly grin creased his transfixed expression.

Auldicia's children were many in number; from all ethnicities. A raven-haired woman with blue eyes and lily-white skin

with a sports bar uniform trudged in behind the Bishop. Looking over his shoulder, he saw the rest of the Treemounts he and
his family had been inoculating with the Dieth darts. Castiana
Treemount, now shaped like an imp minus her breasts and her hips,
trudged in line with her distant cousins with a heavily shadowed
mustache and side burns…side effects from the Estrogen ravaging
Dieth.

Not far behind this Treemount cousin limped Living
Treemount. The former, once statuesque exotic dancer, now
looked like a goat herder. The beautiful red locks that crowned her
head had thinned to only a few dozen good strands pasted in place.
Effects from the Dieth wrecked her body beyond recognition. Living's eyes shifted back and forth as fear and excitement led her
closer and closer to her destination.

Other faintly recognizable faces continued to make the trek
inside the cavern to meet their mother ancestor. One face in particular made him hiss in anger. A man with an uncanny resemblance
to Bose, his dead kindred brother, made him try an unsuccessful
attack. His anger slowly dissipated, realizing the man he saw only
mirrored Bose. City Councilman Cuellar Kellum followed behind
him. He recently took office and worked as a liaison to the San
Antonio Police Department.

A horrible realization set in as Nacio looked at all the faces
of Auldicia's descendants. Many prominent individuals in positions of power and affluence weren't considered when he and his
family began exterminating the Treemounts, and the realization
weighed on him that he and his family would fight them forever.

With the many descendants now gathered at the cavern,

the man might have been a half brother to Bose. The man's build, blondish red curly hair, and signature green eyes made Nacio want to strike the man repeatedly. A smirk licked the corners of the man's mouth as he quickened his pace deep into the cavern toward the now hysterical laughter.

Soon hundreds of zombielike bodies shuffled into the cavern. Mud covered the first few, as if they had bathed in the muck. Again, some of the many female Treemounts that received the Dieth inoculation resembled imps instead of women; waif thin, with bloated bellies, no hips, no breasts. Nacio recognized them as females from the slight female pheromones he scented as they passed him. Other than that, another human would have difficulty distinguishing those females from males.

A shadowy green light up ahead alerted his journey to the vault of the cavern neared its end. Another familiar scent punched him in the nose. Auldicia's arousal wafted up his nasal passages. The centuries old scent of seed from every lover she took into her womb had the smell of rotting flesh mixed in with the natural moisture of the cavern. Instead of retching from nausea, her descendants seemed to gain strength from the scent---taking it in like an aphrodisiac.

She must plan to reproduce with some of these descendants. Why else would she summon so many in one place? I must try to reach Solis once more…Solis can you hear me? Please Sweetheart can you hear me?

Again, wild laughter filled the vault of the cavern. This time it came with a personal warning. "Call her name no more if you wish to see her again." More laughter along with an invitation, "Come to me, Zuri." *Zuri, good looking; a term of endearment I haven't heard for centuries. A name I've resented for just as long.*

The words coming from in the vault seemed to travel for miles. Then, after a short delay, just ahead, a path lined with her servants led to a throne carved out from a portion of the cave. After several centuries, Nacio's eyes filled with the sight of his maker.

Auldicia sat upon her makeshift throne with illustrious red hair cascading down her back, settling at her waist like a cape. Evidently having fed, her skin nearly fully regenerated. Dagger sharp nails protruded from her nail beds, edged enough to shred cowhide. The source of the shadowy green light illuminating the mouth of the cavern beamed from her eyes. Appearing with the likeness of a goddess, Nacio transparently saw her true demon form; serpents on top of her head, talons, fangs, and filth.

Full breasts bounced across a petite rib cage, which sat atop a neat waistline. Anxiously, she uncrossed and crossed her legs, rubbing them together the closer Nacio came. At the foot of her throne, she slowly parted her legs, inviting him between her thighs.

"Don't make me wait another day in this century to receive your touch, Zuri. Come to me now."

"I will not join my body with yours."

"Then I shall join us together myself."

Auldicia defiantly stood, and came down from her elevated throne. Close enough to share breath with him, she took him into her hand and kneaded his testicles. Massaging him, Nacio's head lulled, and his eyes rolled to the back of his head in response to her heated grip. Her wicked tongue snaked in and out of her mouth, as she flicked her taste buds over his Adam's apple. Viciously, she turned her head in disgust and spit. Suspicious, she guided her nose up and down his chest, taking in his scent and then spitted repeatedly.

"Why do you smell like Olinka?

Nacio stood with his chest out and spine stretched taut. Refusal begins now. In no way would he disclose his binding to Solis to the demon female standing before him. Auldicia's unyielding rage puts Solis and all those he loves in grave danger.

"Perhaps your nose betrays you, Auldicia. But even if it didn't, what you seek to possess you will not have."

Tickled even more, diabolical laughter rumbled from the bottom of her throat in victory.

"You're certain of this? Certain I will not command you to do as I please? Certain I will not take your seed from you and give you the heir you should have had centuries ago, before you interrupted my desire?"

She continued kneading his testicles until the heat moistened their surface, making them slick and pasty. Auldicia licked her plumped, glossy lips, thirsting for a taste and a sip of his plasma.

"Zuri, must we fight? You know you will not win. Soon, you will pleasure me until you shout in surrender."

Goading her, Nacio's shaft would not respond to Auldicia's

affections. The crown jutted like an arrow, yet no rigidity held it up to its full-length glory.

"So, you continue to refuse me? Fine, my tongue will do the job for me."

Stretching her tongue through her fangs, she got on one knee before him and coiled her tongue around his flaccid shaft. Her tugging and pulling efforts to arouse him proved unsuccessful. Again, she spit in frustration and shouted to the vault of the cavern.

"Why do I keep smelling Olinka! You dare come forward with the fluid of another female on your skin; an archenemy no less? Your refusal to accept affection is an insult Zuri. Punishment seems appropriate."

Nacio struggled within himself as to what to do since his own voodoo magic is useless. Auldicia loved to punish him in ways that made his nightmares a daytime reality. Upon his first feeding after she made him into a vampire, he had a similar response to her then as he does now. Only now, he rebukes her openly, driving her to the current task. Shouting a directive to the man who resembled Bose, he trembled then stumbled up next to her.

"Get the hot stone ready. It appears Zuri has forgotten his place. Forgotten he must bow to my will, and give in to my demands as his maker…and lover."

On command, the sinister man resembling Bose ventured further into the murky depths of the cavern where light couldn't reach. His heavy shuffling quieted the further away he traveled. Auldicia's gaze fell on Nacio's noodle soft shaft. When the Bose look-alike returned with two small tablet-like stones, smoke sizzled from his hands as they seared from touching the hot stones. Auldicia took the two stones and recited a chant to punish Nacio for his impotence.

"Ill aggamut, Desfonde, Fontodo benanahada, Zuri." *You will pay for your indiscretion, and for your lack of passion, Zuri.* She made certain paralysis, and held him in place, disabling him from any further movement.

No doubt clouded his mind about the fact she indeed planned to punish him for his hatred. After all, a Priestess gets what she desires. He only hoped she would not end his life.

Auldicia took the two hot stones in her hand. Reaching for his shaft with preternatural speed, she placed it between the two stones and slammed them together with his flesh searing between the two sizzling rocks. Nacio screamed in agony while Auldicia laughed at his pain and humiliation. The smell of cauterized flesh filled the vault of the cavern while generations of her descendants looked on and laughed along with their mother ancestor.

"Do you wish to give me your affections now Zuri?"

"Go to hell, you wicked, snake faced witch."

"I've just come from vacationing there. The next time I go, you'll journey there with me. How 'bout that?"

With her patience worn thin with Nacio, aggravation set in. Looking around the cavern and finding no object worthy of her use, she finally settled on a metal barometer previously used by humans in the cavern for humidity pressure readings. The twelve-inch metal casing of the barometer looked strong and unbendable. She reached for the instrument, recoiling and hissing as she regretfully realized the metal casing was silver.

"What trickery is this Zuri?" As she took two steps back, holding her hand in pain.

"You've been gone too long Auldicia. You must understand, you do have vulnerabilities in this realm."

Anguish kicked in and she backhanded him fiercely, tearing skin away from his right cheek.

"Who is this female whore whose fluids you have all over your skin? Hmm? Who is she, and where does she dwell? You will tell me, Zuri, or the consequences will be severe."

Nacio refused to identify Solis or her family history. Anything trivial about his mate acted as information to trap, torture, and kill her. The binding he and Solis had to each other held an irreversible power; they are one flesh. Since he chose Good over Evil, there is nothing Auldicia could change to undo the binding. Even if she continued her attempts to seduce him, his body would continually reject her.

Instead of giving up, she telekinetically picked up the silver barometer. Wrapping his flaccid shaft around her hand, she used her telekinesis to shove the silver up his urethra opening, catheterizing him in one swift motion. Nacio's roar shook the stalactites from the vault.

"Since your body won't rise for me, I made it rise...permanently."

Nacio's shaft jutted erectly from his body with the assistance of his makeshift silver catheter. The folds of his skin continued its limp and rigid appearance. He fell to his knees in agony.

The draping stalactites fell from the vault of the cavern. A sharp, thin one pierced the skull of one of Auldicia's descendants, angering her and causing more torture to befall Nacio.

"Oh look at what you've done to one of my children, you weak pissant. You wail and scream like a spineless serpent. You shall pay for this."

Revenge filled her eyes as she slit her right wrist with a cruddy fingernail. A rivulet of blood ran from her wound. A drop of her blood metamorphosed into a slithering single celled parasitic worm just before it hit the ground below her feet. Gripping his jaw, Auldicia force-fed plasma from her wound to his mouth, allowing him to become host to the slithering parasitic plasma.

"Your lips quiver to be fed Zuri. Drink from me, and find your passion again."

"I said go to hell." Nacio spit the parasitic plasma from his lips.

Furious, she threw a right hook that bled him more. She called to the Bose look-alike and barked a directive.

"You there, what is your name?"

For the first time since his arrival, the Bose look-alike spoke on command to identify himself.

"My name is Ellis Darbin, Mother. I'm here to serve you."

"And serve you will, my dear. Quickly, take him to the farthest corner of this cavern, and shackle him for me. Tightly draw his body in quarters so that I might have my way with him in private."

Ellis Darbin stood shorter than Nacio, but had massive shoulders, perfect for throwing a limp body over them if needed. In this case, only the strong biceps flanking from his torso shoveled Nacio's enchanted body to the darkest area of the cavern.

During her last existence in this realm, Auldicia sacrificed many unwilling souls. Ellis discovered a set of shackles with metal cuffs at the ends of them hanging from the wall. Apprehending Nacio and drawing his body in quarters was easy. The shackles took Nacio down memory lane, back to the torture he sustained at the hands of his maker. He felt her eyes upon him in the distance. She drew closer to him.

"You will remain here until you submit to me, Zuri. I look forward to many nights of passion and pleasure between the two of us from now until eternity." She held his face in one hand as she stroked his sore, throbbing shaft with the other. The silver had already begun poisoning him. Mustering up the little strength he had, he vehemently responded to her advances.

"My soul rotting in Hell is better than you taking my body into yours." He spit with precision of a King Cobra, landing his secretions right between Auldicia's eyes.

"That can be arranged my love." Drawing back her fist, she connected an upper cut that landed in the center of his chin cleft. His head snapped back and forth and finally lulled forward as his black locks cloaked his face. Auldicia's diseased blood and her spell had already begun taking effect. Heat emanated from his sac holding his seed. She planned to conceive a child with him, but he knew it would be an abomination straight from Hell; one he could not allow to live.

"I see your punishments will be many, and they will be my pleasures to indulge in. You will give me a child so that we can rule this realm together whether you like it or not. Although, I believe you will come to like it. Once our child sets foot upon this earth, I will never have to return to face the burning embers in the bed of Vulkus ever again. First, I must seek out this damned female with this stomach wrenchingly sweet scent, and put her in the ground, Zuri. You know I've always been jealous. I will not live in the shadows of a lingering scent. "

Taking a handful of his hair and yanking it from the root of his scalp, Auldicia threw the long strands of black hair in the crowd of eyes staring back at her.

She snapped her slender fingers, and all of her descendants present did a "ten hut", clicking their heels to attention.

"Hear me well. Your summons here is to serve me. I am your beginning and your end. Take a sample of my Zuri's hair, and locate the scent that reeks from his body. Bring the wench to me unharmed…I will finish what she believes she has started with my Zuri. Are we clear?"

Suddenly, the least intelligent individual dared to voice his ignorance, "How do we do that? We don't have any magic, Mother."

In the time it took to draw one breath, Auldicia crossed the distance in the cavern between her and the simple-minded individual and seized him by the throat.

"You dare question me?" A few seconds past as terror marked the man's face. Her beaming green eyes hatefully gazed at the man, almost looking into his soul.

"Speak only when spoken to, ingrate." Plunging her left index finger nail in the left temple of the man, she peeled his skin down the side of his face as if peeling a banana. Bloodcurdling shrieks of pain filled the cavern vault as more bats fled their home from the disturbance.

"What? You still stand before me making this hideous noise?" Auldicia muttered a spell while she fiercely reached in the man's mouth and yanked his tongue forward snapping it from the back of his throat. The screaming stopped, allowing the man only to make smothered grunts as he gasped for air. Swelling surged from his neck up to his face from the injuries she inflicted.

"Now, that's much better," she said, wiping her hands together as if she had just disposed of trash. "I can see you, but I can barely hear you. Much, much better."

Nacio looked on from his shackled prison against the wall, hating the fact he was helpless, and vulnerable.

I must try to contact Solis once more. If not, Auldicia will destroy this realm and everyone in it. Solis...please hear me... With the silver weakening him by the second, telepathically contacting Solis seemed futile as he slipped in and out of consciousness.

The mood shifted in the dark and dank cavern as Auldicia threw the swollen, broken tongued man on the ground. Looking very regal and very deadly, she resumed her place on her throne.

"Who among you can fulfill this request and bring the wench that carries this scent to me? You must be worthy, because you must not fail. The consequences of failure are...severe. Let the consideration weigh heavy on your mind before you accept this task, but you must hurry. I need this task carried out and completed before the next lunar eclipse."

Everyone in the cavern stood motionless as she waited for a response.

"Alright, we can all just remain here until one of you accepts the task. After all, I've waited an eternity...so can you."

†

Dozer pulled the stolen commissary truck off the IH 10 East, stopping on a dirt road in Lake Charles, Louisiana. Childress knew they needed a new vehicle to finish their trek back to San Antonio.

"There's an outlet mall just one more exit down. Dozer, you go to that mall and find a van or something from one of those stores that's delivering a shipment of clothing. Try the one from the Uniform Store so we can change. You got that?"

"Yeah, I got it. What are ya'll gonna do?"

"We're gonna wait for you to return, Cher. And don't you

dare think about crossing me, or you'll have a loose life of misery. You got that?"

"Oh no, I wouldn't dare cross you Childress," Dozer said, shaking her head reverently. "Can Presser and Bula come with me too?"

"Hell naw! You go and come back like I said."

Childress and her crew emptied out of the commissary truck and made a run for the bushes off the dirt road. Once they found a hollow of trees not too far from a swamp, the Treemounts grabbed their heads simultaneously as the auditory summons only they could hear increased. Klein fell to his knees in agony.

"Ouch! Dammit Childress it's hurting! Can't you make it stop?"

In pain like her brothers, Childress squeezed her eyes shut, holding her ears. She felt her blood coursing through her veins as if it were on fire.

"I can't do anything about this noise. We need to hurry up and get back to SA."

Erland began the hysterical laughter that seized him when agitation would set in. Klein immediately responded, by tearing the sleeve of his shirt and stuffing it down his brother's mouth.

"Shut up you damn fool! You gonna get us caught."

Erland began to weep from the noise as it continued its assault on his eardrums. "I miss Justice. Where is he at, Klein?" Erland's stuffed mouth garbled his speech.

"I know it hurts, man, but big brother here is gonna take care of you, okay? We'll find Justice soon."

The mention of Justice had Childress raise her antenna and turn in the direction of her brothers. Her eyes once more had the eerie green luminescence she had the night she became the new family mambo.

"Don't worry about where the hell Justice is at. We'll find him soon and when we do, I'm gonna knock the hell out of him, Cher."

No more than twenty minutes went by, and Dozer returned from her unplanned heist with a Unifirst Uniform van loaded with uniforms of all kinds, giving each of the criminals their choice of persons they wished they could become in life.

Klein grabbed a green mechanic's jumpsuit for Ace Mechanics and Aviation. He selected a White lab coat and scrubs for his weeping brother. Dozer was already in a set of what looked like Pediatric Nurse Scrubs with prints of Sponge Bob over the top. Presser selected a Fireman's uniform, and Bula wore an aviator jumpsuit.

Last, but not least, Childress settled on a Southwest Airline Stewardess uniform. Of course, the skirt was too tight with the seams screaming for release. She tied her hair up in a knot and pushed Dozer to the back of the van with the other Hench Wenches and her brothers.

"Give me the keys, Dozer. I'm taking us home."

Rolling across the San Antonio City Limit on IH 10 made Childress reassess her plan of action. There were scores to settle, and she wanted to have her child back as soon as possible.

It seems like this thrumming is getting a little softer since we're back home, so Auldicia must be in San Antonio. I hope so, because I can't wait to get a hold of Justice and beat his ass. He took my baby and I'm gonna punish him good. Then, I'm gonna find Solis Burkes and finish what she started too. Yeah buddy, I'm in the mood for punishment tonight, and punishment is what I'm gonna give to them both.

Childress followed the now low frequency thrumming. It led her off IH 10, heading north on IH 35 North. She found herself soon exiting on Garden Ridge, heading west on 3009. Driving for seven miles, she finally brought them to a stop at Natural Bridge Caverns. The thrumming shifted to pure raw magnetized power, drawing them to a cavern.

The six fools got out of the van and slowly made their trek across the themed cavern park. A few employees watched as the band of individuals dressed as Halloween characters made their way passed the admission booth and through the entrance to the caverns. A concerned employee tried to stop Childress and charge admission.

"Excuse me, ma'am, you have to pay admission."

Childress turned her green beams on the woman immobilizing in her tracks, "Hey, I remember you. You worked at the hospital downtown where my mama died. You still wetting your pants girl? I guess I scared you pretty good huh?"

When realization of who Childress was hit the poor woman, she immediately lost her bladder control and wet her pants again. This young woman happened to be the one Childress terrorized at the hospital where her mother was a patient the night she came home from prison. Childress caused the woman to wet her pants the night she was on duty at the admissions desk, and now at her new job, terror has found her once more.

"Please, don't hurt me...please!"

"Then get out of my way and let us pass through, or I will hurt you."

Fleeing for her life, the woman quickly stepped aside and ran non-stop down the road leading to the main freeway. She had the good sense to know whatever Childress was doing at Natural Bridge Caverns could not be good. Her only concern now is to put as much distance between her and the impending danger she felt as Childress Treemount made her presence known on the premises.

A long, winding path led from the entrance of the theme park to a wooded brushy area, guarded by rattlers and scorpions. She found excitement driving her footsteps closer and closer to her destiny and her long awaited introduction to her powerful ancestor she was to meet.

"This is it folks! We're going to meet Auldicia."

An innocent question slipped Presser's lips in response to the statement Childress made, "Who's Auldicia? Does she have something to eat, 'cause I'm starving?"

"Shut the hell up, Presser. You don't know who you talkin'

'bout. This is Auldicia, the All-Powerful. She's our ancestor and she's come to help us crush our enemies by giving me her power."

"Well I hope she can give us something to eat, hell. I'm hungry!"

Childress Pimp Slapped Presser two times, with the sound ricocheting off the tree limbs in the distance, unaware that she had just alerted Auldicia to her presence in the distance. All at once, each of them heard the sound of her voice for the first time. She spoke directly to them.

"Come forth children. You are home. I've waited for you all the longest."

Childress drew in a long breath as she put one foot in front of the other and made her way toward the cavern entrance. They all started on their way in when the barrel of a gun chamber clicked, making them flinch in their tracks.

"Yeah, that's them, Sheriff. They haven't paid their admission fee." An overly eager employee had alerted the authorities about Childress and her crew being on the grounds and not making good on their entry fee. The Sheriff made it known he was good and pissed, as he spit a wad of chewing tobacco to the side of where he stood.

"Ya'll plan on going somewhere without payin'?"

Without warning, Klein picked up a tablet-sized rock and threw it at the Sheriff's head, knocking the law enforcement agent out cold. Remarkably, Erland sprang into action by doing his best Jackie Chan moves in mid air and elbowed the male employee in the gut and then crotch. He kicked him so hard, the man fainted.

"Damn, it's amazing what a uniform can do for your self-esteem, isn't it Erland?" Childress sarcastically cheered, as she barked out orders.

"You three wenches get rid of these two unconscious fools. Klein, get that gun and the bullets. You never know when we might need it."

The Hench Wenches grabbed the Sheriff by his feet, and dragged him over the rugged terrain of the trail. They threw him over a ravine and watched his body tumble to the bottom. The wenches were about to give the male employee the same fate, but were interrupted when Childress and her brothers quickly turned in the direction of the cavern.

Auldicia spoke to them once more, "Bring that one in with you…I'm thirsty." Childress gave the directive to Dozer.

"Throw that one over your back Dozer and let's move now."

Auldicia bid them passage into the cavern as they hesitated upon arriving closer to the snakes and scorpions.

"Move aside my pets, and let my children come forth."

The sea of snakes and scorpions quickly skittered to the side, parting a pathway to the entrance of the cavern. Naturally, Erland did not do well at the sight of the pestilence and reptiles guarding their ancestor. Nearly climbing in Klein's arms, he walked with his back against Klein's. The creepy crawlies squirmed and wiggled while they passed through.

"They lookin' at me. They lookin' at me. Tell 'em to stop! Don't you see their eyes on me? Ooh, gracious, ooh gracious they lookin' at me!"

Out of patience and somewhat embarrassed, Childress made her way to the end of their line formation and stung Erland's face with a slap that cracked across his chin and jaw with a pop.

"Shut the hell up damn fool! Those things ain't paying you no attention, now move!"

Erland did his usual whimpering after a good scolding. He sniveled all the way inside.

To their surprise, hundreds of people stood lining the walls of the cavern. All were descendants linked to their family. The family resemblance stood out in some more than others, but the one trait that carried throughout the generations was the eye color. Many of the descendants smiled at them as they passed. but one person in particular did not; Believa Beaushanks. Childress did not hide her disgust at seeing her old friend and partner in crime standing with a full belly against the wall, with her dangling head. Believa looked as if she was about to explode.

"What the hell are you doing here girl? Looks like you got your head caught in a washing machine. This is not your place to hang out at. I thought I made it clear we have no more dealings with each other."

The last time Childress laid eyes on Believa was at the Texas Taste Tease last year. She unleashed a whooping on her that left her face completely disfigured with swelling and bruising. As Childress remembered their last meeting, she giggled to herself.

"I see I didn't quite knock out all your teeth, Believa. You still have a few chairs in your mouth."

With her fatal injuries, she looked liked death warmed over but she was now a vampire who hadn't fed. Difficulty in her speech due to her injuries made her a bit hard to understand.

"I didn't come here on my own Childress. The child I carry is your brother's."

"What? You got knocked up with Justice's baby? Well, well, well…this plot just keeps getting better and better! By the way, where is Brother Dear? We have a score to settle."

Believa stood and grinned at Childress, refusing to tell her of her lover's fate. Childress became distracted at the sight of Believa's fangs, now fully extended due to the thirst for plasma she continues to ignore.

"Oh hell naw! You a vampire too? You mean you let Justice put the bite down on you too? Childress pressed Believa's chest back against the wall. "Where is Justice, Believa? Tell me!"

A now familiar voice commanded Childress to continue her journey further into the depths of the cavern…the voice that held the power to end life itself.

"Continue to come forth, my child."

Noticing only the green rays of light ahead, Childress continued her trek forward. Noting the different facial formations in the rocks, she knew this place held lots of power. She could feel the souls of the lives all around her that no longer called this realm home. Hearing her brothers and the Hench Wenches behind her, she dared to take a breath in this place.

Just ahead, sitting on a throne carved from the cavern rock, Childress laid eyes on her ancestor Auldicia. For the first time in her life, she stood before someone breathless. Childress never felt fear, shame, loss, or least of all regret or remorse. Now, standing before Auldicia, she felt all of those emotions and more.

In her eyes, Childress saw Auldicia as a Goddess, a divine being she planned to worship and serve. Finally, she had someone to look up to, who would give her the respect she deserved. Childress had someone she could look up to and admire. Auldicia commanded her once more.

"Come forth child." Childress stepped forth with caution. So many emotions ran through her, she thought she felt her fingers trembling, so she quickly made a fist to make certain they were not. Her steps were small and precise as she made her way to the throne. Unsure if she should bow, knee, curtsy, or just nod, she played it safe and gave a quick wave of her hand, but she did not speak. Both held each other in the green rays of light their eyes emanated, studying each other.

"What is your name, child of mine?"

Nervous, Childress stammered as she identified herself, "M-my name is Childress…Childress Treemount. And these here are my brothers, Klein and Erland Treemount. We are the children of Frances Treemount. I'm the new mambo priestess for my family. Our mother spoke of you. She called you Auldicia." She quickly pointed to the Hench Wenches, "These are those who serve me."

Preternaturally, Auldicia jumped up and cut Childress across her face with her right index fingernail, and returned to her throne in two seconds flat. She tasted the blood Childress had just spilled for her on her finger. Auldicia tasted a tinge of her own blood mixed in. Childress screamed in pain and fury at the savage actions of her ancestor.

"Yes, yes you are, but you are wrong. You all serve me now, "Auldicia smiled a toothy fanged grin. "It is you whose blood set me free from the depths of hell. It was your blood mixed with the death of at least two others of your family line along with the birth of a legacy. A girl child was born simultaneously to set me free. So, Childress, where is the child you gave birth to? Is she as stunningly beautiful as you are?"

Childress stood before her ancestor now seething from her unprovoked attack. With the power of the magic she experienced from Auldicia thus far, she knew she had to put herself in check if she and her brothers were to survive this day unharmed. Betrayal from her own emotions washed over her. Each second that passed, she revered her ancestor less and less, moving more toward hatred. She knew she had to play her cards right and answer this centuries-old monster with much thought.

"I don't have my child, she's with her uncle." Childress cut her eyes over her shoulder at Believa, still itching to knock the hell out of her for withholding the whereabouts of Justice. Believa stood her ground with her tethered head and sneered at Childress. Figuring out the baby Childress recently gave birth to is of great importance, Believa played a dangerous game with Childress and Auldicia. If what Childress said is true and Justice is now dead, and Solis watched him die, then maybe Solis knows the where-abouts of the baby. One thing is certain. Childress and Auldicia don't know Justice is dead. Sensing more happening from the lack of words and the tension in the air, Auldicia continued her questioning.

"You do not have the legacy in your possession? Why ever not, dear girl?"

More nervous than ever before, Childress felt her heart speed up as Auldicia tilted her head in response, "Well I wanted her to spend some time with him."

A hideous smirk hissed from Believa's broken neck. She knew when Childress was telling a lie. Obviously, Auldicia did as well.

"With her Uncle, is she?" Auldicia rose from her throne, and slowly walked back toward Childress to get right in her personal space to listen to her tell her lie word for word.

"I know you're lying to me Childress. Your heart is pounding as loudly as the summons that brought you all here. You will be punished."

Auldicia connected a right hook to her left jaw that made her teeth click on contact. Once she recovered from the hook, Childress swung a punch of her own. Her fist landed center in the palm of Auldicia's hand.

"What's this? Defensive tactics," She tsked her tongue. What a pity."

Childress lifted her left hand and tried to mutter a spell for strength, but found Auldicia caught her left hand as well. Instead, of getting angry, she smiled and one flick of her wrist sent Childress flying backward, slamming her back against the cavern wall. Writhing in pain, Childress lay on the ground at the foot of the wall.

The noise woke the semiconscious Park employee who escorted the Sheriff to apprehend Childress and her brothers. The Park employee moaned and then began sniveling as the danger closed in around him.

"W-what is this, some kind of cult or something? What are you folks doing in here?"

Auldicia's green eyes flickered over the man. Without warning, an unseen force of telekinesis lifted the man's weakened body and carried him toward Auldicia. Wild eyed and terrified, the man unsuccessfully tried to slip from the grip of apprehension. Hovering in mid air, his body dangled in front of Auldicia.

"Ah, yes, here is my snack. It is so kind of you to join us."

Auldicia's fangs slid from the gums hooding them, with saliva dripping from the corners of her mouth. Looking on in horror, the man screamed and squirmed to break free. She opened her mouth wide, taking the juiciest bite her mouth could gather, nicking the man's artery as plasma sprayed over the ground.

Childress and her crew looked on bleary eyed and in disbelief. She realized how deeply in over her head she was with no way out. The man's body was sucked clean as a chicken bone, with only skin remaining. Auldicia had the nerve to belch after her feeding.

"Ooops, 'scuse me. Ellis, come and dispose of this left over skin and filth. Remains lying around make the bats in here crazy."

"Yes, as you wish mother." Ellis jumped into action, picking up the Park employee's skin remains and dragging them to the entrance of the cavern to dispose.

"Let's see now, where was I? Oh yes, Childress get up and come to me."

On command, the stunned Childress got up and shamefully made her way over to stand in front of Auldicia. Her own hatred of her ancestor expanded with each step she took.

"You don't know where your child is, do you?"

"No. Justice took her from me." Again, Childress glanced over at Believa.

"I see. We need to find the legacy you birthed. So where is Justice, hmm? No one seems to know the answer to that question. Why do you continue to look at that one over there? Bring her to me."

Ellis snapped to action, and grabbed Believa by her arms and brought her forth to the foot of the throne. His jerking motion nearly tore her tethered head from her shoulders. Believa now stood before Auldicia, nervous and terrified.

Auldicia waved her curved nail hand over Believa and her belly. "You are not of my bloodline but you carry someone within your womb that carries my blood. Ahh, I also see you have completed the transition to vampire. You must feed yourself and the child you carry dear. After all, we must continue to spawn descendants.

Slashing her wrist once more after it healed, Auldicia grabbed Believa's dangling head and fed her blood. The diseased plasma hit the back of Believa's throat instantly reviving her. The fetus she carried stomped and kicked inside her womb as in celebration of what its mother received. Taking in the plasma, Believa latched her fangs onto Auldicia's wrist pulling deep draws on the blood offered.

"I see you like the taste and what it does for you." Auldicia smiled as she watched Believa enjoy her sustenance.

Only a minute passed before the sound of bone and flesh regenerating itself in Believa's body filled the cavern vault. Moaning in pain at first, Believa's contorted body, returned to its original form. Damage from the Dieth dart injections slowly began to reverse as well. Her hips and breast returned fuller and more voluptuous due to the pregnancy. Pleased with what she saw, Auldicia smiled.

"Tell me child, what is your name?"

"I'm Believa Beaushanks. I carry the child of Justice Treemount."

"Well now, the plot does thicken now, doesn't it? So now I ask you, where is Justice?"

"Justice is," Believa's confession of what she knew of Justice's whereabouts paused. A noisy grunt in the far corner of the cavern caused everyone present to turn. Nacio began to moan reminding everyone of his presence, and spiking the interest of Childress.

"Oh, Zuri Sweetheart, I nearly forgot you there in the dark, dank corner." Auldicia left her throne and quickly retreated to the area of the cavern where the love her life stood shackled. Childress felt her own eyes go wide at what she saw.

Oh, what is he doing here? It's the vampire we saw with Solis. Now he's here with Auldicia. I want my chance with him. This crazy monster will probably kill us all. I have to think fast if I'm going to survive, but I want to take him with me. I'll use him to find Solis, and turn her over to Auldicia.

Auldicia kissed Nacio's face while he stood enchanted. She slowly kissed down the front of his chest. Again, she reached for his shaft, feeling her spell keeping it stiff along with the silver barometer shoved in the urethra. After the last kiss she planted on his chest, she pulled back and spit in disgust at the scent wafting from his body.

"Yes, now I remember," Auldicia barked, angered and ready for battle. "Descendants, go forth, and find this female who has her scent all over my Zuri. Who among you can bring her to me, so she can receive her due punishment?"

Opportunity has just presented itself, giving Childress a way out of this mess. An opportunity she would not let pass.

There it is…a chance to get back at Solis, and finish her for good. I'll volunteer for this, and we will find her and bring her to Auldicia, and we will get on with our lives. Little did she know, this is only the beginning of a deal with the Devil with a high price which she couldn't default. Childress spoke up sealing her doom.

"My brothers and I know of this female. Her name is Solis Burkes. She and this vampire here had been killing other Treemounts throughout the city last year, and this year too. She lives here. We can find her and bring her to you."

Auldicia listened and weighed in heavily on what Childress explained," They have been killing others of my children. She and this vampire you say?" Auldicia pointed in Nacio's direction, "You say you can bring this wench to me? How soon?"

"Well, we have to get out of here first, but she lives here in town."

Anger lit the corners of her eyes as Auldicia grabbed Nacio's chin. "You have killed some of my children Zuri, you and this Solis Burkes?" Realization dawned on her, "She smells of an enemy I knew long ago. Could it be? Surely it couldn't be? Olinka? This Solis Burkes is a direct descendant of Olinka." Auldicia's wicked laughter boomed against the walls of the cavern, causing her zombielike descendants to chime in along with her. She turned back to Childress and gave her a serious directive.

"Alright Childress, you and your goons must go forth but before you do you must swear allegiance to me." Another slash of her wrist, and the dripping began once more. Her descendants gathered one behind the other to take from her wrist vying their loyalty to their mother ancestor.

"You all will feed from me. Pledging your allegiance, and vowing to destroy all the enemies that have destroyed our lineage." All of them fed. Last in line were Childress and her crew. They all hesitated as Childress stood looking on in disgust.

"I don't want any thank you." Auldicia's eyes looked her descendant up and down, grabbing her neck and she whispered a deadly warning in her ear.

"How impolite, Childress. You've already taken my blood into your body at one time or another. Why be shy now?" Auldicia slammed her wrist to Childress's mouth, as the diseased blood oozed onto her tongue, and down her throat.

Klein and Erland stood next to their sister, watching in disgust. Klein shook his head back and forth as he tried to run for the cavern entrance. Auldicia teleported from where she stood with Childress and cut Klein's escape attempt short, while his bumbling feet slammed his head right into Auldicia's dripping wrist.

Erland tried to ease into his emotional safety guard of catatonia, but Auldicia slapped his face repeatedly until he began doing a wild chicken dance in a circle. A telekinetic force lifted his body up to the vault of the cavern and dropped him face first to the ground. Childress screamed in horror.

"You stop this right now or..."

"Or what? What the hell you think you can do to me, huh?"

Erland's pummeled body twitched and then moved slowly, rolling over on his back. He turned up face first, giving his ancestor the opportunity to drizzle her plasma down his now willingly open throat. By this time, relief settled over Childress once she knew her sibling survived. She stood in awe at the level of power

Auldicia wielded, and she knew her days were few as long as she allowed this monster to roam freely.

How in the world did I unleash this horrible creature on this earth? Me giving birth to a baby is what caused her to return? I've got to figure out a way to send this demon back to hell where she belongs, but I know it'll be a long shot. So I've got to play my cards right.

"Alright, we'll go and get Solis Burkes and bring her back her to you."

"I thought you would see things my way, Childress." Auldicia made it clear death would come on swift feet to those who dared to betray her.

"Don't let the thoughts of betrayal number the days of your life. I expect to have Solis Burkes brought here to me by the next lunar eclipse which should fall on Halloween. If she is not, all those here who have taken plasma from me shall die a slow, agonizing, and torturous death. I plan to conceive a child with Zuri, and free myself from the debt of hell with the sacrifice of a legacy. You will also find your child Childress. A sacrifice will take place with her as the offering to secure my reign with Zuri. Do you understand?"

Childress now knew fear as it washed down her spine. She knew she would burn in hell herself before she gave her child up to this beast. Wherever Justice took the baby was safer than the clutches of Auldicia. Surely, he wouldn't have hurt the child would he?

"Yes, I understand."

"Yes you understand what?" Auldicia mocked as she funneled her hand over her right ear to the response. Childress let out a slow eye rolling breath.

"Yes, I understand, Mother first."

Auldicia's wicked laughter echoed throughout the cavern. "You will set out to find Olinka's filthy waste of a descendant, Solis Burkes."

8

No pain, no gain

The days and nights seemed blended together since the storm came and took Nacio away like a thief in the night. Our home has seen many sorrows over the last several months. Grief seems to follow us everywhere in the walls of the mansion. We tried to look for Nacio, but had no leads as to his whereabouts. It was as if he was sucked right out of this realm and off any radar for me to find him. Sometimes, I thought I heard his voice in the wind, as I sat outside in our garden, but when I turned expecting to see him, of course, he was not there.

My tears have been many, yet the bouts of anger seem to come out of nowhere. I'd find myself shattering drinking goblets against the wall, or ripping our bed sheets to shreds. In a fit of rage, I tore many invoices and receipts that belonged to the Puente Masonry, and discovered in a pile a copy of our marriage license. I traced my fingers over his name repeatedly, hoping it would draw him home, but nothing happened. I tried reaching out to him tele-pathically, and heard no response back from him.

Armando and Patience continue to try to reach out to me, but I have nothing to give them in return emotionally. They bring

Blessing up to my room from time to time. Gosh, she's really grown and she is gorgeous. I often hold her and rock her to sleep, all the while weeping and wishing I had the chance to have a child of my own. Those dreams would never happen. I was thankful to be alive, but felt if death wanted to come claim me, it would have been better than wallowing in grief as I am now. I knew I couldn't continue as I have day in and day out. Something had to change.

One day, Basrick knocked on my door, and I bid him entry. I sat in my robe and pajamas, at the desk in the sitting area. Many Kleenexes sat crumpled up all over the desk and floor. I tried to move some of the rubbish out of the way to try to half way give the appearance of composure. He wasn't buying it.

"Forgive me, Mistress, but I need some signatures on these invoices for the masonry."

I quickly obliged, hoping to return to my confinement to wallow in my sorrow. Instead of Basrick leaving, he stood there holding me in his sky blue gaze. Annoyed, I declared his departure.

"You can go now Basrick, if you don't have anything else." He didn't move. He just stared, making me pissed.

"I said you can go, now."

"I won't go until we get you back. You are needed, and you must get on your feet, Solis."

"You have a lot of nerve coming in here telling me that crap! I lost my husband, dammit. He's gone and he's not coming back. What the hell do you expect me to do?" By that time, right when I thought I had no more tears to cry, the water came like an angry flood. "What the hell do you expect me to do?"

"We want you to live. You would surely dishonor Nacio's memory by putting yourself to death from lack of care."

Basrick struck a nerve, and I got up to take a swing at him, but he only teleported out of sight across the room.

"You get your ass out of here, Basrick. Do you hear me? You leave me alone."

"I won't leave you alone. Your love and kindness brought me back from losing Basira. I won't let you lose yourself, because the sire is only temporarily gone from our home. We will find him, but you can't give up. Please, Mistress, don't give up."

Embarrassed and beside myself, I melted in his arms totally inconsolable. Sleep didn't come easy; often going for days at a time with no rest at all, so this meltdown was inevitable.

"Listen, Mistress, Menlo's sister Urgata is here. She has ex-plained that Childress killed their mother Bureau who was a famed mambo in New Orleans. They plan to exact revenge on Childress for their mother's death. My father and I feel it would be wise for you to learn some of the trade needed to put Auldicia back in the ground and put an end to Childress and her brothers as well. In doing so, we can find the sire, and put things right again. Will you please try?" I thought about his words for a moment.

"Yes. I'll give it a try."

That afternoon, Patience brought me fresh clothing. Making

certain I had bathed and gotten myself together, she combed my hair into a tight bun. I had deodorant on, fresh undergarments, and make up. When she finished the makeover, I looked in the mirror and saw someone I hardly recognized. The reflection showed eyes of someone who had wandered off the path, someone who had been hurt deeply, someone lonely, and yet someone smart. I turned to Patience and tried not to cry.

"Thank you so much for caring. I appreciate all you've done."

"No problem. You know we love you and Nacio both." It had been so long since we spoke his name aloud. Hearing it was like water to a thirsty plant.

"Now, let's go get your husband back."

†

I left my room for the first time in who knows when. The thought of moving about the mansion without Nacio around was too much to deal with. I knew I needed to get on with life to be strong enough to continue the search for him. So, I let today be the day. Downstairs in our living room was Menlo and a strikingly beautiful woman that looked a lot like Childress, only with softer features. Basrick spoke up as soon as my Jimmy Choo's hit the tile.

"Urgata, please meet Mistress Solis Burkes Puente. She and Mr. Puente own the Puente Masonry." I stuck my hand out for salutations.

"How do you do?" I noticed something very humbling about Urgata, a sort of grief she carried everywhere. A deep sorrow she faced all alone. I sensed no danger with her, as I did not with Menlo. She and I hugged in greeting. I also hugged Menlo.

"It's so good to have you back Menlo. I see you've recovered nicely. Please, both of you sit down." I snuggled in the Italian leather seat Nacio and I always shared when there was a household conference. His side was empty, but I carried on anyway as Basrick began to fill me in on everything going on.

"Urgata has some important information for us that could help with our search for Nacio, and to put Childress away."

"Forgive me for my rude intrusion, Mistress. Our mother Bureau Treemount La Deaux was killed by Childress the night she gave birth to the baby you have here in the home, my second cousin. I believe her name is Blessing. She killed my mother in such a savage way, I can't go into it right now, but she must be stopped. I understand your husband is missing. If he is a descendant like me and my sister, or if she turned him into a vampire, it is highly likely that she has captured him and imprisoned him. I do not believe she would harm him, but I am not sure if he is still in this realm."

A fit of rage neared, as I sat on the verge of losing it. I stood up, and began to pace. I felt my fists involuntarily ball up. Before I knew it, I went over to the wall, and drew back my fist to hit the wall. In the blink of an eye, Basrick was there to catch my hand, before the impact crushed it to a pulp. The thought of Nacio in captivity at the hands of his maker was too much to deal with. I wanted to kill her and Childress. Actually, I'm looking forward to the challenge.

"It's alright Mistress, be at ease."

"Forgive me, I don't mean to act out. It's just that I have a score to settle with your kinfolk and the end results are going to be quite deadly."

Urgata looked at me, with a glint of devilment in her eyes. "Those are my sentiments exactly. You have nothing to fear. Solis, just before my mother died, she transferred her powers and abilities all to me, in turn I vowed to destroy Childress. My mother sent me here to seek you out to make my cousin's destruction a reality. She knew that Auldicia had been unleashed from Hell, and she believed you and I as allies can stop her."

"I want my husband back. I want him back now."

"Yes, we will work together to make certain he returns."

Basrick looked on with excitement in his eyes, just as his parents came down the stairs with Blessing. The child slept comfortably with Patience. Urgata looked up and met eyes with Patience. At first, there was some tension from Patience, as she did not part willingly with Blessing under any circumstances and certainly not with another Treemount.

"I'm Patience Caraway, Blessing's mother." Urgata smiled, as tears slid from her eyes. Reluctantly, Patience handed the beautiful baby to her second cousin.

"Please forgive my weeping, but I haven't seen her since the night she was born. It's beautiful to see that Justice had sense enough to bring her to someone who would take care of her. Her scornful mother was about to throw her in the swamp as a sacrifice to the voodoo gods for supreme power. When Justice showed up he took her, and Childress stabbed my mother with the scissors used to cut this child free."

Patience hissed with fangs in full view of what she heard from Urgata. Everyone in the room was on edge.

"My mother wanted us to become allies Solis. It is the only way to stop the impending doom for this world if we don't. I would like to start an apprenticeship with you so that your preparation will be strong when it comes time to battle Auldicia. You will need to carry a weapon, perhaps a sword to utilize against her."

A voodoo apprenticeship educates a mambo, a female voodoo priestess, and houngans, male voodoo priests. The apprenticeship would be a sure way to compare notes and strategize on how to put Auldicia and Childress away, and to get Nacio back home where he belongs.

"Alright, Urgata. I'm willing but we must act fast. I feel we've already run out of time."

"Don't speak that way, Solis. You're only saying that because of the heartbreak you feel now. Trust me you are not alone, and we will fight this together. Not all of us are evil, in fact, my mother had grown apart from my Aunt Frances, Childress's mother. I never wanted anything to do with any voodoo or black magic at all, but it's in our blood. From what my mother understood, it's in yours too. We're going to find a common ground and make certain you save us all."

"I believe you, Urgata. We will fight this evil together, and restore peace to both our families. You are welcome here in this house for as long as you like. Please make yourself at home."

✝

Both Urgata and I went into the basement of the mansion to set up shop. We practiced spells all that night, we worked charms over different pieces of furniture in the home by moving them around, changing the shape of them, or making them disappear. I explained to her my gift of telekinesis. Astonished, she went wide-eyed when I made several objects hover over her head all at once.

In awe at my ability to commune with animals, Urgata stood in amazement when I summoned Nacio's pet Scarlet Macaw, Manolo to come and perch on a bookshelf just above her head.

"When I first met Manolo, Manny as we call him, I was terrified. Honestly, I still am and he knows it so, if he knows it's me calling him, he will just sit perched up somewhere high. When Nacio calls him, he comes directly to his shoulder or finger."

"Your skills are amazing. No wonder my mother knew it was the right thing to do to find you. You will be the one to stop Childress and Auldicia."

"I'm afraid we have problems deeper than that." I muttered. "Justice had a consort before Basrick killed him. Her name is Believa Beaushanks and she was carrying his child. We have a chemical compound called Dieth, Nacio's kindred brother, Bose engineered. We used this compound to try to stop the Treemounts from reproducing more children. Astoundingly, it worked, with remarkable results. The physical transformations of the recipients of the compound took away hip and breast tissue instantaneously, poisoning the female and male reproductive systems. Believa and I fought it out at a local Wal-Mart, and I filled her up with the Dieth, the results weren't so promising because she's now a vampire. I was hoping the Dieth would have killed her, but I have a feeling it might not have worked, because I didn't stick around to see if it finished the job. Bose was a direct descendant of Auldicia's, one of her children actually. She must have turned him right after he was born. Bose revealed this to Nacio when they fought, and Nacio killed him."

"Wow, you're right! If Believa isn't dead and she is carrying a child that Justice fathered, we will need to find the baby before it can be sacrificed. A newborn child as a sacrifice is one of the worst forms of murder all for power. We can't let that happen to the child. If the child survives, it is subject to be evil, only because of the life Justice led."

"I understand. We will need to decide what to do with the baby. We can't let it fall in the hands of either Childress or Auldicia. Would you be willing to care for the child, Urgata?"

"I guess if it came down to it. I've already been mothering our other sister Tahiti's children. No one seems to know where she is. She ran off long before Auldicia's descendants heard the summons."

"I feel I'm ready to battle Auldicia, but I also feel we need more on our side to make certain she goes back to Hell where she belongs."

"I'd like to know more about this chemical weapon you have. Perhaps we could take a look at it and see if it can be changed or mutated to a stronger form to get rid of Auldicia?"

Just then, Basrick and Armando entered the basement. Basrick brought with him good news.

"Mistress, I have an individual that works at the masonry, who could give us some assistance in managing the Dieth and any other chemical make ups." I was a bit leery of anyone new coming into our circle, mainly because of the setbacks we had thus far.

"Is this individual trustworthy?"

"Actually, he is. He's the new foreman over at the masonry named Hymn Platt."

"Has he been vetted yet? I don't want more surprises right now."

"He had already started working at the masonry, before Bose died, and he has done well. His descendants have known us and kept our secrets for centuries; he studied theology and has some contacts all over the world that might be able to give us some clues as to how to battle Auldicia. He knew other generations of our family in Europe who existed after we left."

"Let's hope so he can assist us. We need all the help we can get. Patience won't be able to help much because she's caring for Blessing. So it mainly leaves us." I paused for a moment, and recalled a conversation with Nacio about the new Foreman.

"Hymn Platt is his name? I believe I've heard Nacio mention that name before."

"Well, he's upstairs waiting to meet you so we can get

started."

"Alright, let's go."

†

Before I arrived upstairs, I wasn't quite sure what to expect, but I know I sure didn't expect to see what I saw standing in the foyer. The closer we got to the man I slowly felt my breath leave the closer I came into his presence. Basrick called his name and he turned toward us.

"Hymn, this is Mistress Solis Burkes Puente. She's the owner of the Puente Masonry."

Hymn Platt stood tall with broad shoulders and corded muscles flexing and relaxing in his jeans. Thick masses of curly black hair sat atop his head. His booted feet were an estimated size 12, with a 34-inch waist tapering his V shaped torso. You couldn't miss him in a crowd. We both extended our hands in greeting.

"Pleased to meet you."

"The pleasure is mine." His voice rumbled with bass so deep, he sounded like Barry White on the mansion intercom.

"Let's sit down in the living room."

We all headed toward the living area, with Hymn's heavy booted feet click clacking across the tile. When Basrick claimed he had someone who could help us who happened to be an ex-theologian, my guess would have been someone far older, shorter, rounder, and balding.

"Please have a seat Mr. Platt."

"Oh, please call me Hymn."

"Okay, Hymn. Would you like something to drink?"

"No, thank you, I'm good."

"Basrick, I'll take something to drink." Urgata and Basrick swept out of the room leaving me alone with Hymn---making the room seem extremely small, and awkward. I cleared my throat, attempting to swallow a breath of air. Menlo came in and sat with me.

"So Hymn, Basrick tells me you've been running the masonry?"

"Yes, I just made it to foreman when Mr. Bose passed on."

I hadn't even thought of what details Basrick might have told the staff at the masonry since he stepped in to oversee things. He's been so busy caring for Menlo, he hadn't had much time to spend over at the plant, but he put his every confidence in Hymn. Still leery, I needed to find out more about Hymn. When you first hear him speak, he gives the impression of being a big loving good 'ol country boy, yet you know there is so much more. He had no accent to give away any European heritage.

"How long did you study theology prior to coming to work for us?"

"For the last several years, I've studied at the University of Oxford. My love for the late 18th Century theological study of demonica, fuels my interest to destroy the Obayifo, Auldicia. I discovered in my studies she's killed my family descendants, and I have vowed to see her ashes returned to the pits of Hell once more. Basrick told me you needed assistance running the plant as well as Auldicia's destruction."

So this person is a vampire as well, now I wonder what his agenda is about---what's in this venture for him? His sentiments seemed admirable, yet I was unconvinced, so I continued my inquiry.

"And why would you be so willing to take on such a task?" My tone took on a more accusatory pitch, but I couldn't help it. Detection of betrayal is high on my radar henceforth. We couldn't take another Bose disappointment. "How do we know we can trust you?" Basrick and Urgata returned with a tray of drinks and goblets of warm plasma, just as my cross personality continued to ebb and flow. Hymn picked up a goblet and handed it to Basrick, allowing him to quench his thirst. Hymn continued his same demeanor.

"Well, I understand your concern, Mistress, but believe me what's happened with Bose shall not happen with me. I care too much for the Caraways, and plan to kill this great threat with all the strength I have, no matter what your opinion of me."

Feeling the tension in the air, Basrick quickly interjected to lighten the mood. "Okaaaay, I see we have had the ice breakers. So shall we proceed with what we know?"

I felt that was a good idea. I was about to explode. The longing for Nacio had reached its boiling point. My support came from him. It always had. Now, my support had gone, and I was back to square one again. It's up to me to repair my family and restore my husband. It's almost as if I have nothing left to lose.

Hymn carried a scroll under his left arm that he unfolded on the living room table. Running his hands over the calligraphic text on the ancient looking paper, he began his narrative lecture as we tuned in.

"The Obayifo Auldicia of the Ashanti in Africa owed a huge debt to the demon Vulkus. Her intentions were to get pure souls to seal her reign on earth. When that didn't occur, the demon ripped her from this realm. The damage she inflicted on the generations that followed proved phenomenal. Her bastard children she left behind would wreak havoc on society. They are many in number. You all have discovered some of them have taken powerful positions in political office and other ranks of government, making them especially dangerous."

I hadn't realized the possibility of having more Treemount jackasses in political offices. It would make sense; this would perpetuate the reign of evil, and make it impossible to get rid of them. Auldicia would always have henchmen in the world doing her bidding unless we stop her.

"My understanding is that your ancestor Olinka fought Auldicia at one point during her lifetime---defeating her, and Auldicia cursed Olinka's generation of family members. As one of Olinka's descendants, you carry the will and the power to break the curse and destroy her. Her return to this realm indicates she plans to continue to reproduce and bring more wretched children into existence. She must plan to reproduce with Nacio. His pure soul is one Vulkus would love to have, and it would seal her reign in this realm. She must not reproduce with him, if so she will remain here forever, and Nacio lost forever. With all of her descendants at her disposal, she could assemble an army to destroy Society as we know it."

"I believe she must have returned to this realm with the death of Justice Treemount and the birth of Blessing, the child Basrick's parents are caring for---her mother is a descendant of Auldicia. She is also a voodoo priestess, which makes Blessing a legacy."

"It would explain how she returned to this realm. We must make certain she never gets Blessing in her possession. Should she procreate with Nacio during the next lunar eclipse, all will be lost."

Sitting here listening to Hymn say these things about my husband made me lose it. The thought of Nacio's muscled frame lying in wait for that demonic witch to run her talons over his body made me crazy. Since he and I had exchanged blood, his absence has been unbearable. Tasting his blood made me insanely jealous. Before I knew it, I picked up a two-thousand dollar vase, and sent it crashing into the drywall. Basrick knew he could have stopped my actions, but chose to let my emotions run wild. Menlo and Urgata continued their silence.

"What needs to be done to kill this witch, and the rest of her trash? I need to know, because I feel time is working against us."

"The one thing the Obayifo hates is blood from a legend-ary White Komodo Dragon, a rare species of lizard resembling a white alligator. Legend supports, although not a direct threat to the

Obayifo Auldicia, the Komodo dragon's blood weakens her. Its blood is like acid, literally eating away her existence. The trouble we will run into is locating one. They are primarily located in Indonesia, but it's only the blood of the White Komodo that will do. We need to open a portal between the Realm of the Living and the Realm of the Condemned. To do this, we will need to invoke the spirits and contact Vulkus himself, to come and get his possession." Basrick knew time is of the essence.

"I will begin the search for this lizard, and pray that we can locate one." Armando's voice called out around the corner as he walked in with Patience and Blessing in tow, coming in on the tail end of the conversation.

"We will need extra caution my friends, and turn Auldicia's custody over to Vulkus immediately once the two realms are open. We don't want Vulkus to return to this world and claim any of us."

I still needed more to go on besides the fact the blood of a reptile can weaken her. I wanted her ass dead…again.

"Once we find the Komodo Dragon. We need to make certain that she returns to Vulkus and cannot return to this realm. If Blessing's birth and the spilled blood of other Treemounts set her loose in this realm this time, what's to say she can't use another child from another Treemount birth to return again?"

Hymn looked at us and finished his explanation. "Whatever resources we have available to us now will help us. I've seen the Dieth you've been using to inoculate the descendants, we can continue its use, but we also need to fortify it with some of the things that will stop her physical regeneration, and shackle her soul back to Vulkus. Her last apprehension took place at the hands of Vulkus. As a lust demon, he made certain her body only sustained minimal damage from traveling through the membranes of the two realms. Receiving flesh burns from the Hell brimstone fires, Auldicia's body regenerated easily---keeping her seductive curves intact to entice the lust demon."

Armando added his input, making a valuable point to wipeout Auldicia's regenerative ability.

"The Dieth we have in our possession already has a major impact on the physical appearance causing internal and external deformities on contact. The chemicals can be altered to add more erosive effects to stop her tissue from regenerating."

Finally, I felt we had a plan and action to get Nacio home, and to send Auldicia back to her waiting demon bedmate. Still, even though we had the plans in motion, I knew we needed someone with information on mixing the right amount of chemicals. Bose left notes on the Dieth recipe, but mixing more poison into the vats we have could be lethal for those of us that are human. I knew just who had the information I needed.

"My Uncle Nuke can talk me through engineering a chemical for physical decomposition that is safe. You guys can survive, but we might not survive a HazMat situation if those chemicals got loose."

Hymn continued with things he discovered over the years in his research on Auldicia and her existence. Much of the needed notions for her destruction are not readily within our grasp. The White Komodo Dragon blood will take us on the other side of the world. Nacio's absence is enough to send me to Hell, just to have him home. With things the way they are, me going to Hell to save him might so be a reality. Hymn's next words felt like a punch in the gut.

"Theology rebukes all forms of vampirism. As cliché as it might seem, Holy Water---a special Holy Water mixed with silver---burns the skin surface of a vampire with the fury of brimstone fire. Such water existed between the 15th and 18th centuries. Many scholars spoke of this blessed water as the end weapon used to fight vampirism when the church discovered its existence long before doctrines on vampirism became available to those realizing its detriments."

Again, I lost it. Pacing, the floor until if felt as if my heels chipped pieces of the mortar out of the tile. My adrenaline spiked, dipped, and coursed through my blood like Rose thorns.

"What? Silver spiked Holy Water?" I couldn't get over how outlandish Hymn sounded. "Well let's go to San Fernando Cathedral right here downtown and get some Holy Water and then go get my husband back." Hymn's face looked less hopeful than when he walked in. Then he confessed.

"Well, Mistress, it's not that simple. The water we need is located in only one place in the world. The required water resides deep beneath the Vatican floor---blessed by Pope Pius II."

"Rome? We have to go to Rome? Seriously? Hymn you're kidding, right? Hymn we don't have that kind of time. I need my husband now!"

"I could lie to you, but I won't." Hymn stood with his

voice raised an octave. "This is not something that will happen overnight. If we're not careful, one wrong screw up, one miscalculation, could seal our fate with Auldicia remaining here forever."

Time ticked away, and with every minute gone, I felt Nacio's fate becoming more and more doomed. Urgata spoke up, letting everyone know Childress owes a debt to the voodoo gods.

"Solis, remember I told you Childress is indebted to the gods for my mother's death. Punishment must be rendered." Urgata slammed her fist down onto her knee. Everyone's temper flared.

"Oh, she'll get her punishment. Urgata we are going to hex a special mix of Dieth for Childress and her hotcake ass, to make certain she has no more babies. We lucked out and had Blessing brought to our doorstep, but I doubt seriously if we'll have such luck in the future. We must leave immediately to get started retrieving what we need, yet I don't want to stop looking for Nacio, or Childress for that matter." Armando stepped up with coordinated plans awaiting my confirmation.

"Mistress I will continue to look for Nacio, so don't worry about that. It will also allow Patience to remain here with Blessing. We can't take a chance on Blessing being outside of the protection of the glamour Nacio and I put over the mansion the night of the storm. Things could get a whole lot worse should Blessing's whereabouts be detected."

"I agree. Menlo you are still not quite 'fight-ready' yet." Menlo cut her eyes in my direction and took the defensive.

"The hell I'm not! I'm not letting you all do the work and

sit back and watch. You have things twisted, Solis. My cousin killed my mother. Her dumb Hill Billy ass has let loose a Hell Cat on society, and you expect me to sit and recuperate? Hell to the "no" ain't happenin'!"

"Menlo, I couldn't stand to lose you as well. I want you to be safe. Plus, we need all the help we can get." Her gaze continued, as she paused to collect her thoughts. Menlo had done extremely well since her gunshot wound, mainly because Bose had bitten her prior to her receiving the wound. This blood exchange between the two helped her survive the life threatening injury.

"I can stay here with Basrick. I'll make a few calls to the PD, and follow up on leads on Childress and the other two fools to find out if they've been spotted. Urgata can help with whatever else needs to be done." Urgata gave a quick nod and reassured things would continue as planned.

"This would give me an opportunity to check on Nayphous and my boys. I can only imagine what they must be thinking with losing their grandmother and all. I've only talked to them briefly. Tahiti's children have undergone lots of trauma since she ran out on them. She's probably where ever Auldicia is. That means it's up to you two to get the things we need." Urgata looked at Hymn and me. Menlo jumped to her feet, and readied for action.

"I'm going to the library to make a few calls to get a few leads." Menlo left the room, anxious to get started on her investigation.

Urgata glanced at Hymn and me with a hopeful look. He turned in my direction and brought his point home.

"Solis, do you know why your fate would have you as the one to defeat Auldicia? Why you have to complete this task as the chosen one?"

I quickly shook my head 'No', but thought it interesting to shed some light on the subject.

"Your ancestor Olinka, descended directly from your ancestors that practiced only worshipping the good in those around them. Her sole purpose involved stamping out evil, just as Auldicia's sole purpose involved spreading evil, filth, and disease. The age-old epic story only you are in the direct line of those ancestors who existed closest to divinity Solis. No matter what you've endured here on earth, your purpose called you to be a keeper of order and good. Although overwhelming, you are the chosen one to carry on your family name, and the only one to end this reign of evil and terror."

With Hymn having spoken those words to me, I stood in shock. I certainly didn't look forward to this task, and had been hoping to live my life with Nacio. My admonishment for shunning this task had already come from the deceased spirits of my relatives, making it clear I had no choice.

"I see. Well, when you put it in those terms, Hymn, there's nothing I can do but move forward."

Menlo returned as quickly as she'd left, and her expression showed irritation. "My new partner explained Childress, Klein, and Erland got busted in Louisiana a few weeks ago."

"Thank God," I sighed, interrupting Menlo with the rest of her bad news.

"There was a jailbreak in New Orleans, about a week after their apprehension, and now they're at large again. Ten to one, they have come this way, if they haven't made it back to Bexar County already."

"Dammit, here we go again. Okay, from here on out, we all carry loaded Dieth pens for anyone of Treemount descent. I'm going to carry one of the swords we have in the library. Urgata, before we leave I need you to work a spell on the sword. Once we return with what we need, I will dip the sword in the silver traced holy water---making it a special weapon of destruction for Auldicia." Basrick stood next to his father and smiled. As the deadly, killing machine predator, he liked what my words implicated in slicing Auldicia's head clean off her shoulders.

"Sounds like a plan to me. I'll get started on the flight arrangements."

My anxiety continued to heighten, but I had to gather my wits to complete the task needed to get Nacio back.

"Good. We pack and leave next available flight out."

Hymn gave a curt nod, as well as the rest of the household. I needed time to myself to get my head together and decided to turn in for the night.

"Hymn, please feel free to chose from our suites upstairs. Basrick please show everyone to the rooms. Goodnight."

†

As soon as she returned to her suite, Solis locked the door immediately and looked around the room. Patience had taken the time to sneak in and clean up the place, leaving the bed turned down with crisp new Egyptian cotton sheets. Running her hands over the comforter, she closed her eyes as heated images filled her mind of a time she made love to Nacio.

Hazel filled his eyes and desire filled his heart. Erect and ready to fill her, she straddled his hips, and sank down on his shaft. The slickness of her loins made his entry easy, making her cry his name, as she threw her head back in ecstasy. His crown filled her so much that she felt him in her abdomen, taking all of him in one smooth movement.

Placing her hands on his cemented six-pack, she rode him long and steady---teasing him and making more wetness seep between her thighs. Her breasts bounced and floated over his face, taunting him more. Loving the feel of him filling her, she eased up once more, sliding him out of her, all but his crown, and then plunged down with fierce accuracy, taking all of him again. A stream of juicy wetness washed over his hips as he drew more from her, wanting all she had to give. She gave to him freely.

Needing more, Nacio flipped her over, making her ride backward saddle. Agile and extremely limber, Solis completed a horizontal split over his hips, sinking down over his crown making them both hiss pleasure from their lips. Readily accepting again, her piston movement took on a rhythm that started slow, but grew in cadence, making his crown wetter with each plunge.

Knowing she drove him to the edge of release, Nacio needed to be in control and present to his bride what she longed for, only what he could give her. With preternatural speed, he turned her over on her hands and knees, then spreading her legs he drew in a whiff of her scent, making him crazy. Placing his finger between her legs, he stirred the cream her body so easily made for him. His fangs eased from under their hood as he fought the urge to break his vow and give her his immortality. Instead, he extended his tongue and dipped it into her steamy folds, lavishing the moisture and lapping it over his lips, intoxicating himself.

Breaking away from him only briefly, Solis turned and grabbed a handful of his shaft, pulling it into her mouth. Taking a long draw on his flesh, she took as much of him in as she could, tasting the clammy moisture that settled over the surface of his crown. Her suction drew cries from him that let her know he belonged to her.

"I will love you all the rest of the days of my existence, Solis. Nothing will ever change that." He spoke after one last lap of her wetness, and then urgently guided himself into her from behind with a sluicing sound that shook him so much that he once again fought back his release.

Solis took her nail and cut the palm of her left hand. She reached back and fed her blood to his lips. The taste made him moan with a slow rumbling in his chest that began to build. One last penetrating stroke and Solis broke water like a crested dam as she came all over his crown, down his shaft, dripping over his sac. Her cry and his moan of release bellowed throughout the room, shaking the walls of their suite, rumbling the columns and drywall. The seed he gave her mixed with her own copious fluid, wet the bed in a soft drizzle accenting the love they shared for each other. No-

where near sated, Nacio grabbed his shaft readying it for another
round of love for his mate.

"...all the days of my existence."

Driven by the memories of the love she made with her husband, Solis moved the crotch of her panties to one side as her finger descended between her thighs to stir her emotions once more. Finding her silky pearl, the slick fluid washed from her walls as she whimpered in ecstasy. The pad of her finger strummed the ball of her clitoris like a guitar---making her own sweet music to keep the tears from stinging the corners of her eyes with grief. She lifted her hips and spread them, allowing deeper entry of her finger as she probed the ridges and smooth surface of her inner walls.

Her breasts fell to the sides of her chest as her nipples stood firm and erect, resembling small doorknobs waiting for someone to turn them. The hair around her lips carried her scent, and absorbed the moisture her finger stirred while she continued indulging in pleasure. She slowly withdrew one finger, shining under the dim light of her lamp, and brought it to her lips. The tang she tasted reminded her of a sweet kiss she shared with Nacio.

Adding another finger to work her pleasure, the volume of wetness soon pruned her fingers to wrinkle as her G-spot sent her hips high in the air as she climaxed repeatedly. Stroking her finger up and down the wet folds of her sensitive lips, her arousal moistened her from front to back. The puddle beneath her hips grew and spread into a pasty circle over the new sheets Patience applied to her bed earlier in the evening.

Laying in the wetness, Solis turned her head and wept softly in her pillow. Shame and desire had overtaken her, leaving her empty and burning for him. The idea of the unknown made it impossible to sleep. Grief settled in to lullaby her to a fitful rest.

†

Two hours passed as Solis tossed and turned. Awakening in the middle of the night, she went to her closet and found a plastic bag with a single strand of red hair she retrieved the night she and Childress fought. During the fight, she grabbed a handful of red hair from Childress just before she slammed her head down on the curb in front of her grandparent's home. During the fight, Klein and Erland threw a Molotov cocktail to blow the house up. Heading to the bathroom, she found a lighter, and worked a spell vowing to punish Childress.

"Childress please know that I plan to make the rest of your days on earth Hell. You have destroyed my family, and punished others. It is now your turn, and the misery you've inflicted on others will be returned to you tenfold. You killed my grandparents, you encouraged your brothers to rape me, and now you and that monster ancestor have my husband. You must die."

Solis hit the light and watched as the single strand of hair caught fire and burned to nothingness in her sink. She washed it way, with a final chant.

"I'm coming to get you Childress."

Satisfied she completed her spell, she dialed her Uncle Nuke who managed the Laurence Funeral Home and Sunset Services. Her thoughts continued to roll through her mind on the discussion she had with Hymn and Basrick about eviscerating Auldicia's body. Uncle Nuke would surely know about the stages of decomposition and the chemicals needed to increase the process. His caller ID let him know to greet her on the first ring. He picked up, and the conversation commenced as if he had just hung up with her.

"Here, here, what's going on?"

"Nothing Uncle Nuke, what's happening?"

"Awww, slow boogie. What's happening with you?"

"Uncle Nuke, I need to know exactly what chemical will increase the stages of decomposition on a body."

"Why, you need it for school or something?" She hadn't exactly told her uncle she wasn't in school the last semester and a half. She needed to come up with something quick to tell him. The less he knew made it safer for him.

"I need to know what you know because I have to make up a formula of a batch of my very own chemical to accelerate the decomposition process." She couldn't lie to her Uncle Nuke---not too much anyway.

"Well, let's see. There is stage one, Initial Decay, that brings with it Liver Mortis; the bruising after death first sets in. Then stage two, Putrefaction that brings bloating to the abdomen. Then you have stage three, Black Purification, known as advanced decay."

Uncle Nuke paused, and then smacked his lips happily,

washing down a gulp of his Miller Light. He continued his cliff noted lecture.

"With this stage comes what's called 'Skin Slip', because the skin slips off the bone. After that, comes stage four, the Butyric Stage or Fermentation Stage. You see, as the body breaks down, it takes on a smell like cheese. Stage five is Dry Decay, or the Skeletal Stage. This stage of decomposition can take years. It's where bones can turn into fossils."

"I need to make up a chemical formula that gets to the end of stage four ASAP."

"Well, hell, if that's all you need, just get you some Hydrochloric Acid and be done with it. There's no faster way to have flesh fall off your bones than to use acid."

Of Course,she should have thought of it sooner. "Oh thanks, Uncle Nuke. I'll see if I can't get some." His conversation always ended with a caution.

"You be careful out there now, you hear girl? We've been real busy lately on top of the bodies we've received from the tornado, we've had some come in that looked like they still have that serial killer on the loose. The bodies have no blood or plasma, and here lately, bodies have been coming in without the three F's; no fat, no fascia, and no fluids in them. Whatever's going on is dangerous. I'm mean real bad business, Solis! Please be careful."

"I will Uncle Nuke, I love you. I'm out." She hung up the phone, and fought tooth and nail for sleep.

†

Hymn stood with his head against his suite wall, listening to Solis first moan in pleasure, then whimper in pain. He said a prayer of peace for her.

"Father, please let her find comfort soon."

Making his way over to his bed, Hymn knelt at the bedside and continued his Psalm. As tears flooded his eyes, "Father, please give me the strength to watch over Solis, give her the courage to face her destiny, as I find the courage to give into mine. Keep her out of harm's way, and let us return to you safe and sound. In Jesus name Amen."

Hymn drifted off to sleep with his mind searching for ways to fulfill the needed task.

9

For the cause

Waking up the next morning, Solis found it easy to get her life-threatening journey underway. After a quick shower and simple grooming rituals, she readied for battle. Finding a skin-tight Black Matrix jumpsuit, she acknowledged how easily the leather slid over her smooth curves. Grief had carved away nearly 25 pounds, and she stood before the floor to ceiling length mirror; sexy, curvy, and in fighting shape like a newly dubbed Ninja. The leather of the suit, poured over her hips and thighs, giving her a deadly, sinister look; letting you know she intends to take no prisoners. She slicked and cinched her hair into a bun, revealing her beautifully arched eyebrows and almond shaped eyes, finishing with radiant skin. She finished packing then set her luggage at the door. One special suitcase with Dieth darts that resembled Insulin Pens, sat neatly packed with a double luggage lock near the handle.

Satisfied with her travel clothes, she completed her look with spiked, pointy-toed, black, Jimmy Choo, kick-your-ass boots. With the last track of zipper in place on her right boot, the phone in her suite rang. Basrick had just brought the car around front.

"Mistress, your 2 hour check in time is in 30 minutes."

"I'll be down in a minute Basrick. Thank you." She looked down at the beautiful 3-karat, red diamond ring Nacio gave her.

"We will reunite with each other soon, my Sweetheart." Opening the door, her reflexes caught her off guard as Hymn stood with arms crossed over his chest outside her door, waiting for her to enter the hallway, reaching for her luggage, greeting her easily.

"Good Morning, Mistress. How did you rest last evening?"

"I've seen better evenings, Hymn. Thank you."

Grabbing the colossal luggage from the entry of the suite, Solis noticed Hymn's cowboy boots---black, newly polished Eel Skin boots. They complemented a pair of black jeans, charcoal grey shirt, and a black Stetson broke down over his left eye. The scent of Armani Diamonds Cologne lingered from him shoulders. Moving to one side, he cleared the path at her feet, as they entered the hall toward the staircase.

"You look ready for the journey."

"I just want this over with as soon as possible."

"The end will come soon enough." Hymn rushed them down the stairs and out the door to the waiting Cadillac DTS. They both got in the car, and just before the car pulled out from the mansion driveway, Basrick gave a warning.

"Once you two are outside the protection of the glamour, you must take caution. If Auldicia has gathered her descendants, she might have them on the lookout for you, Solis. Once we get to the airport, check in immediately and keep moving to board your

flight. You are in first class to board first." Shoulders tense, Solis
readied for another life-altering journey.

Few words passed between them for the duration of the
trip, but adrenaline prickled through Solis as she tried to remain
calm. Looking up at the sky that covered their mansion and driveway, she saw colors resembling the Aurora Borealis, the northern
lights. Nearing the end of the two-mile glamour covered driveway, the colors faded marking the end of the protective magic.
Basrick's knuckles tightened on the steering wheel while his foot
hit the accelerator. Doing his best to get them there as quickly as
possible, the engine of the DTS roared while the front end jerked
forward, stretching out and eating up Highway 281between the
mansion and the airport.

Solis blinked as the drive made the scenery along the Highway smear to a blur in the windows. Drawing a long breath, she sat
stunned at the destruction of the Wal-Mart where she and Believa
battled it out. Debris and roof rafters lay to one side in a pile, as
City Public Works cleared the dangerous debris in the parking lot
of the demolished store. The monster tornado took out several
other buildings along the way. So much has changed since the day
of the storm. In reality, it meant since Auldicia had returned to this
realm.

The short ten-minute ride left no time to enjoy the comfort
of the luxury sedan she indulged in each time she rode in it. Basrick soon brought the car to a smooth curbside stop.

"I'm going to hang around until you call me to let me know
you've made it passed that gate. Clear?"

"Clear. I'll call as soon as we make it past the checkpoint."
Solis nodded and waved goodbye to Basrick.

Hymn slipped out of the car and went around to the opposite side to open the door for Solis. Slinging her purse over her
shoulder, Solis slid her hand into his huge palm to help her out of
the car.

"Let's go in this way Mistress. We need to get checked in."
Hymn quickly escorted her to the Southwest Airlines Counter for
baggage check-in. Solis made it to the counter and reached for her
identification. The ticket agent asked to see the identification card.

"Hello ma'am," the woman's southern drawl took the lead
in the conversation. "May I see your identification please?"

Solis quickly handed the woman her identification, and
in return the woman handed Solis a baggage claim. Repeating
the pattern, the ticket agent swiftly handed Hymn his identification card along with a baggage claim. The two worked their way
through the now thickening crowd toward the gate. Luckily, Solis
and Hymn wound their way through a snaking line to clear the
gate. The TSA agents ran a tight ship, getting carryon baggage
through scanners and using the hand held wand to assess any carryon weapon danger.

Hymn walked in front of Solis, taking off his Stetson and
placing it in a content bin. He held his arms out as a petite Brunette ran her wand over his tapered V mid-section, leading all the
way down his muscular thighs. The petite woman took her time
slowly running the wand just over his crotch. Hymn smiled at the
woman, raising his left eyebrow.

"Looks like I'm all clear." Hymn rocked back and forth on his booted heels. The Brunette smiled back at him happily and winked seductively.

Solis took two steps forward underneath the metal detector. The TSA agent, whose nametag read Delareaux, ran her wand over Solis's shoulders, not finding anything nor did the siren sound, yet she stood in Solis's way not allowing her to pass. Agent Delareaux drew in a deep breath, smelling the air and personal space around Solis like a dog hot on the hunt. Solis stepped forward, and still the agent wouldn't step aside. Irritated, Solis confronted the woman.

"Is there a problem?" The agent stepped right into her personal space and drew closer--- escalating the situation.

"Yeah…there's a problem, and you know just what it is." The woman's eyes were jade green as they gazed at Solis. Instantly, she knew she just had a confrontation with one of Auldicia's descendants, possibly dispatched to harm her. The green-eyed Brunette made her intentions known when she refused to step aside and let Solis move forward with the rest of the boarding crowd. Without drawing too much attention to herself, Solis pushed passed Agent Delareaux in a huff. Quickly catching up to Hymn on the other side of the gate, she whispered her plan of action, and placed a quick call to Basrick as promised.

"Hymn, that green-eyed hellion who just groped you fits the description of one of Auldicia's descendants."

"I suspected but wasn't sure. Come to think of it, she winked after she sized my package up pretty good."

"I'm going to place a call to Basrick. I might need his time-rippling skill in a few moments. I'm going to lure her to the restroom to avoid an all out confrontation that might involve police; then we're screwed. I can't let anything stop us from boarding the plane to California."

Just a few steps past the boarding checkpoint Solis grabbed her cell phone and called Basrick, who loyally awaited notice of her boarding.

"Basrick, we've just been frisked down by one of the descendants. I'm luring her into the women's restroom. Be on standby, to place a ripple in time within the next ten minutes."

"Will do. I'm on standby."

Hymn looked at Solis and started to intervene as Agent Delareaux conveniently slipped away from her post at the checkpoint. Solis placed her hand on his firm chest muscles, and slightly shook her head declining any intervention. After all, she could handle herself.

"I got this Hymn. Wait for me over by the tarmac, and we'll board together as planned."

"I can't allow anything to happen to you. I won't let anything happen to you."

"Trust me. I can handle this wench. Wait for me over there please."

Following instructions, at first it appeared as if Agent Delareaux planned to follow Hymn to a secluded corner for some quick pillow talk. Hymn quickly split off from Solis as she made a pit stop in the restroom. Agent Delareaux followed her lead and closed in on her, entering into the women's restroom.

Solis put her purse down on the sink counter and waited for her assailant to arrive. The sound of knuckles cracking from the hands of the agent echoed off the tiled walls, as her booted heels came to a stop. Slowly, Agent Delareaux stood face to face with Solis.

"That's a mighty interesting scent you carry, Solis Burkes. Mother First is looking for you. She says you've been rolling in the hay with something that belongs to her." Continuing to crack her knuckles, she smiled insidiously.

Missing Nacio and pissed off to no end, Solis responded the only way her emotions would allow her to. "Yeah, well tell Mother First to kiss…my…entire…ass."

Solis lunged forward connecting a powerful right hook, sending Agent Delareaux slamming into the hand towel machine on the wall---a cut split open on her head and blood spewed. She followed up with a missed upper cut, as Solis bobbed and weaved to one side. Delareaux's anger made her imbalanced, causing her to reach for a concealed box cutter in her back pocket. Waving the box cutter in a circular motion in the air, she taunted and teased.

"Oh you think you're tough, don't you? Just wait 'til Mother First, gets a hold of you! You're going to be squealing for mercy, and there shall be no mercy." She swung and missed, giving Solis the opportunity to kick her in the gut; stuffing it in far enough to crack a rib. Already sore, the agent's back slammed into the tiled wall, knocking the wind from her lungs.

Frustrated, Delareaux simply threw the box cutter, nicking Solis with a flesh wound on her upper arm. The sting startled and irritated her.

"Damn that stings!" Before she could blink, the bloody agent charged her grabbing her by the throat. Unusually strong, with similar agility like that of a vampire, the woman attempted to crush her windpipe. Solis found the woman's strength amazing, wondering if magic fueled her muscles.

"Mother First has big plans for you. Oh yeah, you haven't felt pain until she puts it on you! You just watch and see."

Right then, Solis knew she had to make a life or death decision. She had never killed anyone before, but she understands how quickly self-defense justifies the rational for taking someone's life. The decision came quickly.

With her assailant merely inches away, Solis head butted the woman, knocking her backward. Stunned, the woman scurried to her feet, just as Solis completed a 360-degree fan kick. The kick brought the golden Jimmy Choo heel across the woman's neck, ripping a happy face smile between her two carotid arteries. Delareaux grabbed her wound while blood spatter decorated the walls, pooling at her feet. Dropping to her knees, the sound of her shattering kneecaps crunched on the floor as she fell forward splashing in a puddle of blood.

Satisfied Delareaux stood at Death's door. Solis quickly grabbed a hand towel and wiped away any flesh that clung to her four and half inch heel. Timing the disposal of the body just right, she hurried out of the restroom and placed a call to Basrick.

"Now, Basrick go ahead and put a ripple in time. Fast forward and put us on the plane."

Outside in the parking lot at San Antonio International Airport, Basrick held his breath, closing his eyes, and everything around him sped up to a blur. Solis hurriedly blended in with the blur around them, and she and Hymn boarded the plane without any problems. The dead TSA agent's body lay in cold blood for the cleaning crew to discover. Nothing would implicate Solis, nor would any security camera footage disclose the assailant of the horrific crime.

Solis sat in a seat next to Hymn. He held onto his Stetson during the flight. Looking at Solis in astonishment, he took a deep breath and let his shoulders relax in the seat.

"I guess you can handle yourself pretty well. What will the cleaning crew find when they go in there?"

"A bloody mess." Those were the only words she used to describe her first kill. Her thoughts reflected on the events of the last few minutes.

Life is so precious. You can't waste any time living your life. None of us knows when our last day to breathe comes. I didn't know myself for one moment when I took that woman's life. I didn't know myself, because…I liked the rush I felt when I took her life…I liked the power. For once in my life I didn't have to play the victim. I'm going to find you Nacio, and I'm going to kill Auldicia…and Childress. Her obsession to kill them both grew with each minute that passed.

†

An irritating scream came from the women's restroom near the C Gate at San Antonio International. Airport Police as well as the San Antonio Police Department came rushing down the terminal corridor to find the deceased Agent Delareaux sprawled faced down in a pool of her own blood.

Delareaux had a sister, LaMaze, who also worked as a TSA agent. She had just clocked in when the commotion exploded down the corridor. She too had received orders from Auldicia to hunt down Solis. Another TSA employee ran to stop her from entering the bloody crime scene. She received confirmation of the victim's identity; her screams joined the chaos. Knowing her centuries old ancestor would not like this news, she had to inform her of the events that occurred. This incident would surely cause an uproar making the strike against Solis imminent.

Reporting to Auldicia took top priority over following the speed limit as she weaved in and out of traffic, nearly rear-ending an 18-wheeler. Swerving to miss a deer standing in the road caused her to hit a rock, shredding her tire. Without missing a beat, she continued at top speed and drove on the tire rim with sparks scorching the road. Arriving at the gates of Natural Bridge Caverns, she hopped out of the car and left it smoking on three wheels.

Her quick pace and heavy footsteps kicked rocks and brush clearing a path to her ancestors cavern. Coyotes howled at the moon, while she entered the presence of Auldicia. Rotted flesh greeted her as vicious flies swarmed and buzzed through the humidity and mold. Several yards deep within the cavern Auldicia's green eyes beamed like spotlights on her. She must have just finished feeding because another human carcass lay at her feet underneath her rock-carved throne. Hissing after a strong burp, Auldicia's interrogation began.

"Did you find Olinka's filth?" Identifying Solis as 'Olinka's filth' rather than by her name served to remind those around Auldicia of the hatred she held for her nemesis. LaMaze, sucked in a quick breath before she answered.

"My sister must have found her because she is now dead, and Solis escaped." LaMaze began to weep as she hung her head low. She shook her head back and forth as grief washed over her. "Her throat was cut open."

"Did you say Solis escaped?"

In the far corner of the cavern in the dark, a semi-conscious Nacio opened his sunken eyes. Silver and mercury from the barometer Auldicia shoved into his urethra turned into liquid poison, which seeped from his tear ducts---burning his face. Listening to the drama unfolding further between Auldicia and the descendant, he knew how she rendered punitive punishment during her rage.

LaMaze nodded her head. Her weeping continued.

Auldicia stood, stepping down off the throne, offering comfort to LaMaze for her sister's tragic death.

"There, there, you poor dear." Extending her arm with long talon like fingernails in a comforting gesture, she stood still. LaMaze leaned in to receive the affection from her ancestor. Her weeping turned into uncontrollable sobbing.

No warning sound or words came within the next second before Auldicia looked into the young woman's eyes and wrapped her right hand around her throat---crushing her windpipe. Air escaped the woman's throat sounding like a teakettle whistling as LaMaze screamed her last breath.

"You dare fail me? I said bring Solis Burkes to me!" Auldicia raged, and dropped the limp body to the ground. "Now you and your sister can be together once more."

Ellis squinted in horror as the teakettle hiss from LaMaze finally ended and death stepped in to collect.

"Clean this rubbish, and leave it for the bats outside, Ellis. I want you to go and bring Olinka's filthy waste to me. Do you hear? Do it now, or risk ending up like this one!" Auldicia pointed to LaMaze lying dead at her feet. With her neck squished, eyes bulging, and face frozen, she looked more like a tablespoon lying on the ground.

"Right away, Mother First."

Not wanting to gamble on his life, Ellis quickly obeyed and set out to find his ancestor's enemy…his enemy.

Nacio continued his helplessness in silence. Feeling his dread, Auldicia went into the darkness, slowly drawing closer to him. Holding on to the little strength he had, he couldn't flee which made his anguish worse. She slithered up behind him, washing his left ear canal clean by flicking her tongue inside.

"I want you now, Zuri, and you know I get what I want."

Taking his shaft in her hand, she pulled the skin of his shaft downward, forcing the silver barometer from his urethra---giving him a slow relief from his toxicity. She removed one poison only to replace it with another.

"Ellis, bind his arms with the silver chains." Ellis turned around and moved swiftly to fulfill his task.

"Now leave us. I do not wish to be disturbed."

Ellis scurried out of the cavern to begin his mission of finding Solis. The other descendants already had a jump on their assignment with little results. Delareaux and LaMaze are now dead.

"It's time for you to give me your seed, Zuri."

Auldicia wrapped her right leg around Nacio's waist. She guided his shaft between her legs, and into her rotten folds. Completely mounting him with her other leg, she draped her body around his, and allowed herself to indulge in pleasure. With her preternatural strength and speed, she allowed her body to make long steady strokes up and down his shaft.

Throwing her head back in ecstasy, her climax shook loose several stalactites from the cavern ceiling. Unbeknownst to her, the cry of pleasure caused lightning to strike from underground, reaching up from the depths of Hell. The electricity from below destroyed stalagmites as they stood in place, but now turned to dust. The force of the electrical surge threw her body against the jagged wall behind her. Cursing the name of Vulkus, she knew her captor's jealous rage shook the ground below her feet.

"Damn you Vulkus! You have no power over me in this realm. Leave me be! I have no love for you. Getting my freedom from you shall come soon enough." She returned to straddle Nacio's waist and continue her rhythm.

Nacio whispered to the great demon below while Auldicia cursed him.

"Great Vulkus, I vow to deliver this hellion returned to your clutches for imprisonment for all time."

His continuous trance rendered him helpless, while Auldicia rode him until his skin tore from his flesh. The silver in his body made regeneration nearly impossible. After taking her pleasure then dismounting him, she reached out to touch his face.

"We will rule together my love."

†

A buxom blond flight attendant with extra black mascara plopped in the corners of her eyes approached Solis and Hymn with a courtesy cart. Slowing it, she smiled cheesily at Hymn. Her low cut Dolce & Gabbana blouse folded allowing the split between her plentiful bosoms to greet Hymn's flushed expression. Solis sniggled to herself as the flight attendant's too-tight skirt rode up her thigh, doing her best to flirt. The Texas twang drawled her words.

"Do you need anything, anything at all? Just call me, hear?"

"I'm good, ma'am. Thank you much." Hymn tipped his hat to the top-heavy flight attendant.

Solis sat surprised. Hymn turned down the country bump-kins overt advances without a second glance at her assets.

"Wow, Hymn! You gonna turn down that opportunity?"

"She's not my cup of tea. I like my tea steamy and hot. That one's a little too cool and open if you get my meaning. Besides, my focus is on one thing only. That's getting us to Indonesia safe and sound."

The flight took them to California, and then their connecting flight took them straight from LAX to the far pacific island of Flores, Indonesia. Both Solis and Hymn had an opportunity to look at every in flight movie aboard the plane. Hymn had been snoring softly under his black Stetson. Solis found it a bit more difficult to find peaceful sleep. Her dreams carried her to strange places, with Nacio either just ahead of her or several steps behind her. Exhaustion from the chase in the dream left her weary.

The flight attendant gave an overhead call. "Please fasten your seatbelts we'll be landing shortly."

Hymn awoke ready for action, and began planning their navigation to find the White Komodo Dragon. "This big lizard can be found on the inland shore on this Island of Flores. Once we find it, we can get our loot and go."

"Will the lizard be hard to apprehend?"

"I doubt it. However, you can never be too safe."

†

The travelers touched down on the Island of Flores. Many of the natives drove cabs similar to the ones you see in Japan. Solis had never traveled to this part of the world, and left most of the navigation up to Hymn. Once he identified a half way trustworthy cabbie, he explained he needed to make it to Komodo Island. Since this island sat tucked away between Bima and South Flores, they knew they had to make haste to get what they needed. Solis voiced her apprehension.

"Are you sure this man is going to lead us to the island? He looks a bit shifty eyed."

"Just what do you mean by shifty eyed?"

"Well, for starters he keeps looking at your hat as if he plans to pull a snatch and run stunt. Second, he's moving a little too much for someone who should be focused on getting us to our destination."

"If it makes you feel better, I can ask him how long it will take to get where we're going."

"Yes, I'd feel much better." Solis gave Hymn a sharp look and folded her arms as she waited for the Indonesian man's response.

Hymn, began speaking what few words he learned in the native tongue of Manggarai and Malay…not knowing many. He played the role of a lost tourist very well. He convinced the man to take them where they needed to go. Money spoke many languages to communicate their needs.

"Our journey is a long one; just at the base of those mountains on the island in the distance." Hymn looked at Solis with his left brow arched up high over his eye, and his lips pursed in frustration.

"Well, guess we'd better get a move on. Lucky I brought my hiking boots." Solis had never really been on a hike before and guessed it would be best to brace this as a new experience. It didn't matter what she had to do. She needed Nacio back at her side, and she planned to get him back by any means necessary, even if it meant going to the ends of the earth.

The two made their way across Flores, which went well into the nighttime hours. The little half jeep, half Volkswagen vehicle bounced and threw them about the open cabin so hard that Solis actually found a light bruise or two. They finally made it to Komodo National Park Hotel.

The Hotel buzzed with travelers from far and wide. A couple with an Australian accent argued about what time to leave for the next gaming expedition. An Aborigine male with native clothing stood at the desk speaking what one assumed were curse words at the maitre'd. The hotel staff kept pointing at the two-inch thick mud encrusted underneath his toenails and dangling from his feet. One assumed the argument centered on the filth caked to his body. Basrick had made reservations for two rooms under Solis's name. A local man checked them in and called for the bellhop to show them to their rooms.

Pleasant scenery at the hotel caught the eye of the guests. The pool drew most of the attention. It led to the beach, but the beautiful view ended with the pool. The beach on the other side of the pool hosted lots of rubbish.

Arriving at their rooms Solis noted the rooms were side by side, which proved a good thing since she had never been to the other side of the world, unlike Hymn. He had studied theology around the world, and felt safe enough to count this place as one of his travels. She bid Hymn good night.

"Thank you, Hymn. I'll see you in the morning."

"I bid goodnight to you too, Mistress."

Solis saw the bed in the center of her suite, and swan dived straight in the center of it. Jet lag claimed her body, and sleep seemed best for her. Stripping every piece of clothing off, she dropped a trail to the bathroom and just as she dropped her bra, she noticed a connecting door to Hymn's room. A little shocked but not overwhelmed, Solis resumed her plans for a hot shower, anticipating a pillow under her head.

The first two days there on the island turned up empty. They ventured out alone without a tour guide within the first 48 hours after arrival, and found themselves going in circles and coming no closer to completing the task than before they left the states. Solis and Hymn talked more and strategized about the different sightings of the Komodo dragon over the years. The island natives knew of the White Komodo, and explained they needed to get to Komodo Mountain. The two made plans to strike out and go there the next day.

The evening set in and the two sat in the Dining Hall. When the waiter came to take orders, Solis ordered a Seafood Fanfare from the menu. Not having paid much attention to his eating habits until now, she noticed Hymn ordered the same entrée. Solis asked Hymn about his theological studies around the world.

"So I take it you've been to this part of the world before?"

"Yes, I've been to this part of the world a few times. There are many religions in this part of the world that are very interesting to me."

"Do you feel we all live in sin and fall short of goodness?"

"Yes, I do believe that."

The waiter had gone for only a short time, when he returned with their food. Solis sat in shock and bucked her eyes when she saw him pick up his silverware, and slice into his fish, and bring it to his mouth. He ate it, identifying Hymn as a human.

"Oh, I didn't know you ate. I guess…I mean…I thought you were a vampire."

Hymn continued to smack and chew heartily before giving her an answer. She watched as his mouth formed words.

"You thought I traveled as part of the same species as the Caraways?"

"Yes, yes I did."

"Well, I'm human, Solis. If you remember, the night we met. I explained my family knew the Caraways from Europe. The members of my family, who knew the Caraways, are from two and a half generations ago. My family knew them, and knew what they were, and kept their secrets." He whispered low to keep the level of privacy.

The things Hymn disclosed to Solis made sense. It fell in line with the age Nacio claims and the age the Caraways claim during time they became vampires.

"As I mentioned, I took an interest in theological studies, and made it my life's quest. My family left generational wealth at my disposal. I've enjoyed many experiences in my lifetime. "

"You never wanted a family or children?"

"Well, I just thought those things would come with time. I never felt a rush to get those things."

"I guess I just thought you were immortal like them."

"Nope, I'm as human as you are. If you stab me, I'll bleed. If you kill me, I'll die."

The two finished their meal and continued to talk, and learned trivial things about each other. Neither of them pried about the other's love life. The night ended quickly.

"Well, Hymn, I guess it's time to turn in. I've enjoyed talking to you. We've got a complicated task tomorrow."

"Yeah, we do. We have to get an early start."

"Goodnight Hymn."

"Goodnight Mistress."

†

A steaming hot shower put her right to sleep. Her longing for Nacio's embrace began once more, as a dream carried her right into strong arms that felt good.

Her naked body reveled in his touch. She stroked his face, and soon found herself stroking his shaft although his physique felt different. She knew every inch of his body, but thought nothing of the change she felt in his touch. The girth in his shaft had a thickness that filled her wet folds on contact. Even with her generous moisture, it took two shoves for him to enter her body, leaving her breathless and then whimpering for his rhythm to begin.

Yes, the difference in his touch made her weak; made her want more; made her ache for more. Devilishly, he snuck his hand between her legs as the other held her left leg at a 45-degree angle, both legs in mid air resembled a television antenna. He slipped his fingers fluidly over her clit making her arch her hips to him. A cry slipped from her lips, making her juicier.

"Nacio, I need you." Her whispers continued as his rhythm increased along with the sweet little circles he made with his fingers. Crying out again, she called to him once more.

"Do it again, Sweetheart." Solis slit her palm with her fingernail to feed him her plasma, just as she opened her eyes to climax. Instead of seeing Nacio...she saw Hymn's face as his release washed down her hips in a warm stream. "Hymn", she called out.

Solis was startled from her sleep, sitting straight up in bed. Her saturated pillow felt cold from her sweat. Her muscles continued with spasms. She reached for the comforter and fell back with her hands overhead. Once again, the tears came, and they were angry ones. She wept herself back to sleep.

Just on the other side of the connecting door. Hymn stood with his back against the wall. He had been fighting his stiff erection for the latter part of the last hour. Hearing Solis cry out in ecstasy repeatedly proved unbearable. His wide shaft strained for her hands to touch him there, standing out from his groin like a flagpole. Sweat began to drench his body as well. His sac hung like a weighted anvil.

Did I just hear her call my name? Is it me giving her all that pleasure in her dreams? Oh, I can't stand this. I'm going to knock on this door to make sure she's alright. Damn it, I can't go in there like this. It would be death for me to look upon the Sire's wife with lust in my soul. Oh Father, please purge me of this lust, and let me restore the Sire back to his spouse. I can't take this agony anymore. I'm going to knock and make certain she is unharmed.

Hymn raised his hand to knock, but stopped short once he heard her weeping. He knew sleep would return to her, whether peaceful or not. Sleep would not come as easily for him; not with a flagpole leading his body around the room.

Hot to his touch, he held his shaft in his grasp---barely getting his hand around it. He lifted his flesh as the tip seeped and moistened his stroke. Hymn moved to the side of the door, and braced his free hand against the wall, getting a firm footing as he held on. Each stroke tighter than the last, his release bubbled to the tip causing his hot fluids to splatter against the wainscoting. His hips bucked as his seed kept his body in a state of tremors for several minutes. He quickly moved over to the bed, the crown of his shaft sliding over the comforter. The slightest touch caused another pressurized round of seed to spew from his crown, prolonging the tremors and increasing his desire for Solis. Soon, wetness covered most of his bed. Completely exhausted, Hymn rolled over on his back and soon his shaft gave way and loosened from its rigidity. Sweat moistened his curly hair to lie flat to his scalp, and the rest slid over his pillow. His limbs loosened after his release forced him into a comatose like sleep; sleep that saved his soul from committing sin and receiving death.

"I beg you, Father, please save me."

✝

The next morning the sun rose high in the sky. Hymn jumped to his feet, and then made a mad dash for the shower. He had to get downstairs before Solis did. The thought of facing her after his solo session last night made him shake like a leaf. He couldn't disclose his feelings for her. Something that cataclysmic had the potential to end his friendship between with the Caraways, and last but not least…death.

Their journey today takes them to the top of the largest mountain on Komodo Island. The legendary White Komodo Dragon would lie in wait in its lair, as they pursue the task of acquiring some of its blood. Ultimately, they meant the animal no harm.

Hymn started out of his hotel room and headed downstairs to the first floor. Once outside, he knew they had lots of ground to cover today. Around back, poolside of the Hotel stood the cabbie that taxied them to the hotel. He had the duty of tour guide for the day. Working on getting in his right frame of mind for the trek, Hymn sat and enjoyed coffee while he waited for Solis to arrive downstairs.

†

Greeted by the early morning light of the sun, Solis sat up in bed from a fitful night of rest. Confused, she recalled the strange dream of making love with Nacio. What started out as a dream of passion and desire, turned into a nightmare of deception and evil.

What is wrong with me? I don't understand how I would mistake Hymn for Nacio in my dream. His body is entirely different from Nacio's. Sure he's handsome and all, but I could never betray my beloved; I won't betray my beloved! Could it be I'm missing him so much that I've confused Hymn's chivalrous and protective stance with Nacio's demeanor? No matter, this is strictly Business. Hymn Platt is here to get my husband back and that's it. End of story.

Solis jumped in the shower, and wore her hair in a high cascading ponytail that dusted her shoulders. A three quarter length sleeve white cotton button down, Rider jeans, and lug style hiking boots served as the ensemble she chose to wear for the journey. She said a quick prayer and headed downstairs. Stepping into the lobby, she looked out on the patio and saw Hymn and the cabby that escorted them to the Hotel sitting poolside. A bit flushed, she kept her conversation short and businesslike with Hymn.

"Good morning Hymn. Did you sleep well?" Hymn seemed a bit jittery, but answered her by jumping to his feet and tipping his hat.

"Good morning, Mistress. Well, we have a long journey ahead so we'd better go." Nervously, Hymn jumped to his feet and waved motion to the cabbie, for their departure. He nearly left in a rush, appearing distracted. Solis nearly had to run to keep up with his pace.

"Are we in rush for some reason?"

"Well, Mistress I know how you want to hurry and get back to the states, so we need to make a move. We still need to journey across Asia to Europe, so the sooner the better." He couldn't help but notice how snuggly her thighs fit in her jeans as she stood in front of him. Entertaining thoughts of her naked body would not help with the task at hand. Solis simply nodded and slid into the Volksjeep looking SUV, and prepared her mind for her journey to the top of Komodo Island Mountain.

After driving 20 miles across the island, the Volksjeep bumped and sputtered to a stop at the valley foot of Komodo Mountain. Hymn jumped out, and grabbed his handheld telescope to look up the path that scaled up the mountainside. Their destination came into view at the top of the big rock. Hymn sprang into action.

"Alright, our goal for today is to make it to the top of this rock. The legendary White Komodo is in that cave. Once we get in, we'll need to tranquilize the animal, siphon the blood, and move on. We don't want to stick around here at night."

Solis grabbed the bags packed with climbing ropes and tents to pitch a small camping ground. Once they pitched camp, Hymn instructed the cabbie, who only identified himself as Dong, to remain at the camp until they returned. They traveled with only a medium-sized bag with three hunting knives, tranquilizers, water, syringes, Dieth darts, and two small flashlights. Hymn kept his darting eyes away from looking at her butt as she traveled in front of him along the narrow winding path. Taking two steps for every one of his, she purposely kept ahead of him to widen their distance. They spoke few words, traveling silently.

Solis took a chance and asked how he enjoyed his night in his suite. "So Hymn, how did you sleep last night? My room felt somewhat hot." Feeling his shaft respond to the first word spoken from her mouth, he allowed his steps to fall back from hers.

"I felt only cool drafts from the wind." He lied to keep his responses short, not wanting to engage in any conversation. He feared his growing erection would disclose his real feelings."

Trudging in the hot sun for what seemed like hours, they reached the end of the path, only to find they underestimated their journey. Hymn's destination proved accurate, but they stood flabbergasted at what they saw. The path abruptly ended a few short feet from where they stood. A weak looking bamboo tied wooden bridge stretched approximately 150 feet across an estimated 750-foot ravine. Their destination continued on the other side another 400 feet. Solis froze when she saw her obstacle course.

"Dammit, I hadn't prepared for this. I hate heights."

"Don't worry. We'll make it in time for Sake back at the

Hotel." Hymn tried to jest to keep her mind from the task before
them.

From looking at the rickety bridge, they couldn't take any
chances on having one of the ropes break from the added weight of
the equipment they carried. A unanimous decision to leave some
of the weight behind came quickly. Solis took the lead in front
of Hymn, and started crossing the bridge. Hymn soon followed,
listening for sounds of snapping rope as she put her weight down
on the planks.

Both of them crossed the raggedy bridge in a heel to toe
manner, carefully distributing their weight equally. Solis crossed
the bridge first, making certain her traveling partner followed
closely.

"Looks like we made it. Now let's hope we get what we've
come for."

"Roger that."

With 400 more feet to go, they had nearly made it to the
opening of the cave, when Solis noticed a large marble sized
mosquito that flew with the velocity of a slingshot. She ducked the
pest picking up her pace, when suddenly Hymn shouted.

"Run, Solis, Now!" A buzzing swarm of marble sized vec-
tors came at them from the direction of the cave. The thickness of
the swarm blackened the sky, forcing them to run into the darkened
unknown of the cave. Solis kept moving to escape the predators.

"Don't worry, I'm running." She kept her pace as they
sought shelter in the mouth of the cave. As quickly as the blood-

sucking mosquitoes appeared, they were gone. Still swatting away at their attackers, they took note of white glowing eyes in the distant darkness. They knew they'd made it to the right place. Now only equipped with the small handheld flashlights, syringes and tranquilizers, they had to get their harvest quickly.

At first, Hymn thought wind blew through the cave, but soon realized several Komodo dragons hissed as they lined up to greet them---ready to attack. Solis stood ready in her defensive stance.

"Oh boy, here we go Hymn. Are you ready?"

"Yeah, I'm ready. Let's do this carefully. You know they're pretty stealthy."

"Yeah, I know that. Just distract them while I try to fish out the White Komodo."

"How are you going to do that? It's not like he's just going to come to you." Hymn dodged the long tail of one Komodo, careful to avoid its bacteria poisoned red saliva dripping from its mouth.

Solis only took seconds to figure out a plan. She already had the loaded tranquilizer gun at the ready, but she didn't want to use it on any Komodo except a white one. Hesitating proved dangerous for her as she narrowly escaped the snapping jaws of one of the angry residents, jumping on the top of rocks to move out the way.

Hymn let loose his frustrations and started firing the tricked out insulin pen disguised tranquilizers to slow the predators. The force of the propulsion and the strength of the needle had to penetrate the density of the Komodo's skin. One agilely moved out of range, causing Hymn to miss his target.

Running and dodging the animals only seemed to take them deeper and deeper into the cave. Solis held tight to her flashlight, but soon stopped short with a gasp. A good 20 feet ahead of her, a White Komodo Dragon lie draped across a raised platform. Solis stood in amazement, as the grand 10-foot monitor lizard turned its head in her direction, and hissed loud enough to have the sound echo up and down the walls.

"Hey Hymn, I've found him…and he's pissed."

"Yeah, I bet. I'm coming your way. I've got four knocked up with tranquilizer. They'll be down once it kicks in."

Solis moved in closer to the animal. It started to hiss louder, sliding down off the rock, and moving towards her. Standing still, she tried to reach out to the animal, by communicating with it. She sent a telepathic message, hoping for some acknowledgement.

"We come in peace. We seek your help. A sample of your blood holds power where I come from to help rid us of evil. Will you please help us?"

Pissed, the White Komodo gurgled up some of its toxic saliva and spit directly at Solis, narrowly missing her arm. Soon the reptile stood up on its hind legs nearly standing to the vault of the ceiling.

"I take that as a 'No'." Hymn looked on as he took notice of more movement behind the white Komodo.

"We have to move quickly, Solis. He's called in reinforcement."

Behind the White Komodo, several others took up flank on either side of it, all slapping their tails from side to side hoping to disarm the two intruders holding their tranquilizers.

"I'm going to have to nick him in order to get a sample. Let's draw him closer toward the front of the cavern, so we can get out of here." Solis and Hymn slowly began to take steps backward, causing the White Komodo to follow them.

The aggravated White Komodo dropped on all fours and lunged at Solis. Anticipating the attack, she had no choice but to throw the knife slicing a piece of flesh from the animal. Hymn fired another tranquilizer at the animal. The other Komodos fell back for only mere seconds. Solis and Hymn moved in quickly with the collections vials to harvest as much of the Komodo's blood as they needed.

Solis collected the blood with great caution---careful not to touch any of the animal's blood. Capping the last vial, Solis stood as Hymn warned of more danger.

"Uh…we need to move. There are other things moving in here. It seems our buzzing buddies are back with friends."

Startled at the loud roaring buzz echoing off the cavern wall, Solis looked back in the distance of the cavern to see a black floating swarm of mosquitoes and flies. The flies sensed the White Komodo's blood and took formation to find it. Hymn took no chances on safety, and planned to go for their escape.

"Let's go, we can't afford to take anymore bites in this environment."

"Yeah, let's make a move."

Not a moment too soon, they collected their vials and made a break towards the mouth of the cavern to the way out. The black swarm of mosquitoes and flies swooped down and took flight towards the retreating intruders. By this time the tranquilized, Komodos returned to consciousness. The swarm continued gaining velocity Solis and Hymn swatted and flicked at the pestilence attacking them. Hymn's long stride passed Solis, as he rushed back to the rickety wooden bridge.

"Keep running, Mistress! We have to reach the bridge."

"Don't worry, I'm right behind you."

She turned to look over her shoulder and found one of the Komodos who obviously hadn't been tranquilized gave chase, and hungrily snapped its jaws at her ankles. The faster she ran only made the Komodo, swat its tail and gain speed as well.

"I'm almost to the bridge. Keep running, Mistress!"

Hymn's booted foot hit the first plank of the roped bridge to cross the ravine. His weight caused the bridge to rock and sway side to side, as if it were angry for the disturbance.

The swarm of pestilence fiercely followed Solis, as did the brown Komodo who insisted on having her as a salty snack. Hymn had nearly made it across the bridge when Solis finally made her first step. She picked up her pace, jumping onto the first plank as the Komodo snapped one last time. Luckily, he only bit into the air.

Running as quickly as her heavy stride would take her, she ran across the swaying bridge as her weight compounded by the crosswind made the journey back across to the other side of the ravine nearly impossible. The middle of the bridge appeared sturdier.

Hymn made it across successfully, and looked back to make certain Solis wasn't too far behind.

"That's it Solis. You're almost home."

Solis had a few more steps to take to make it across from the middle of the bridge. Taking her next step sent her foot through a plank. She grabbed onto the worn ropes, clinging to them for dear life. Her bag hung across her neck, but the hunting knife she had slipped and fell into the 750-foot great beyond beneath her.

"Hymn, help me please!" Her scream echoed between the two mountains. In the distance across the ravine, she heard the Komodos hiss wildly, as if cheering for her to fall into the ravine to her death. The crosswinds blew her dangling body back and forth, making her look like a flag blowing in the wind.

Wasting no time, Hymn sprang into action. Re-crossing the bridge, and taking great care not to break any other planks, he tiptoed out to where Solis hung on for life.

"Grab my hand, sweetheart! I've got you. I won't let you go. I promise. Just grab on to me."

Solis grabbed his hand while he slowly began to pull her

up. Hoisting her to his level, she held onto his shoulders. They made a futile attempt to stand up, causing one of the ropes to snap sending them both over the edge of the bridge. Now they both hung suspended over the ravine.

"Hymn the entire bridge is giving way! Hold on!" Solis screamed as the entire bridge came loose from the Komodo dragon's side. The entire planked bridge let loose and sent them careening into the side of the cliff. Hymn tried to twist his body so that he would absorb all of the impact as they slammed into the side of the cliff.

"Hold on, Honey, we're going to hit pretty hard once more."

Their bodies bounced from the impact, and dangled over the side of the cliff. Fortunately, neither of them received a concussion from the impact.

"We should be able to climb up the side of the cliff. Hold onto my neck and shoulders, and I'll pull us up."

"Okay, I'll hold tight."

The two made it to the top of the cliff, with their hearts racing. Minutes passed as they caught their breath, and processed everything that had happened. Solis noted all of the mosquito bites she had over her legs and arms. Hymn lay on his back scratching all the bites he received as well. His back ached, and he probably had a few broken ribs for his valiance. Solis felt lucky to be alive.

"Thank you so much for saving my life, Hymn. I'm forever in debt to you."

"Think nothing of it." He lay still as the pain from the impact set in.

"How bad is your pain? Can you walk?"

"Yeah, I got it." Hymn held his breath as they started down the hill back to the Volksjeep to get them to the hotel. When they arrived, the tour guide escorted them into the vehicle and rushed them back to their accommodations. Solis found her anxiety stirring as nightfall set in.

"I'm ready to leave this island, and move on to Europe as soon as possible."

"Well, I'm ready when you are."

✝

Getting Hymn to the hotel took the last reserves of her strength. The tour guide helped Hymn to his room after the hotel physician examined him. Ace bandaging was applied after he took a steaming shower. He lay in bed with his back propped up against several pillows.

Solis knocked on the adjoining door to visit with her life-saving traveling partner. Hymn lay in bed with only the lower half of his body covered. The rest of his body shimmered in the light over his bed. His curly dark locks lay slicked to his head. His head rested against the headboard with his closed eyes.

"Hello, Mistress. I'm just resting my eyes a bit."

"I just came by to say thank you for all your bravery today. I'm so used to Nacio saving me. It felt strange to have another man so close to me."

Hymn's face flushed as he slowly opened his eyes and blood rushed to his shaft. Solis stood before him still fully dressed from earlier today. She hadn't had a chance to get cleaned up.

"It's no trouble at all. In fact, I liked saving you today." Now totally embarrassed that his shaft started its usual recourse of rising whenever she came this close to him, he quickly grabbed the comforter up over his ribs. Folding his arms over his lap, he made an effort to cover his snaking shaft, keeping the crown from sneaking out from under the covers.

"The doctor said you'd be just fine in a few days. I've called Basrick. He's rearranged our flight plans to leave right away in the morning. I hate to rush your recovery but..."

"Absolutely! We need to leave as soon as possible."

Solis walked over to his bedside, and kissed his forehead, unknowingly sending shudders up his spine. His straining erection attempted to stand, but he held his restraint. She noted his uneasiness, and fluffed his pillow.

"Are you in a lot of pain? I can get the doctor to come back in here?"

"No, please, I'm okay."

"Alright then, we fly out tomorrow. Goodnight."

"Goodnight." She left the room, heading through the adjoining door.

Hymn reached over to his nightstand to get the ice pack he made up for just this occasion. The icepack would help deaden his erection. In his mind, the heat and stiffness of his erection proved he could melt the few ice cubes in 15 seconds. He had to do something, because he could not risk lying in bed hard as rock another night. He couldn't lie in bed in this kind of shape, especially not after her legs were wrapped around his waist while they dangled from a rope 750 feet in the air.

"Father, please let me make it through the night."

10

Mother Love

Nacio remained shackled with silver chains to the wall of the cavern. With his strength reserves depleted, he needed blood, but didn't want to take any more blood from Auldicia. He could feel his chances of ever seeing Solis again becoming nil. A strange tickling sensation crept over his shoulder. A familiar feeling he knew all too well. Auldicia's textured tongue slid over his skin. She probed his body, taking in his scent and kissing his navel. Her tongue trailed its way to his groin, filling her hand with his sac. Her vile touch reminded him of how much he wanted her annihilated. She sensed his alertness and pulled his face to hers.

"I want you back in my life, Zuri. We will rule together once I destroy this Solis Burkes…or Olinka's filthy waste as I like to call her."

Nacio knew if he wanted to see his wife again, he must think of some alternative to getting Auldicia to destroy herself and her descendants. He decided to come up with a plan that would help destroy the hierarchy of power from within.

"How do you plan to rule when you have a descendant that

wants me as much as you do? Have you not seen the way Childress looks at me? In her mind she plans to do things with my body only you should as my lover."

Auldicia's fierce gaze held him paralyzed. She did not stutter, mutter, or utter a word. Getting up from her comfortable spot next to Nacio's cold frame, she began pacing the moist floor. Ready to strike at an invisible target, she turned on her heels and addressed him with venom in her voice.

"What are you saying to me, Zuri? That Childress, a peasant of a girl, would dare strike against me, and wants you as a lover? I will twist her head from her bones. I will dismember her limb from limb."

This reaction from Auldicia gave Nacio hope. He wanted her to respond in this manner. Hoping to get her to turn on Childress and her brothers while he worked on a plan to get free, he needed to get Childress alone and weave the same web of deception. With the silver removed from his body, he knew he could start to regenerate. He continued weave his deception with his unwanted suitor.

"Priestess, I need plasma."

"My own is not enough to sustain you, my love."

"As sweet as yours is, we both need fresh plasma. I need you to go and get us fresh plasma."

"You can have access to one of the descendants, and take as much as you like."

"No, my love, I need…we both need fresh plasma or we

will die. Please go and get some and bring it back to me." Nacio pretended to slip into a state of unconsciousness. The opportunity to have a chance alone with Childress held the key to success for his plan to have the two witches turn on each other.

"Only I can give you what you need, Zuri."

"Yes my dear, but I will not be able to give you what *you* need if I am weak. I need blood." After Nacio explained this, Auldicia considered his meaning.

"You're right, Zuri. The lunar eclipse nears, and we will conceive our child. You are correct. You need strength, and muscle for me to take you in my body on the night of the eclipse. I will get blood for us, and deal with Childress when she returns with Olinka's filth. I will eliminate them both, and no female shall look upon you again."

If Nacio could have vomited, he would have. The thought of entering Auldicia once more disgusted him so much, he nearly blacked out once more. Childress lying beneath him gave him the same disgusting feeling. His arms ached from the silver binding Ellis used to shackle him. He continued to amuse Auldicia, in hopes of her leaving within the next few seconds.

"I will leave for my hunt now my love, and when I return we will resume our love games." Childress flicked her reptilian tongue across his lips and teleported away. As soon as she left, he found himself praying for Childress to return with her brothers.

†

Regaining consciousness after an undetermined amount of time, Nacio caught the scent of sour underarms and sweaty feet. He slowly opened his eyes to find Childress ogling him. Evidently, Auldicia hadn't returned, or the sound of ripping flesh would have awakened him. Childress sashayed over to him, and then whispered in his ear. Her crew hung back a few feet.

"I've been watching you since I first saw you with the weak tramp, Solis. What do you want a woman like her for, Cher? I know how to make you feel good." She rubbed her hands over her moon-sized butt in an attempt to entice him. Again, nausea would have set in on his stomach if his body produced gastric juices.

"Don't you care if what will happen to you or your brothers if Auldicia returned to find you in her comfort zone?"

"Hell naw! I'm not scared of her. I can blast a few rocks myself in this here cave. I want you, and I plan to have you."

"How are you going to do that Childress? You're a fool if you think you can beat her. I tell you what, if you beat her, you and I will go somewhere and spark a fire with each other. What do you say?"

"Oh I can beat her, but what if I don't?'

"Well, you need to make sure you can, because I can tell you where your child is…but you have to get us out of here. Can you do that?"

"Quit playing with me, vampire. Where's my baby?"

"Uh, uh, uh…not until you get us out of here."

"You better tell me, or else."

"Or else what?" Standing in the distance toward the mouth of the cave, Auldicia stood with two victims, one male and one female. Her strength overwhelmed her victims as she nearly crushed their limbs dragging them toward him.

Childress stood before her ancestor, eyes as big as tea saucers, shifting back and forth, knowing Auldicia could throttle her body against a pointed stalagmite that would kill her instantly. Her distance to Nacio would cause problems for her as her jealous ancestor stood questioning her motives.

"What are you doing standing there next to Zuri, Childress? Are you trying to screw with what belongs to me?"

As the treacherous skank she had always been, she turned on Nacio to save her own butt. Quickly formulating a convincing lie, she opened her mouth to instigate trouble that would surely shake the cavern well into the night.

"He and that tramp have been killing other Treemounts or poisoning them. We know because several of them have come up dead, right Klein and Erland?"

The two Treemount fools stood with their hands in their pockets. The Hench Wenches held a blank stare. They had joined the hunt to find Solis, but their efforts turned up cold. Standing and nodding like Bobble heads showed their only talent.

"Yeah, Mother. Our other family members turned up dead because of them Nacio. He killed them."

Erland had actually mellowed out. Small firelight sat at the corner of his mouth as the joint he smoked blazed in the half-lit cavern. His mouth formed words, but no sound followed. Erland had gone out and scored some weed instead of finding Solis. It seemed he would get his throttling before Childress. He made a poor attempt at responding to his sister's inquiry.

"Uh, Mother First. I uh…I uh…I uh…," his smoke induced high, withered Auldicia's patience. "Uh, you want some weed?" Erland questioned sorely, offering Auldicia his sloppily rolled joint.

Auldicia crossed the cavern and shoved the joint down Erland's throat so hard, he bit his own tongue trying to apologize to her. Little puffs of smoke filtered out of his ears, as he swallowed the lit joint.

"You find this amusing do you?" She took her fingernail and cut a gash down the side of his face. Horrified, Childress stood still and then threw her hands in the air to work a spell to stop Auldicia. The sound of her failure ricocheted throughout the cavern as Auldicia snatched a handful of red locks from Childress. The ripping sound made Klein cover his ears. Childress looked at her ancestor contemptuously.

"Don't hurt my brother! I just told you this vampire has killed your descendants, and you hurt Erland? What the hell is wrong with you?"

Auldicia did an about face, and turned to run upside down on the cavern wall. She looked like a blur, and by the time her feet hit the ground again she was standing behind Childress. Taking one hand, Auldicia slapped Childress in the back between her shoulder blades. With a scowl across her face, she fell to the ground, scraping her knees.

"You truly think you can beat me, Childress? I have centuries of strength and knowledge that you cannot begin to comprehend, child. You covet what's mine; my power, my knowledge, my influence and boldly...you want my lover."

Childress tried to deny the things Auldicia spoke of, but her eyes didn't blink during their confrontation. She did want those things; power, knowledge, and most of all...Nacio. If she had him, she knew everything else would fall into place. He held the power to give her the happiness she craved. Auldicia smiled, as she sensed the covetousness within Childress, recognizing it was like that of her own.

"If you think your insignificant powers can stop me, I'll give you that opportunity to prove this. If you cannot beat me then you and your brothers will die. You will need to return Solis Burkes to me, and you will need to demonstrate your power and ability against me. The only way you could possibly destroy me is to find your child. Then you must sacrifice her to the voodoo gods and take reign over this realm. If not, you and your siblings will die."

Nacio knew Auldicia's rage would eventually put an end to Childress. He didn't have much time, to get an escape plan together. His body would not be able to stand anymore of Auldicia's poisoned blood. If his body did not respond to her sexual advances, she would surely punish him in the same manner she used to after she turned him into a vampire. He knew Solis's chances of survival were slim to none. The lunar eclipse would soon be upon

them, and Auldicia planned to conceive a child with him. That ter-
rible fate could not happen. Playing Auldicia's little game would
buy him some time, but not much.

"Lover, please give me some plasma. I need my strength
to serve you the pleasure you require. But, I cannot pleasure you if
my hands remained shackled. I long to touch you, my love. Please
untie me." Nacio had gone from disobedient prisoner, to doting
lover. The silver shackles prevented him from regenerating and
teleporting. Regaining his strength had to come quickly to fulfill
his other priorities. Solis remained safe as long as she stayed at the
mansion with the other vampires. If she left the protection of the
glamour, she increased her chances of Auldicia finding her. While
unconscious, he thought he heard someone say they spotted Solis at the airport. If this is true, then Solis has started her journey
to find him. He continued to coax Auldicia into playing his little
game.

"Priestess, your lover needs you. Please provide me with
some nourishment." Hearing her lover's cry for her made her
work quickly to give him what he needed. She spun the male and
female victims around to face her. She shoved the female victim in
front of Nacio, causing him to open his mouth and bite---drawing
large gulps of plasma. Auldicia spun the male around and hyper-
extended her jaw to put the biggest bite on the man possible. The
bite sounded more like a chomp. She finished off her victim, sip-
ping fat from his body until only skin and bone remained---leaving
only the limp carcass behind. When Auldicia saw that Nacio did
not finish his feeding the same as she, immediately she finished the
female off for him.

A smile spread across her face as wide as the opening of the cavern. She barked out an order, with a punitive warning.

"If any of you return to this cavern without Solis Burkes, you will pay with your life for your insolence. That's a promise. Now leave us. Oh…and Childress, you'd better find that child of yours. If you don't…you will find your ass skewered and slow roasting on an open fire as a sacrifice. Do you understand?"

Childress shook her head.

"Do you have any questions?"

Still shaking her head, she stood frozen.

"Do I make myself clear?" Childress began trembling as Auldicia finally finished her declaration.

"Find her or you all will die a slow and most painful death a human could possibly imagine."

Childress turned on her heals, but then thought quickly and turned around to point at Nacio. That's when Auldicia crossed the cavern and grabbed her by her jaw. Dialing her finger in a circular motion, she cut the other side of her face, sketching a huge gash in her right cheek. Blood dripped to the ground like a broken faucet.

"What is it that is so important to you to dare speak against Zuri? Hmm? You think I would give up the love of my life for someone as wicked and covetous as you Childress? You are the worst of the worst, and I'm just the one to punish you for what you've done."

Childress wanted to tell Auldicia that Nacio knows where

her child is and that he is probably in on her whereabouts. Again, the contempt she had for her ancestor wouldn't allow her to disclose this information. The life of herself, her siblings, and her child were at stake. She knew sending Auldicia back to Hell took precedence over anything else. Her baby girl's safety must remain undisclosed. Childress stood before her ancestor and continued to play dumb.

"I just wanted to mention, he looks like he is going to blackout."

"Don't worry about his well-being. He's mine, and I will take care of him. Don't let me catch you touching him again. I mean it Childress! If you are caught doing so, you will be a one-eyed Cyclops from henceforth, because I will rip one of your eyes from its socket and let you see what you look like. Are we clear?"

"Yes." Auldicia stood with her back straight and funneled her hand over her ear---prompting Childress to finish her acknowledgement. She paused as she did this. Childress obliged her request.

"Yes, Mother First."

Childress and her crew quickly turned and exited the cavern. She threw a nasty glance back at Auldicia. Once she left the cavern Auldicia turned on Nacio, rattling her raging fist in his face.

"Did you kill my descendants, Zuri? Why wouldn't you tell me?"

Nacio took a chance and told another lie to save his own life. "Justice spoke ill of you Priestess, and I punished him for it."

Nacio knew the choices he made would have a major impact on his life henceforth, should he conceive a child with this witch. He knew he had to save Solis, and if lying with Auldicia meant having to do this, so be it.

"You know the price for insolence, Zuri. You must pay." Auldicia raised her hand to strike him, but found she could not and stopped by these words from his lips.

"Come Priestess, and give yourself to me. Conceive my child...our child."

A smile followed her beaming green eyes. A long pause captured her surprise at his submission, as she dropped the thin dress she wore from her body. Her body responded so willingly to his voice, that Nacio noted a hint of trembling in her hands.

"We have little time to spare Priestess. The lunar eclipse approaches us."

"I'm yours, Zuri. Take me and give me your seed."

"As you wish."

With the silver barometer removed from his body, Nacio did his best to will his body to respond to hers. The sickening sound of her body lubricating from his touch made him want to dismember her body with his hands, but he knew he could not. Making certain Solis had protection took priority as his only concern.

Forgive me Solis my love. What I do now is for our future, if I am to return to you. If I cannot return to you, then I will go to Hell and burn before I let Auldicia harm you, or Childress for that matter.

Auldicia took his shaft in her hands once more, now admiring the diameter of his crown. She stood in awe, anticipating him entering her.

"Take my body, and mark me," she commanded, sliding down to meet his glorious body with her own. She soon found her body would have to adjust to taking so much of him into her, and it would take several strokes before she could accept all of him.

Nacio did well not to flinch from the horrible smell that emanated from her womb. The sickening scent of hot raw sewage and rotting flesh filled the cavern air. Her strokes began slowly as she accepted more of him, then finally all of him. Licking her fangs caused her to thirst for him, as she rode on to ecstasy.

To his surprise, Nacio found his fangs responded to her as well. He had already taken her blood into his body, and her blood calls to his body now. He wanted to flip her off him, but he could not. Silver poison sat stagnant in his blood, keeping him under steady sedation. He would remain in his current weakened state until all silver left his blood.

Auldicia's hips soon bucked, and she reached a soppy climax. The smell worsened as she came, throwing her head back in victory. The tryst gained nothing for her. Nacio never reached a climax. Watching her now before him, reminded him of an animal.

If Auldicia ever knew how beautiful my wife looked, she would truly want to skin Solis alive. The creature that sits before me now, who wants my seed will never get it. I have to leave here before the lunar eclipse. The descendants cannot find Solis. I pray

Armando and Basrick have found some way to penetrate this barrier to return her back to Hell.

After her climax, Auldicia fell off Nacio's lap. Feeling like she had accomplished something, she stood hoping to feel her usual instant conception. Rage quickly replaced her elation as she realized the lubrications that saturated her thighs were hers. No trace of Nacio's fluids mixed with her own.

"What happened to your seed?" Auldicia's shock didn't surprise Nacio. In fact, he anticipated her mood and followed up with a calculated response, while disgust weaved in and out of his thoughts.

"I miss touching your skin, Priestess. *You are such a vile witch.* I cannot stand not to fill my hands with your curves. *I want to snap your spine in half.* I've longed to smooth my hands over your skin. *The screams of you dying will fill my ears with music.* I cannot do these things shackled like an animal. *I plan to push your body into the fires of Hell myself.* Please free me."

Auldicia took her hand and wiped the folds between her thighs, disappointed the magical conception had not taken place.

"Are you playing with my emotions, Zuri? Is it so wrong to want to be with you forever? You are my one desire; my only desire that would make me walk through the fires of Hell so I could be with you. Why will you not give me the opportunity to give you a child?"

Nacio paused before he answered her, dangerously playing with the strings of her non-existent heart. Answering carefully, he tried to rekindle the smoldering embers of desire she had felt seconds ago.

"Fret not dear. We have all night to enjoy each other."

Auldicia's smile returned once more. The love games started over once more.

11

Keep it to yourself

Solis made certain to take extra precautions after the last airport fiasco. Hymn seemed unusually quiet. The painkillers he took last night had him knocked out. The medicine had him snoring like an avalanche. Today, he heel-toed it pretty quickly through the gates, not taking any chances on getting caught up in any unexpected skirmishes.

They boarded the plane on time without any problems. Solis packed away samples of the White Komodo's blood in her luggage---keeping them disguised as insulin pens. Basrick made contact with them prior to leaving, and gave them directions for their journey. Solis felt confident getting in and out of the Vatican would prove less treacherous than frolicking in the cavern back in Indonesia. Hymn would know just where to go to get the things they needed. The trip took several hours. The time sitting still gave Hymn the rest he needed for the next part of the journey.

"What we need is in the basement of the Vatican. This Holy Water happened to have the blessing of Pope Pius II. This particular Pope served in the 1400s. It's said he had dealings with Dracula himself. He knew what could drive a vampire to the gates

of Hell. He made certain to have Holy Water that could burn a
vampire to the bones. That's the water we need to have Auldicia
returned to Hell. We have to get it or we will suffer the consequences of her existing in this realm."

"I understand, Hymn. As long as she's here, we run the
risk of Vulkus returning to wreck havoc. When we land, I'll phone
Basrick, and let him know he and Armando need to get to the
masonry to start mixing the chemicals to poison Auldicia. We'll
need to make certain Urgata has returned from Dog Water Swamp.
I need her to help with the spell for the sword to open the plane
between the Realm of the Living and the Condemned."

Hymn sat deep in thought, contemplating if he should
remind her of the dangers they face should they fail at their attempt
to send Auldicia back. Tension and worry had settled in her shoulders. When she worried, she tended to hold her eyebrows a little
higher with a line running down the middle of her forehead.

Throughout all the time he'd spent with her, he'd never
heard her laugh. Yearning for the day he heard the jovial melody
from her voice would earn her his undying devotion. He would
continue to remain stranger to these feelings he has for her; sincerity, courage, valiance, lust, desire, passion. Along with these came
danger, deception, and damnation. He couldn't bring himself to
betray the trust of the Caraways.

His own selfish feelings would ruin the trust in his friendship with Basrick, not to mention Nacio. Getting into Rome and
getting the Holy Water should be a simple in and out task once
they landed, but he also knew he had to plan for any trouble if it
came up. Time continued to run out. Each day that passed by in

which Nacio had been gone, the lesser his chances of returning home to Solis. Still with several hours to go before their landing, Hymn settled off to sleep. His dreams took him back into her arms; smelling her hair, his lips blazing for hers, his shaft straining to reach inside her.

Solis saw Hymn had drifted off to a rather audible sleep. He murmured, even whimpering at times, and other times flat out speaking.

"You feel good…love it…need you…mine."

Although asleep, he made it clear he enjoyed making love to this mystery person in his dreams. From his sentiments, this person met his needs very well. She couldn't help but eavesdrop on his passion. Listening made her ache for what only Nacio could give her.

I need my husband right now. Tasting his blood has damn near driven me crazy with need for him. Listening to Hymn moan doesn't help. My crazy dream about Nacio turning into Hymn, and vice versa, doesn't make sense. This poor guy must really care for this female. He hasn't stopped praising her skills. Whatever he's dreaming about is making his body respond while he's asleep.

While looking at Hymn's crotch, she noticed the imprint under his jeans crawling down the inside of his thigh. Instead of turning her head, the swollen imprint under his jeans kept her entertained with naughty thoughts, causing a jolt to shoot straight to her groin. Leaning over in the opposite way, she tried putting distance between her body, and Hymn's growing bulge. Her response nearly overwhelmed her, she fought the urge to reach out and touch him.

What's wrong with me? I'm truly losing my mind! We need to hurry and get to the Vatican City. I miss my mate, and I won't rest until he comes home. Why can't I stop looking at Hymn? This is insane!

The indicator light on her cell phone showed she received an email. This helped to break up the impulsivity she felt sitting so close to Hymn. Her heart skipped a beat as she read Basrick's urgent message:

Need you here soon. Menlo's liaison informed her, at SAPD there have been several bodies discovered dumped along the IH 35corridor, horrifically decayed. The medical examiners explained no fatty tissue connected to the bones...all missing, with only skin left. Auldicia takes random victims and feeds on them. Urgata fears the nearing of the lunar eclipse. Something big will occur on that night. My father continues to look for Nacio, but no luck. My mother continues to care for Blessing. She too fears something awful on the horizon. You must return home soon.

~Basrick~

With their estimated arrival time to Rome in three hours, Solis needed to organize her thoughts. Hymn continued to sleep, and she didn't have the heart to disturb his dream. Basrick's news would surely upset anyone receiving it. They needed all of his stamina to take them underneath Vatican City to retrieve the Holy

Water blessed by Pope Pius II. Pondering the outcome of this venture, Solis hoped for the best. Auldicia's descendants probably have gathered from all over the globe by now. She knew she needed to guard her life carefully until she could stand before Auldicia and get Nacio back. In her heart, she felt time sifting away from her happiness with each minute passing by.

I wish I knew where to look for you, Sweetheart. Can you hear me? Nacio, please answer me. I need you. I will find you and bring you back home. That's a promise.

†

Landing in Rome, Hymn opened his eyes and greeted Solis with a hypnotic stare. Although he had slept for the last several hours while traveling across the globe, jet lag drained his strength. The more he roused, the more he remembered his dreams of the closeness he shared with her. Fantasies filled his mind, bordering on obsessions. The new struggle between what's right and what's wrong had started to take its toll on his conscience.

I plan to express my feelings to her. I can't go on this way for much longer. She deserves a life with children and stability. I don't want her to have to go through any more pain. Oh dear Father, she's not mine for the taking, but should her husband not return I would give my life for her happiness.

Solis sat next to Hymn with a flushed face. Torn between disclosing Basrick's devastating news about Auldicia and lingering in his noticeably heated gaze, she chose Basrick's news. Her own embarrassment about her lingering eyes a few hours ago caused her hesitation when it came to explaining Basrick's news.

"Good Morning, Hymn. We've just landed. Basrick emailed me a few hours ago. Things are getting worse back home. It appears Auldicia's cruel actions have increased in violence. Several John Doe bodies have turned up along the IH 35 corridor. He wants us home as soon as possible."

"Don't worry, Solis. I know the layout of Vatican City well. We will want to blend in with the rest of the tourists. In doing so, we'll book a tour of the Vatican along with the rest of the tourists. I won't let you down." Hymn reached out and took her hand in his. They both looked down at their hands together. He rubbed small circle over her knuckles, causing her already flushed pallor to wash away completely.

Protesting silently, she pulled her hand from his and retreated to the far corner near the window as the flight attendant called for them to empty the plane. Solis quickly grabbed her overhead bag. She tried to figure out a way to get to the center isle to exit the plane, but realized she couldn't without pressing her body against his. Attempting to distract him, she tried to get him to stand up into the rushing traffic of people exiting the plane.

"I need to call Basrick to make certain we have ground transportation." Disappointment settled over Hymn's face, as she pulled away. His expression conveyed his thoughts held a deeper need; one she could not fulfill. His smoldering half-lidded blue eyes said it all. Not only did she have to make certain to watch out for Auldicia's descendants attacking her, she also had to make certain not to give Hymn any mixed messages. She added her own misguided emotions to the list of potential foes she had to fight off.

Getting to the Vatican and back home couldn't happen fast enough. Once off the plane she took larger strides to widen the distance between the two of them. No more than a few words passed between them.

"Hey Solis, slow down. What's the rush?"

"What's the rush? I want my husband back, Hymn, and I can't seem to get this trip over with quick enough! Do you understand that? I want my husband back."

Startled, Hymn stayed two steps behind Solis, only stepping in to speak Italian when needed. He knew she didn't have ground transportation lined up and would have to acquire it after they left the airport. Somehow, he knew his gesture of holding her hand on the plane struck a nerve with her, and now she put up a wall between them; exactly the opposite of what he wanted.

Rome had beauty she never knew. Sadly, she had hoped Nacio would have taken her to the places she traveled to thus far; therefore she couldn't appreciate the beauty of it all. A cloudless sky showed all the exquisite architecture of the city; informing visitors of its rich history. Once they received their belongings, a taxi drove them over the remarkably constructed Ponte St. Angelo Bridge. Cars bustled and honked back and forth over the bridge getting busy onlookers to their destination.

Hymn pointed out during their ride, they were now crossing the Castel St. Angelo. He explained the connecting passage led directly to the Vatican and it served as an escape route for getting the Pope to safety in times of harm during war.

They arrived at the gorgeously constructed Hotel Alimandi

Viale Vaticano. Hymn quickly paid the driver. Keeping her quick
pace as she did at the airport, she grabbed her luggage containing
the White Komodo blood, making certain it sustained no damage
from its preservation packing on the plane. She hurried into the
Hotel, leaving Hymn to lag behind her. Again, she took notice of
the swank hotel and travelers from around the world. An American church travel group, stood a few feet over from them in line
to check into the suites. She instantly knew their nationality due
to one girl standing in line with an American flag on her t-shirt,
and how she dropped the 'ing' from each word she spoke; an east
Texan, no doubt.

Basrick made the hotel arrangements here as well. Solis
prayed for no more connecting suites. There needed be no more
easy access to each other. The bellhop came and escorted them to
their rooms. Both suites were side by side. Solis almost cringed.
Hymn looked at her just as they each opened their suite.

"Solis I have something I want to tell you." Even as he
stood five feet away from her, heat rolled off his body like a campfire.

Solis continued to work the key card to enter her room as a
distraction to keep from listening to what he had to say.

"Hymn, please don't. I've very tired, but I'm ready to get
this tour over with. We need to get home. Please understand that.
I need you to call and get an itinerary so we can get to the Vatican
at once. Please understand my urgency."

They stood silent in the hallway. Looking into his glisten-
ing eyes as tears welled, Hymn simply nodded to her.

"As you wish...Mistress." He stepped inside, and gently closed the door.

Shocked at his sentiments, Solis realized the gorgeous man that stood before her had tears in his eyes. She didn't want to hurt him. She'd never been torn between two men before, and she didn't trust her emotions. She opened her suite, entered, and closed the door. Relief hit her pretty hard when she noticed the walls to her suite didn't have an adjoining door to the suite next door. Falling onto the bed, she lay flat looking up at the ceiling.

I can't believe myself, but I couldn't let Hymn say the words I know he planned to say. I'm in love with my husband, and I can't be tempted. I won't be tempted. We need to get this Holy Water and leave. I feel so foolish coming to the Holy See with lust in my heart and grief on my mind. Then again, I could be wrong. What if Hymn hadn't wanted to express his feelings for me at all? What if I'm the only one with lust in my heart? I'm only human. Yes, that's it...human. My attraction to Hymn is a human emotion, but I won't betray my husband, even if he is not human. Maybe I'm being too hard on myself and Hymn. I'll apologize later. Soon, she drifted off to sleep.

†

Solis awoke to the sounds of knocking on her door a few hours later. She went to the door to find Hymn dressed in his usual boots and jeans, smoldering sky blue eyes, clean-shaven, his Stetson broke down low over his left eye, and a smile as wide as Texas. If she didn't know better, she would have sworn he wore cologne laced with human attraction pheromones. How else could she explain the wild growing attraction between the two of them? His cologne wafted in through her doorway, nearly knocking her off her feet causing her to swoon.

"Good afternoon, Mistress. Are you ready for the tour of the Vatican?"

All Solis could do is nod in response, still too taken by the sight of his tall tanned frame in her doorway. Her response to him deepened his smile.

"Mistress, I want to apologize to you for my forwardness earlier. My actions showed poor judgment, and I don't want to upset you, or cause you more pain."

"I apologize to you, Hymn. My short temper seems to get the best of me these days. Please forgive me."

"No apology necessary, but we do need to get going. We have to catch but 49 to take us to the Basilica. The Holy Water we seek from Pope Pius II is there, and we must hurry before the tours end for the day."

"I'm ready."

They left the hotel and caught bus 49 as Hymn explained. Solis lost her breath as she saw the grandeur of the Holy See. The tour guide spoke of the Swiss Guard that guards the Vatican. Amazingly, the guards are all Swiss males, between the ages of 19 and 30 years and from Roman Catholic families. They have stood guard over the Basilica for centuries. As the tour guide continued to speak, Hymn chimed in her ear talking about Pope Pius II. Humidity from his breath gently warmed the top of her ear, sending shivers down her spine.

"Pope Pius II is considered a Renaissance Pope, crowned at the age of 52 on September 3, 1458. He later died on August 14, 1464. His remains are noted to have been buried in the Patriarchal Vatican Basilica there," Hymn pointed at one building. "Then his remains were transferred to the Basilica Sant'Andrea Della Valle during Pope Paul V's reign, so we are challenged by two different locations to search for the Holy Water."

Solis turned and looked puzzled. "So we will have to search both places then."

"I'm hoping we find it at the first stop we make. We need to leave here tonight Hymn."

"I understand, and that is our goal."

The tour bus stopped in front of St. Peter's Basilica. The Constantinian architecture beautified the structure. Popes have interred at the Basilica for centuries. The first Pope, disciple St. Peter's remains lie directly under the altar in the beautiful church. Entering the structure, she noticed the Basilica's dome. The tour guide estimated the dome diameter at 137 feet. Just as they continued to walk, Solis stood stunned at the Sistine Chapel ceiling.

Hymn allowed her to walk ahead to take in the heart stopping site of the chapel. Standing in awe at the sight, he allowed her a moment alone. Solis looked at the chapel as tear streamed down her face.

This beautiful painting reminds me of the first time I saw the painting of Jesus and the children Bose did at the mansion. Seeing this only made her home sick and even sicker for Nacio.

"Hymn, please take me to the Patriarchal tombs. We know what it is we're looking for. We need to get the water and go."

"The tombs are just up ahead. Once we get there, we can go to the basement, and we will follow the flow of the crowd. The water is at the foot of a tomb in a small challis. The belief says, even though Pope Pius II is interring, the water placed at the foot of his tomb continues to receive his blessing."

"Okay let's work, and hopefully luck will come our way to find the challis here."

The crowd shuffled along the narrow walkways going further and further down into the ground underneath the Basilica floor. When they finally stopped, the tour guide pointed out they stood exactly 33 feet underneath the floor and directly above them stood St. Peter's Altar. The remains of the great saint sat behind a wall. The tour guide explained St Peter's upside down crucifixion. Scholars knew the bones they'd found belonged to St. Peter, because of the missing foot bones. During crucifixion, the guards chopped off the feet to bring the body down from the crucifixion site.

After passing through St. Peter's entombment, they soon found themselves in the area of the Scavi, or excavation site, where the Renaissance Popes interred. Satisfied they'd reached their destination, Hymn steered Solis away from the crowd to the foot of a tomb.

"Mistress, this is it. This is Pope Pius II." Behind a rope and at the foot of the Pope's tomb stood the challis Hymn mentioned. They lucked out, and their search ended.

Solis needed a distraction to use her telekinesis to get the challis open to get some of the Holy Water.

"Hymn, go to the front of the crowd and come up with some sort of panic attack so that I can concentrate on getting the Holy Water from the challis."

"Will do." Hymn went to the front of the crowd as Solis stayed behind. She eased her way closer to the rope and to the tomb's end. Concentrating on lifting the challis, she focused on raising it and sending it forth, hoping no one would see her attempts. The challis slowly shook just as Hymn started shouting out in horror in the worst British accent she's heard yet.

"Help me, oh help me! I'm claustrophobic and I can't stand the dark!"

As planned, the crowd rushed over to see what started the commotion, giving Solis the time she needed to empty the challis of its contents. Growing up in a strict Baptist home, she knew she had to make things right for what she'd done. Once she completed the task, she closed her eyes and prayed for forgiveness.

"Father, please forgive me, because we need this water to save many lives. I love you Lord, please go with me."

The crowd had built to a small mob around Hymn. Elbowing her way to the middle to get Hymn out of harm's way, she noticed a particularly striking man with red hair and vicious green eyes. The man seemed unconcerned about Hymn, and soon his eyes fell on her. Not wanting to stare, she assured the crowd of her partner's behavior.

"Sorry for the trouble. He hasn't eaten and needs to get some air." As if on cue, the crowd rushed them both out of the tomb and to the upper level. This put lots of distance between them and the man who looked like he could strike at them at any moment. Solis whispered to Hymn about the danger lurking a few feet behind them.

"There's a descendant mixed in the crowd over your left shoulder. We will need to get lost in this crowd as soon as we hit the surface, okay?"

"Got it."

Once they hit street level, Hymn and Solis both rushed toward another crowd of folks, running in the opposite direction of the Basilica, hiding behind a column in St. Peter's Square. Solis didn't want to take any chances, and readied herself with a Dieth dart.

"I brought along a little extra something just for this occasion. There he is."

The redheaded, would be assassin came right out from below to street level looking disheveled and lost. Hymn steadied himself behind Solis, and then at the last minute pulled a Superman stunt. He jumped out from behind the column and alerted the descendant to their location.

"Hey man you lost? You lookin' for someone?" Livid,

Solis snapped at Hymn.

"What are you doing? Are you crazy? Now he's coming right for us!"

"That's exactly what I want."

The descendant quickened his pace, and soon followed them down an alleyway. Reaching a dead end, Hymn turned and pulled a loaded Dieth dart out and fired, hitting the descendant diagonally in the left carotid artery. A thin spurt of bright red blood showered the tiled ground below. Solis knew they had to make headway getting back to the airport at once.

"Let's go. We can't waste anymore time. Did you have to do that? I had him as a target and could have taken him out. Now we need to get back to the hotel and head for the airport right away! I'll contact Basrick and have him on standby to change our flight immediately."

"I did what I had to. I didn't want to lead him any further down the alleyway. There are lots of Bishops from all over the world turning these pillars, and anyone could have seen us. I've been here before, remember?"

"I just wished you'd warned me first."

"Well, contact Basrick, but it might be some difficulty getting out of here this soon. We might not be able to leave until first thing in the morning."

"I hope not."

"Oh come on, I don't think there will be anymore trouble.

If you'd like, we can check into another hotel."

"No, if I leave then I'm leaving this country on foot, if I have to. We'll stay the night."

12

Draw the line

By this time, they headed back to the hotel on the same bus that brought them there. The lobby seemed less busy, as the night set in over Rome. A full moon set low in the sky, and moonbeams danced on the Tiber River, making for a romantic night, and trouble for Solis. Her stomach growled and she knew her appetite edged toward 'out of control'. Hymn knew she hadn't eaten, and asked her to dinner.

"I'm sure hungry. We need to eat something. Let's go down and eat some of the best Italian Food in the world."

Hesitant, annoyed, and hungry, Solis turned Hymn down flat without a second thought. "No thank you. I'll be dining in my room this evening."

Again, he hit her with his sultry half-lidded eyes. Taking the declination in stride, he nodded and went to his room.

"Until morning, Mistress."

"Goodnight Hymn." Angry with herself, Solis sat quietly on her bed pondering the events of the day. Rather than let her mind linger for too long, she decided to call Basrick. She dialed, and Armando picked up the phone, going straight into the conversation.

"Solis, is everything okay?"

"Yes dear friend. We've found the Holy Water blessed by Pope Pius II. I wanted to know if there was any way for us to leave here tonight. I'm ready to come home."

"Basrick and I had hoped for you to come home sooner when we made travel arrangements, but the earliest flight out is 8 am tomorrow. Again, is everything okay?"

"Yes, I just want to get this over with to bring Nacio back home, and to send Auldicia back to Hell."

"I understand, Solis. Try not to worry. Nacio is wise and well aware of Auldicia's trickery. He'll do what he must to survive. Don't forget that."

"How are Patience and Blessing?"

"They are well, and Blessing grows each day. Her eyes aren't lit up and dazzling as they were the night all this happened, but they still have a shine to them."

"Continue to protect her, Armando. How are Basrick and Menlo?"

"They too are well. Menlo continues to follow up on the bodies that keep showing up in different areas around town. She's keeping her eyes open for any signs of Childress and her brothers. Is Hymn alright?"

Solis knew she had to tread carefully in answering Armando's question about Hymn. She couldn't give any indication of the turmoil raging inside her head, or he would know instantly. She pressed forward in a smooth transition.

"Yes he's fine, he's gone to eat. Listen, Armando, you all need to be on the lookout for any of the descendants. Their eyes are unnaturally green like Blessings have been over the last few months. If you find them, use the Dieth on them immediately. Hopefully, if Auldicia is putting the bite on any of them, she will have some of the poison in her system as well until we can load her up with it."

"Alright, we'll look out for them, but you watch yourself as well."

"Also, make sure Urgata returns by tomorrow night. I need you all to go ahead and get things ready at the masonry. When we get back, we need to mix this stuff right away. Have you all found the hydrochloric acid yet?"

"Yes, we have it mixing in the largest vat at the masonry, ready to go upon your return."

"Good, she and I will chant a hex over the vat, and over the sword we keep in the library to tear open a seam between the Realm of the Living and the Realm of the Condemned to send Auldicia back. She can also take Childress with her as well."

"Yes, that would bring Patience a lot of peace if Childress were gone from this world."

"Well, I'm working on it, Armando. I'm working on it.

You take care, and we'll see you tomorrow night."

"You do the same, Mistress."

Speaking to Armando reassured her things would work out. By this time she could no longer ignore her hunger.

I guess my anger about this entire situation made me take my frustrations out on Hymn. Maybe I will go to dinner with him and clear the air. It seems like this Hell sent journey is nearly over.

Going into the bathroom, she quickly showered and freshened up and changed into a clean pair of jeans and a shirt. She ran a few strokes of her brush through her hair. She gathered her wits to go and have 'the talk' with Hymn over dinner. She opened the door and stepped outside into the hallway, and stopped short at what she saw.

A tall, shapely Blond had her arm looped through Hymn's as he closed the door to his suite. Her waist long curly hair draped over her back, and bounced each time she moved. She wore blood red lipstick and black Christian LouBoutin shoes with shiny lacquered red soles. Hymn's charm and stunning looks caught him a real catch this evening, similar to the Flight Attendant that flirted with him when they left San Antonio. With breasts the size of two cantaloupes, and cleavage cut low enough for a 50 cent piece to get lost in, she stood smiling as Hymn caught sight of Solis standing in their direction. He stood there shocked, and Solis…well she was pissed.

"Hello, Solis." Overwhelmed, Hymn stood between the two women, and eventually, stammered out an explanation. The blonde widened her smile.

"We were…we…were headed to get some dinner. Would you like to join us?"

Her anguish proved difficult to hide. She couldn't determine if she had interrupted a sexy interlude between the two of them, or if they planned to come back and have one. Her mind told her both scenarios were true, and she quickly covered her emotions, and stammered a response.

"Oh no, I'm going to get some ice for my drink." She continued to stare at the blonde. Hymn broke the silence, and introduced his busty companion.

"Solis, this is Bella Donna Verlonni. She's been a contact of mine in Rome for many years. I saw her in the lobby a few moments ago, and we're headed to dinner…just now."

Solis found it amusing the way he stammered and felt he had to justify his acquaintance with Bella Donna. The two stood quietly as Solis excused herself.

"You two have fun. I'm going to bed early."

Bella Donna spoke and bid her goodnight in a heavy Italian accent.

"Have a pleasant night, and pleased to meet you."

Solis didn't waste any time retreating back to her room. If she were an Ostrich she would have put her head in the sand. Hymn and his hussy left the corridor. Solis listened as they departed, and soon as she heard the elevator doors close, she left her room. She waited a few seconds to make certain they were gone. Still flustered, she went downstairs, straight to the registration desk. Just as she approached the desk, the manager saw her and put on the biggest smile ready to take her request.

"How might I help you, Signora?"

"I need to change my room. Some newlyweds kept me up last night."

The manager smiled as he raised his eyebrows up and down, and quickly granted her request. "Might I send the bellhop to assist you with your move?"

"No, Signore. I can handle it. Thank you."

From across the hotel restaurant, Hymn looked over his wine glass, and saw Solis at the registration desk. He excused himself from his dinner guest, and rushed over to where the manager stood.

"My traveling companion was just here speaking with you. Is everything alright?"

The manager asked for identification and made certain, Hymn had indeed traveled in with Solis before answering his inquiry.

"Yes, Signore. The Signora Puente requested a room change."

"A room change? I have to look after her and I must know what room she has retired to."

"You must discuss that with her, and I cannot....," Before the manager could continue to decline Hymn's request for Solis's new room information, he slipped him a handsome Euro that got the information he needed. Knowing he needed to check on Solis, he returned to excuse himself from Bella Donna.

"Please excuse me, Signorina, but I must retire to my room for the evening. It appears Signora Puente is not well."

"I see." Bella Donna sat with a jilted look, and offered to retire with him. "Should I retire with you?" She stroked his fingers across the table, hoping to stir his loins for an extended visit throughout the night. Always the Gentleman, Hymn turned her down as gently as possible.

"It has been a most memorable evening, Signorina, but I must make certain Signora Puente is well. I bid you goodnight."

Bella Donna took the news fairly well, though she's not used to getting the boot, especially not to a married Signora.

†

Solis sat in her room, eating her room service meal. Finally getting her emotions in check, she lay in her bed wishing for the time to pass by. Boredom had taken its toll on her, and she sat in the windowsill, overlooking the Tiber River. Her new room gave her the stunning view of the river. Consumed by her thoughts, she fantasized about the wonderful reunion between her and Nacio. Interrupted by a knock at the door, she took her time responding. She looked out of the peephole, and saw Hymn standing alone. She opened the door and watched his large frame strut right past her.

"Why did you switch rooms without telling me? I'm responsible for your well-being, you know."

Standing with only a robe on, Solis flinched as he turned on her and demanded an answer to his question.

"I wanted a room with a better view, and I like this one quite nicely." She watched as Hymn circled the room.

"I've known Bella Donna for years, and I've never once had a tryst with her. I only went with her tonight to have dinner and that is all." His voice had raised at least two octaves.

"You don't owe me any explanation. I just wanted to change rooms, which is totally my business."

"Your business? I'm responsible for you, Solis! You could have told me if you weren't comfortable in your room!"

"You make me uncomfortable, Hymn!" She blurted out her discomfort with the gorgeous blue-eyed man in her room. "I want you to leave right now!"

Hymn continued to circle the room. Suddenly, he brought his feet to a stop and turned toward her. "Why? Why do I make you uncomfortable?" He'd walked over to her now and stood in her personal space...a dangerous place to be.

"Answer me, Solis! Why do I make you uncomfortable?"

She hesitated before answering. She started anticipating the impact her words would have on them both. "I don't want to be close to you. Please leave."

Hymn continued to close the distance between them. Large

volumes of heat rolled off his body, making her weak. The conversation she feared having most came to fruition, and nothing she did stopped what he said next.

"Damn you, Solis! Look at me. I ache for you, and in your presence, I want to give myself to you completely. I don't know how this started, only that I don't want you to hurt anymore. I need you to understand, I didn't come to this decision lightly. I know what is at stake here, and you must know I've craved you since we first met. I want to give myself to you and protect you."

Solis stepped away from Hymn as he stepped in closer. Shaking her head, she screamed at Hymn, wanting to keep her distance.

"You get your ass out of here, Hymn…and don't come back!"

He stepped up to her, reaching out to her, but her sharp bark sent him out of the room.

"I said get out!"

Hymn slowly walked past Solis, leaving the door to her suite open. She watched as he walked to the elevator. Just before he stepped into it, their eyes met briefly, extending the ties of longing between the two of them.

Hymn rode the elevator to his room two floors down. His heart raced, as his temper flared. Desire overwhelmed him and fueled the fire to his emotions. He reached his suite and slammed the door. Stripping down, he calmed his nerves with a cold shower.

The cold water did little to curb his erection that snaked down the inside of his thigh. A pair of gray warm-ups lay at the bottom of his suite case. He fished them out, and put them on. Lying on his back atop of the bed proved the only comfortable position since the slightest touch sent his shaft straining forth. His appendage stood high above the waistline of the warm-ups.

He continued to lie on the bed listening to the sounds of his watch chime. The erection he nursed and the urge to stroke his body overwhelmed him causing him to give in. One touch of his crown, caused a moan so deep within his throat he hardly recognized the sound of his own voice. Hymn jumped to his feet in a rush, as he sprang for the suite door. He flew out the door to the staircase in only a pair of dark gray warm ups, with his shaft stiff and at attention leading the way.

Climbing the stairs two at a time, he reached the floor to her room. Knocking softly, he laid his forehead on the door, hoping her ears would remain deaf to his pitiful plea to enter. To his relief and surprise, Solis opened the door. Immediately, her eyes settled on his erection, nearly making her mouth water. Nervously, she licked her lips.

Without an invitation, Hymn boldly stepped into her suite. One sweep of his arms, and her body pressed against his. He slammed his lips into hers, without giving her a chance to protest or to breathe. His shaft pressed into her abdomen, making her loins moist and full of guilt. She pushed her hands between the two of them, and pushed his body away with all her strength.

"Why are you doing this? I didn't ask you to come here like this."

"I can't help myself. When I look at you, I want to give you everything. I can give you the life humans share with each other, not traipsing halfway around the world to get yourself killed over a vampire, Solis. I want to protect you, and give you children and a home. I need a place of my own to settle down, and I want you...I want you! My family has watched over Nacio and the Caraways for decades. I've read about my forefathers, and Nacio and the Caraways. That's not the life you deserve, Solis. You'll be long gone before they will, and the cycle goes on and on. I know you want a life, and I know you want love."

"You don't even know me, because if you did, you'd know I'm in love with Nacio and he loves me. You are making yourself a target of his rage, and when he returns he will come to harm you."

"If he comes home, Solis...if he comes home! This thing with Auldicia is no small matter. Everyday she's in this realm makes things worse for mankind. If she has Nacio it's highly likely he won't be returning. She very well might have already condemned him to a live of servitude with her. It's how their species survives, and it's no life for you. You must accept this reality, Solis."

"It's you who must accept the fact I'm bound to him. I don't have to accept anything from you!"

"Yeah, well, why did you kiss me? Don't pretend you didn't...because when I kissed you, you kissed back."

"You came to my room with your body hard as a rock. I have not, in any way, led you on to believe I wanted anything to do with you! You came as a guest in our home and I will not be a whore in your arms! Do you understand me? Now get your ass out of this suite right now, or so help me I will scream!"

"Solis, please, I want you. Can't you understand what I'm telling you? You're in danger as long as you live this life."

"I'm married, and Nacio is the life I choose. Get...your... ass...out...of here!" Solis pointed toward the door."

Hymn walked out of her suite still rock hard, and jilted once more. He knew a hard night waited for him once he returned to his suite. With his anger nearly out of control, he sat up all night waiting to depart the country, headed home. He dressed himself with difficulty stuffing his unbendable erection beneath his zipper. Although only a few hours stood between him and sunrise, he truly had a long night ahead of him.

Solis sat on the corner of the bed, out of breath and sweating. Hymn's words rang out in her ears.

"I can't help myself. When I look at you, I want to give you everything. I can give you the life humans share with each other, not traipsing halfway around the world to get yourself killed over a vampire Solis. I want to protect you, and give you children and a home. I need a place of my own to settle down, and I want you...I want you! If he comes home Solis...if he comes home! This thing with Auldicia is no small matter. Everyday she's in this realm makes things worse for mankind. If she has Nacio, it's highly likely he won't be returning. You must accept this reality, Solis."

Part of what he said hit home. She did respond when he kissed her. Treading dangerously, she knew at any time she could make a costly mistake, putting her bond to Nacio in jeopardy. She wanted to leave and get home, so she packed her things and dressed for the morning departure.

†

Sunshine streamed in through the beautiful view of her suite. Today, she headed home to get her affairs in order. The sun gave her hope after surviving a restless night once more. Hymn made his intentions known to her, and guilt she carried for kissing another man nearly drove her to tears. His affections gave her the determination to do all she had to do to get Nacio home.

She freshened up and made her way down to the registration desk for checking out. Over in the lobby, she saw the points of Hymn's booted feet sitting by the curb, checked out and ready to taxi to the airport. He heard the resonance of her voice and stood. She finished checking out, and wheeled her luggage out to the curb. Hymn grabbed his luggage and followed. When the taxi pulled up, she immediately started to load her luggage, but his strong hands interrupted her grip. Their eyes met briefly, as he finished loading his and her luggage into the trunk of the taxi.

Just one look at her sent his heart raising. Whenever in her presence, he always had a semi-erect shaft that stiffened simply from the scent of her hair, leaving him mercifully at her whim. He'd revealed his heart to her last night, and it now belonged to her...completely. In all the years of theological study, he thought he understood the definition of sin and forgiveness, but the things he wanted to do to Solis surpassed any forgiveness. He wanted all of her, and willingly risked his friendships, a centuries old family allegiance, and even death all for her. Strangely, he didn't fear Nacio. In fact, he wanted to challenge to champion this woman to win her heart.

The quiet ride to the airport passed without words spoken between them. The worry line that zigzagged down her face, between her eyes, boldly appeared in its usual place. He wanted all this to end, and knew it soon would. A great distance stretched between their bodies as they sat in the taxi. In an attempt to speak to Solis, he found his words cut short as her cell phone rang. Basrick began a conversation that drowned any efforts of conversation between Solis and him.

"Basrick, what's up? Yes...okay...In Austin? Yeah, sure... straight to the mansion...got it...we'll be there in a few hours. Yes, I know tomorrow night is the lunar eclipse. So everything is ready? Alright. Thank you, and I'll see you all soon."

Disconnecting he call, Solis finally turned in Hymn's direction to give the high points of the conversation. "Basrick has rearranged our flight plans to land at Bergstrom Airport in Austin, Texas. He feels this will throw the descendants off our trail, since one of them attacked me at San Antonio International, they'll expect us to return home at that airport. This change in plans will allow us to drive home, and go straight to the masonry."

Hymn did his usual nod, but did not speak. That took Solis by surprise. She knew he would have some remark to give, but he remained neutral and did not speak. In fact, no more words passed between them at all, except a polite thank you here and there. They boarded the plane and flew several hours over the Atlantic Ocean. Solis fell fast asleep. Her mind warped through several passionate dreams sending her through multiple orgasms. The last one shook her so hard, she awoke with Hymn gently touching her face.

"Hey, are you okay? You squirmed quite a bit, and I wanted to make certain you could relax. Do you need anything?"

"No thank you. I'm fine."

"Listen, Solis I wanted you to know that…,"

"Please don't say anything more, Hymn. We've both said a lot already, and I just want to get home."

She turned her head to look out over the dark ocean. His heavy, magnetic gaze made her want to say things she knew she would later regret, such as she wanted to wrap herself in his embrace, and watch him slowly undress while standing in front of her. No, she couldn't say those things out loud and remain bound to Nacio.

Admittedly, she realized she didn't trust her own judgment in this situation. It seemed as if some evil force worked secretly to destroy all her happiness. Something evil worked to make her want to put her lips to this man's mouth and lay with him. She knew she had to resist this urge, but found she got weaker and weaker each day in his presence, and each day of Nacio's absence. Regressing back to her old way of life, getting involved with a different man every other month, would not happen again. Taking responsibility for her actions started the night she married Nacio and nothing would change that it.

Since assuming responsibility for her actions has become her new way of life, she has special plans for the rapist, Klein Treemount. Solis obsessed over her actions.

Oh yes, Klein. I have a special gift for you---one you'll remember me by...forever.

13

Take a dose

Their connecting flight touched down at Bergstrom Airport. Alert and on the lookout for any descendants, Solis and Hymn grabbed their luggage and shuttled to the nearest rental car kiosk. Once on the move down IH 35, she called Basrick one last time.

"Basrick, we have ground transportation and should be home within the next 90 minutes. Is Urgata back yet?"

"Yes, and she's here now. We'll head straight for the masonry and prepare the mix so all you'll have to do is bring the main ingredient for the spell."

"Great! We're on the way."

Hymn ignored the speed limit and struck out on IH 35 with speed that had fire coming out of the tail pipe. The meager Ford Focus could only do so much to meet their need for speed. Time sifted away each day of Nacio's absence, and Solis needed him. A few miles outside of the Bexar County line, Hymn spoke leaving her speechless.

"I wanted to let you know, as soon as we get to the masonry

our business is complete. My plan is to turn in my notice of resignation to Basrick, effective immediately. I'll leave once you and Urgata have cast your spell. I will burden you no further, Solis."

"But you can't just leave! What about Auldicia?"

"We've acquired what's needed, and everything should go well."

Frustrated and shocked, Solis began shouting nearly on the verge of tears.

"You can't just leave, Hymn! We need you...I need you!" Having said those words, Hymn served off the highway onto the shoulder of the road, and slammed on the brakes.

"Dammit Solis, I can't stand this! I can't stand the weight of your presence on my heart. Every time I look at you, I want you. The smell of your hair, your skin, every damn thing makes me want you! I can't have you and I cannot stand it. Please, let me go."

"But we need you."

"That maybe, but do you want me?"

Solis froze, knowing she had to choose her words wisely. The high price to pay from words spoken too hastily often led to grief, which hurt those you cared for most.

"Answer me, Solis. Do you want me?" Silence.

"I thought not." His blue eyes held her gaze, waiting for her response. He stared at her lips waiting for the words to give him hope, yet none came.

"Alright, just as I thought. You can't even answer me, but I'll tell you what. I'll make you a deal. I'll stay and help you fight Auldicia. After that, I'm gone…no questions asked. Got it?"

"I understand."

They rolled into San Antonio and headed straight for the masonry. It felt good to see the sky over the city. As she passed the Roy Richards Road exit, Solis felt her soul stir. For the first time in months, she felt a glimmer of hope her husband still lived.

"Keep driving, Hymn, and hurry. The lunar eclipse happens tonight, and we need all the preparation we can get."

They turned down the narrowly paved road to the Puente Masonry. Just looking at the structure made her heart ache for Nacio. Menlo's car sat parked in front, which meant the rest of the family had gone inside. The masonry had closed, leaving them alone to do what they needed to send Auldicia back to hell.

Hymn led the way down to the sublevel of the masonry, which stored the huge vats full of Dieth. They needed room to spread out into a circle to cast the spell. Armando brought with him the sword Solis and Urgata needed to hex in order to open the plane between the two realms. They all hugged Solis, with Hymn in tow. Armando and Basrick greeted her first.

"It's good to see you, Mistress," Armando spoke. "It's good to have you home."

"We've missed you," Basrick chimed. "The vats are ready to go."

Urgata and Menlo hugged and kissed her cheeks. Menlo started first.

"I'm glad your back. I thought I would have to find and kick Childress in her ass all alone."

Urgata went straight to business.

"I have the spell ready, and the sword is ready for preparation."

"Thank you both." Armando and Basrick shook Hymn's hand. After their sincere handshake Solis witnessed, she couldn't help but think of the ulterior feelings Hymn kept for her.

If these vampires knew you wanted to have me as your own, they would mix you into that huge vat with the acid.

Right when Solis finished her thought, Armando's expression changed and he held her in his gaze. Knowing his keen telepathic senses probably picked up the tail end of her self-talk, she quickly crowded her mind with battle plans.

Hymn sensed her uneasiness and quickly excused himself to get the luggage from the rental car. Solis needed to strategize to get the plan into action to find Auldicia, but first needed to mix the ingredients they retrieved from their trek around the world.

Reaching for her suitcases, Hymn grabbed it from her hand and walked it up a ramp to a 10-foot high plank over a vat that turned continuously. The potent smell of the chemicals clued bystanders to its lethality. Solis commanded Urgata to join her in pouring the contents into the vat.

"Urgata, we need to pour the blood of the White Komodo and the Holy Water of Pope Pius II into the vat. Armando and Basrick, have you loaded the Colloidal Silver and Dieth into the mixture?" They both nodded.

Urgata stood to the side of Solis as the circle to cast the spell formed. Armando and Basrick circled the south point of the vat. Menlo and Hymn filed in from the east and west point, while Solis and Urgata stood to the north of the vat. Armando held the sword ready to dip it into the mixture, curing it to open the realm membrane. Urgata and Solis began their chant to cast the spell. Solis started, and then Urgata followed.

"Tonight we stand underneath the lunar eclipse. Let the voodoo gods Agwe and Guede summon the one to claim Auldicia from this realm. Let him come and take her back to the depths of Hell where she belongs."

"Akba, vendoto, sefweh, bundaloo, Rogato, Vulkus dumba-loo Auldicia. Come and stake your claim, Vulkus. Receive Auldicia back to your possession."

The chanting continued as Solis poured the blood of the White Komodo Dragon and the Holy Water of Pope Pius II from the Vatican into the vat. Soon the contents of the vat sizzled, coming to a rolling boil, yet no heat convection blew through the room.

"Armando, dip the sword now. Do it now." With preternatural speed at his disposal, Armando stood dangerously close to the vat, reaching far over the edge. He let go of the sword, and telekinetically allowed it to submerge itself under the surface of the mixture. The ordinary sword remained submerged for as long as Solis and Urgata continued to chant.

When the chanting stopped, everyone looked at each other. Solis looked each of them in the face, as the mixture of the vat turned colors, from silver to blood red.

"It's working. We need to hurry, because time is running out. Whatever Auldicia plans to do, it will take place tonight." Menlo spoke then readied herself for action.

"The question is, where do we look? I mean, Armando has tried looking throughout the city, but we haven't had any luck."

Solis remembered what she felt as soon as they crossed the Bexar County line. For the first time in months, she felt hope and knew Nacio hadn't left the realm. Her eyes lit up in response to Menlo's question.

"When Hymn and I came down IH 35 near Roy Richards Drive, I felt something like Nacio's spirit. That feeling let me know he still lived. The TSA Agent that attacked me at the Airport kept mumbling something about 'Mother had plans for me' or something of the sort. I say I become bait and go back there. If they knew I left, surely they'll expect me to come back through the Airport again." Basrick stepped in.

"Of course. That reason alone is what made me tell you not to fly back through San Antonio International. This could work, but it does have risks Solis. I don't want to risk any harm to you. The sire wouldn't dream of it." Hymn averted his eyes to the floor at Basrick's reference to Nacio.

"Once I'm at Auldicia's location, you all can track me to the location with my cell phone GPS. You'll need to have the chemical mixture and the sword with you."

As Solis spoke of the sword, the rolling boil that surged from the vat rumbled and brought the sword forth. The magic of the chant and the blessed Holy Water extended the length of the sword at least a foot. The gleaming blade shined underneath the ceiling fluorescents, while the hilt sat firm with a golden edged grip.

Solis smiled as tears welled in her eyes. "The chant worked. I believe this magnificent sword demonstrates we have the favor for victory this evening, and Nacio's return will happen."

Solis used her telekinesis, and summoned the sword toward her. She extended her hand to the hilt. Armando cautioned her about the lethality of the mix.

"Careful. It just came out of the mix with the acid. Perhaps I should hold it to test its safety?"

With hope in her eyes and faith in her heart, Solis continued to extend her hand to the sword's hilt, unafraid of a burn to her skin. The sword found its way into the palm of her hand. She held it firmly, and touched the renewed artisanship of the blade. As she familiarized herself with the blade of the sword, her touch significantly retracted the blade. Another touch and the blade extended to its renewed length, making it easily concealable. Armando noted the power Solis wielded in her touch.

"I believe it's clear. You will carry this weapon forth into battle tonight, and victory belongs to us."

Again, Hymn's eyes darted back and forth in doubt, causing Solis to cut her lids low, narrowing her eyes in his direction. Feeling her own frustration starting to boil, she finalized their plans.

"Patience will remain at the mansion with Blessing as planned. I'm sure Childress wants the little one for her own evil-doing, and a battle is no place for a baby. In no way shall Childress have access to Blessing."

"I agree," Armando voiced. "We will need to look out for other vampires. Auldicia has had plenty of time to create more monstrosities, and we must take precautions."

"Yes, this is true. Hymn, will you please assist Armando and Basrick in loading the contents of the vat into two of the mixing trucks?"

He masked his doubt with a quick nod, and then moved quickly. Solis noted Armando's expression as Hymn moved toward the outside of the masonry. With keen intuition and senses sharp as a tack, not too long from now, Armando will sense the change in Hymn if he hadn't already. Even so, he couldn't mention the subject at this point, not with the task before them.

"The plan is to drive the trucks to the location. Armando, can you and Urgata glamour the noise they make?"

"Yes, that is wise. Surely Auldicia would have sense enough to know danger lurks if she hears the infernal noise these machines make." Urgata conveyed her thoughts as well.

"We cannot make mistakes. Once the port of the two planes opens, we have to get Auldicia pushed through. We cannot take a chance on Vulkus tearing through the plane and remaining here. His very presence would wreak havoc beyond reason. We have to act fast. I will assist Armando with the glamour," Hymn finally spoke up, and offered his assistance without having instructions given to him.

"I'll drive the first truck, given I know its maneuvering capabilities." Solis looked his way.

"Thank you, Hymn. Your assistance is appreciated."

Everyone stood ready to move into action. Solis gave her final instructions and warnings for safety.

"This is an all out battle. Strike to kill. My personal targets tonight involve dealing with Klein Treemount. Menlo, I'm sure you and Urgata have a few choice moves of your own in dealing with Childress. I'll take the leftovers from that ass beating. We must all work to subdue Auldicia. On my word, the mixing trucks must release the chemicals. If any of the descendants have turned to vampires, the mix will destroy them. Make certain you all have your Dieth darts at the ready for those human descendants. We have to destroy their reproductive system; males included. Are there any questions? Let's move out."

With everyone receiving their instructions, they sprang into action. Solis chose to ride in the truck with Basrick and Menlo, careful not to stir more tension between her and Hymn. In no mood to have her senses probed, she also avoided riding in the truck with Armando. They didn't have time for 20 questions, and she needed all of her strength and courage to get her husband back from the hell-sent, bitch dog that imprisoned him.

As the calendar had it, the lunar eclipse had begun. The moon hung high in the sky, large enough to reach out and touch with your hand. All the men loaded the chemical mix into the mixing trucks to flood over Auldicia during the confrontation. Urgata's wisdom held true. They couldn't make any mistakes. The cement mixing trucks have a payload of a quarter of a ton, filled with a major biochemical hazard traveling through San Antonio streets. The potential catastrophic danger to the populous would be immeasurable.

Now, as Solis headed into battle for her husband's soul, she sent a silent prayer to her loved ones on the other side, asking for guidance and strength.

"Mama and grandma, if you can hear me, please help me bring my husband back home. I need his love. Please help us."

Basrick and Menlo smiled at each other as Solis finished her prayer. Within minutes, they arrived at the Airport, ready to use Solis as bait to lure them to Nacio and to lure Auldicia back to hell. Basrick parked at the Airport Shuttle parking. Solis got out of the truck and walked over to the shuttle bench to get her final ride into the airport. She walked toward the bench, turned around, and held up her cell phone. This provided the reassurance to them she had what she needed for them to track her location. Solis mentally prepared herself as the shuttled dropped her off curbside at the Southwest Airline Terminal.

Alright, let's try this again. When Hymn and I walked through the gate, our nasty little TSA agent friend tried to shake me down. I don't have a ticket to board a plane so, my guess would be to linger near the checkpoint to see if any fellow descendants spot me. I'm guessing it won't take long, so here it goes.

She moved closer to the checkpoint in hopes of having a descendant identify her, and move in for the capture. A narrow set of benches stood near the checkpoint. She sat in place for a few moments, communicating with Basrick and Menlo as they waited parked at a remote location outside the airport.

"So far, nothing," Solis checked in. "I'm still wandering up here on the departure deck. I'm going downstairs to the arrival luggage pickup station."

"We copy that, and we see you here on the GPS."

"I'm headed downstairs now. With the Bluetooth device turned on, you'll know the moment they have me."

"Got it." Basrick confirmed. She heard Menlo's voice through the speakerphone.

"Good Luck Solis, and be careful."

"I will, and see you guys soon."

Just as she wrapped up her last check in, Solis took notice of a crowd of distinctive green eyed folks. A man with an uncanny resemblance to Bose led the pack. She tried to relax, and not look too apprehensive, but found relaxing easier said than done.

"Basrick can you hear me," she whispered." I've just spotted them; a crowd of four at 12, 3, 6, and 9 o'clock. They have fanned out to surround me. Here we go."

"Copy that. We're on standby."

Basrick gave the order to move out on his cue, once movement occurred. The convoy of trucks revved their engines waiting for movement. Solis breathed deeply, and she prepared for her apprehension. She watched as all of the descendants moved in on her from different directions. The one who resembled Bose reached her first. His disguised 'Miss, do you have the time?' approach behind his lacquered smile indicated he had more on his mind than asking for the time. Solis had the volume turned up on her cell phone, so Basrick and Menlo heard every word as the man spoke.

"Solis Burkes? Mother First awaits your arrival."

"And just who is Mother First?"

"Auldicia, bitch, now let's go." A nasty piece of work this man was. He even shoved her when he enunciated his point.

By now, Solis determined the human descendants had vulnerabilities leaving them open for a vicious ass whooping she could do on all four in five minutes. However, it would defeat the purpose. She needed them to apprehend her in order to find Nacio, so she carried out her plan. Hating to sound like the cliché damsel in distress, she asked a question that would surely get her assailant violently angry.

"Where do you plan to take me?"

Without giving a response, the man tightened his grip on her arm, and hurried her through the crowd in front of the arrival and departure curb. The assailants whisked her away in a tricked out black Jeep Cherokee, screeching away from the curb. One of the descendants stood approximately 6' 9", weighing a minimum of 380 pounds, so getting into the Jeep proved difficult. In their presence, she realized the descendants eyes glistened and held an unnaturally fluorescent glow. The dead TSA Agent and the red headed man they ran into in Vatican City had similar eyes, probably entranced and brain washed. The one who looked like Bose insulted her further.

"Mother First plans to feed you to Vulkus himself, but first she's going to punish you good."

"I haven't done anything to your mama." The remark earned a slap to her face from a female descendant sitting next to her. A reflex response from Solis slapped the female descendant right back, leaving a bloody nose and a loose gold tooth. The commotion caused the Bose-like descendant to swerve and slam on the brakes.

"Stop this foolishness now, or you will regret your actions! You'll regret them anyway." He ended his sentence with a sour, diabolical laugh, which made a tremor run down her spine. She took note of the direction they traveled. Sure enough, they traveled up IH 35 and exited near the very spot she felt hope reenter her heart. She knew her beloved would soon return to her embrace.

They exited 3009 Roy Richards Drive, and headed west. Her confidence continued to grow because her entourage convoyed not far behind her. The Jeep traveled approximately 7 miles, and then hit a dirt road. Dips and bumps rocked the Jeep, throwing her back and forth between the bloody female she hit and the 6' 9" simpleton. When he leaned over on Solis, his weight completely immobilized her.

Auldicia's descendants possessed a cruelty that never

ceased to amaze Solis. On the way to Auldicia's lair, the Bose-like descendant hit a bucking deer that leaped in front of the jeep. The descendant hit the deer in the hindquarters flipping it 180 degrees over the hood, flinging it into a cactus, piercing its body with several needles.

"Hey, can't you try to drive a little more carefully?" This time, the giant man next to her shoved his pillow soft elbow into her side. Another reflex response from Solis caused her to take her right index finger and poke him in the eye. The big wuss started crying. Bose's twin wasn't pleased.

"Shut up, damn fool, and keep your mouth shut! We don't want to upset Mother First." The head descendant placed a call notifying someone of her capture. She knew from her own experience the descendants looked for her in many places, including half way around the world in Vatican City. As suspected, the descendants resided all over the world. They had set out to find her.

"Tell everyone we've found her. Plan to meet back at the location for the ceremony," the descendant commanded, telling the rest of them to return to the cavern where they headed now.

The bumpy ride ended with a jerk of the brakes. Recognizing the area as Natural Bridge Caverns, Solis audibly expressed her amazement.

"This is where you all have been vacationing? At Natural Bridge Caverns in the woods? From the looks of you, I guess you couldn't get a room at the Grand Hyatt." Solis made certain to let the Bluetooth eavesdropping Basrick in on her exact location. She knew to win the battle ahead she needed all her strength because

Auldicia would not take defeat lightly.

The foul mood descendants snatched Solis out of the car. Although the road trip ended, they started a hike down the side of a mountain that trailed to a cavern. A loud flock of squawking vultures flew overhead, circling what looked like human carcasses from a distance. Solis knew this place held her captured husband. Her heart pounded as her hopes soared to new heights in hopes of seeing him alive.

She checked her surroundings, making certain to notice the path and everything on it in case she has to make a quick escape. In high hopes, she prayed the GPS would reliably lead Basrick and the rest of the crew directly to this place. In strike mode, she stood at the threshold of the dark cavern.

14

Breakthrough

"The time has come, Zuri, for us to conceive our child together. The lunar eclipse is high in the sky, and I must conceive within the next 12 hours. I've enjoyed our love making. It's something I've dreamed of for centuries. It makes me proud to know you plan to give me your seed now."

Nacio's body now lay shackled on a sacrificial altar. He knew what occurred in the next hour would change his world permanently. If Auldicia's spell worked, and they conceived a child, he would lose Solis forever. If needed, he would sacrifice himself to keep Solis out of harm's way. He played along, hoping to buy himself more time for a miracle to occur. He quickly thought of a lie to throw her off, before the rest of the descendants returned.

"Yes, my love, let's conceive our child, and rule this realm together. We must hurry because Childress plans to give her body to me as well. She denies having feelings for me. You must watch how she looks at me."

Auldicia climbed up to the sacrificial altar, and looked him straight in the eyes. "Yes, Zuri, I know Childress covets you, but you belong to me. And I shall punish Childress more for having any thought of giving her body to you. Think of her no more."

Auldicia began to chant as she took Nacio's shaft in her hands. Her firm grip worked in conjunction with the spell to harden him to full length. Straddling his lap once more, she slid down onto his crown to take him inside her. Her gums retracted from her fangs, displaying them in full view. Her rhythm started slow and soon increased in pace. As much as he hated what took place, he knew he had to play along in the charade, so he began to move his hips with hers, bringing her to one thunderous climax after another. Opening her jaw wide, she bit him, sending a rush of his blood down her throat.

Staying in character, Nacio again pleaded with her to release him.

"I need to touch you Priestess. Please release me."

"I plan to release you once our child is conceived, Zuri, so please make sure you give me what you need for your release." Blood sprayed from her lips as she spoke. She continued grinding her hips, catching his forward thrusts. An hour later, she still had not conceived.

Nacio bucked harder and harder beneath her hips, all the while knowing he'd never conceive a child with this demon witch. After her last climax, she dismounted his hips to give herself room for the conception to occur. Still nothing, and Auldicia came to realize the possibility of what stymied her conception.

"Zuri, have you bound your soul to Solis?" A sincere expression of pain and anguish covered her face. She moved slowly toward his face, waiting for his response. Her scream demanded and answer.

"Did you bind with her?"

Nacio only stared at the vault of the ceiling, as Auldicia wailed. Her cries shook the dirt as she held herself and sank to the floor. From the volume of her cries, one would have assumed she lost her soul. Her wailing soon turned to a heart-wrenching moan. The vow of a marriage bind, forfeited any magic she could conjure, making her efforts to conceive a futile attempt of what she wished could be.

"How could you, Zuri? My love for you is greater than my soul. How could you bind to a mortal? What purpose would it serve? You belong to me and now you have given your soul to a mortal? Your punishment shall begin now."

Auldicia searched for the silver barometer she used to catheterize him. Taking it in her hand and burning herself in the process, she held it high over her head and stabbed him very close to his heart. Nacio lay in agony. He cried out as the silver barometer seared his skin, releasing a cloud of black smoke in the cavern. The glory of her figure and facial features changed, bringing forth her true form. Talons stretched from her fingernails, while her toes turned to hooves. Her beautiful legs turned to hindquarters. The metamorphoses revealed her true form to Nacio and those descendants entering the cavern returning from hunting for Solis.

Her voice took on the tone of a demon. "You knew damn well I could never conceive if you bound your soul to another; and a mortal no less. You have mocked me for the last time, Zuri.

Your face shall never see this realm again under the moonlight. Since you have deceived me, you shall take my place in Hell."

A fierce wind kicked up in the cavern, blowing dirt and sand in the air. Bolts of lightning struck beneath the cavern floor, disintegrating stalagmites in various parts of the cavern. Many of the descendants returned from the expedition, and walked straight into madness. The first few descendants that entered the cavern met their doom when she grabbed one at a time and bit them multiple times over their bodies, draining them of all the plasma in their body, only allowing a few ounces to remain. The bodies dropped to the floor and began withering away, thus starting the initial transformation to vampires.

Auldicia continued her thirst binge through the crowd of nearly 200 people in the cavern until she reached Believa. Her guttural tone sounded almost incoherent as she spoke. Childress and her crew stood silent and listened.

"You carry the child of a Treemount in your womb. Give me the baby for the sacrifice, and then I shall break the bond Zuri has with Solis. Then I can conceive his child. No one will stop me."

Believa stood baffled at what Auldicia meant. When she did not step forth and do what Auldicia commanded, the unexpected happened. Believa's insolence further enraged Auldicia, making her cast a spell to start labor. Believa fell to the ground, allowing the contractions to push her unborn child from her womb. Childress stood off to the side and smiled at the pain Believa felt, but it also caused a letdown, and her own breast milk flowed once more. The stream of milk leaked outside of her shirt, causing her to step back and retreat into the shadows of the cavern.

Believa's body twisted in pain as the labor caused her to tremble and shake. Her abdomen moved and squirmed as the child Justice fathered fought to make its way into the world. No one helped deliver her baby, as it crowned its head amid the wind and flying dirt. Believa's screams echoed throughout the cavern. Auldicia stood silently as the birth neared its end.

There amid the dust and muck, a male child lay between Believa's legs, bloody and covered in dirty. Auldicia came and picked up the child in her arms, yanking the afterbirth from Believa's womb. Another scream came from Believa, as Auldicia cut the umbilical cord with her talons.

"Let me hold my baby. Please give him to me. I need to see Justice and I know the baby looks like him…please!" Her plea to hold her son went ignored. "Please! His father is dead, and he will never get to know him."

The news of her brother's death sent the surviving Treemounts into a free fall. Childress shed one single tear, and then hatred shattered her emotional exterior.

"You mean my brother has been dead all this time, and no one admitted to it?"

Klein and Erland both lost composure. Klein started pacing, as Erland cried and laughed simultaneously. Klein cursed Believa.

"Tramp, you knew Justice had died, and you're only now saying something about it? Who killed him?"

Auldicia held the crying newborn in her arms, taking it to the sacrificial altar Nacio's body lay upon sizzling from the silver in his wound. Klein's question went unanswered until Nacio drew strength enough to answer the question with an untruth. He did not want the Treemounts to know Basrick killed their sibling. Knowing if he did not survive this night on this lunar eclipse, he knew the Caraways would care for Solis, and he would not put Solis at risk any further.

"I killed your rotten brother." Klein lunged for the altar, when an unseen forced snatched him backward, throwing him at the wall. Auldicia admonished him for attempting to approach her sacred area.

"You will stay exactly where you are Klein Treemount and watch as a true Priestess brings forth life."

Believa's screams became louder as Auldicia held the child high over her head, and began a chant of doom for the child. Irritated at the high-pitched hissing Believa made, and showing her fangs, Auldicia teleported to the ground and looked at her. She handed the baby boy to Childress to hold while she held Believa in her gaze.

"Your services as an incubator are no longer required." Auldicia raised her hands as orange flames set Believa's body on fire. Soon the hissing and shrieking noises faded. Only crackling fire and howling wind echoed in the cavern. Klein and Erland stood open mouthed at what they witnessed. Neither of them made another sound in fear of the same ill fate. Briefly distracted, Auldicia regained her thought process and began her sacrifice protocol once more, only to experience another interruption.

The wind carried a scent she recognized from long ago. The citrus smell stopped her mid-sentence as she laid her eyes on the figure standing in the cavern threshold. Ellis had returned with Solis in tow. Solis carried the scent very similar to that of her ancestor Olinka, whom she'd fought centuries ago. Auldicia stood smiling with her fangs sharp as knives to greet her enemy's descendant.

"At last. We finally meet." Briefly, Auldicia stood in her true form, but soon allowed those to see her in her curvaceous human form once more. She dared not look like the monstrosity of her true self before this beguiling female who shared the bloodline of her enemy. Ellis spoke the unnecessary introductions as the tension in the air thickened.

"Priestess Auldicia, Mother First, I give you Solis Burkes Puente." All the air left the cavern at his last spoken word.

Nacio snapped his head in her direction to behold his bride. Joy, love, and shame overwhelmed him at the sight of her. Solis immediately sensed his presence and looked at him from afar. Overjoyed to see her husband, his smile gave her the courage she lacked to start the battle to send Auldicia to back to Hell. She spoke her first words to the female demon that morphed into human form.

"It's strange, but I thought you'd be bigger than you are. You look nothing like I'd imagined." Her facetiousness jabbed at Auldicia irritating her.

"And you look every bit like I imagined. You are Olinka's filthy waste. So it is you who has wed my Zuri; you who have taken away my right at conceiving a child with him?"

Solis had the Bluetooth device on, and listened as Basrick cued her to strike.

"We're here Solis. On my count." She continued to toy with Auldicia waiting for the perfect moment to start her offensive. The sword in its retracted size fit in the inside pocket of her shirt on standby.

"According to history, you've had several men and several children, all of which are standing amongst us now."

Klein howled in at what Solis said to his ancestor. "You gonna let her talk to you like that?"

Auldicia turned in his direction. Hearing everything over the Bluetooth Basrick started his count.

"In three, two, one, now, Solis!"

Grabbing the Dieth Dart special mixed for Klein Treemount, she telekinetically flung the dart straight at his jugular vein. The chemical mix in the Dieth did the usual physical altera-tions, but for a male it had the opposite effect. Klein fell to the ground, curled up in a fetal position.

"What the hell did you do to me?" The reaction caused him to have muscle spasms, which then flattened him on his back. The drastic transformation held everyone's attention. Klein's crotch squirmed underneath his jeans, while his testicles shrank. His two reproductive organs retrograded into his abdomen, causing excru-ciating pain. As a promise to herself, Solis carried out her plan to punish her rapist. She had Klein Treemount castrated; retribution for raping her years ago.

Childress held on to the baby in her arms as she stepped further and further away from the mayhem in the cavern. She pulled Erland by the hand as she eased her way toward the opening in hopes of a quick getaway. She had watched as Auldicia roasted Believa, and she couldn't take a chance on having another of her siblings killed. Erland crowed like a rooster, when Klein went down. The devastation of realizing Justice died still hadn't quite settled in yet.

Auldicia grabbed Solis by the throat, raising her in the air. Startled by her preternatural movement, Solis didn't anticipate her offensive move, and struggled to get free.

"I have to kill you just for the filthy blood that runs through your veins. Go to hell and tell Olinka hello for me would you?" Tightening her grip on Solis, Auldicia commanded the bloodshed to begin; roaring in the wind.

"Descendants…attack!" The trance like descendants made their way towards Solis.

She fought to get free, and eventually took out a Dieth dart, plunging it into Auldicia's hand. The silver ignited her skin causing it to burn on contact. Solis slipped from her grip and fell to the ground, just as Basrick and Menlo came crashing through one of the cavern walls, and Armando and Urgata came through the other. Childress and her brothers turned back toward the mayhem in the cavern with the rest of the descendants when she heard the trucks crashing in. Hymn followed behind Armando's truck to block the exit leading outside.

Menlo and Urgata saw Childress and ran toward her. Menlo had her gun drawn and her finger on the trigger, trembling to pull it.

"Just where the hell do you think you're going Childress? It's too bad this is the first time in years we've   seen each other, and looks like you're going back to jail…for the murder of Bureau Treemount La Deaux." Menlo's gun held several large, silver bullets. The La Deaux sisters looked like two coyotes waiting to skin a meal. Unaffected by their stance, Childress stood and smirked at her cousins about her dirty little sin of killing their mother, Bureau. She handed Believa's newborn son to Erland to hold, calming his nerves. Erland continued to back away toward the cavern entrance, now humming to the infant and protecting its head. Childress goaded her cousin, throwing salt in their wound of losing their mother.

"The question is what the hell you think you're gonna do to me with that gun, Cher? I beat your asses when we were children, and I can sure do it again now."

Urgata and Menlo looked at each other and shrugged their shoulders. Menlo fired her weapon just as the earth shook. Childress took a bullet to the right shoulder---knocking her down as the earth scattered the descendants in all directions. Menlo kept shooting sending fatal shots to her cousin's weak Hench Wenches. Dozer, Presser, and Bula collapsed from bullet wounds, ending their lives and short-lived freedom. The sisters looked up to see their wayward sibling Tahiti running amid the chaos. Urgata called to her.

"Tahiti, where are you going? Tahiti come back here, you

have children that need you."

A fiery hiss came in response. Menacingly, Tahiti snapped her fangs at her sisters as she started approaching them, "I don't have children anymore, and I'm coming to feed on you two."

Urgata screamed as Menlo fired her gun at their sister. Tahiti had started the transition to vampire. Menlo had one last bullet to fire. As she looked at Urgata, her sister gave her the nod to take their Tahiti's life. Menlo's silver bullet cut Tahiti down as it embedded in her heart, exploding out from her back. Urgata's heart wrenching cries rang out in the cavern. Menlo knew the anguish she felt, as Tahiti's children no longer had their mother.

Auldicia's skin crackled, burning to ash. The noise acted as a distraction for Solis to pull her sword. One touch to the blade and the sword extended to the size of a magnificent weapon to complete the task. Without any hesitation, Solis swung the blade at Auldicia, cutting her right arm from her body. She didn't hesitate and struck another blow, only to miss her left arm, but cutting off her left hand instead. A chant came to mind, and Solis started the words to send Auldicia back to Hell.

"Maalak gothra, lembeck aldood, Vulkus. Maalak gothra, lembeck, aldood. Return for your possession, Vulkus, return for your possession."

Auldicia began screaming when she heard Solis speak the words to call the owner of her soul to claim her. With no way to cast a spell, Auldicia knew her fate had changed, and soon Vulkus would come for her. Solis commanded her entourage to release the chemical.

"Release the mix now!"

The descendants began to flee, but discovered they no longer had their freedom. Hymn had his truck preloaded with the chemical weapon mix; blood from the White Komodo Dragon, Holy Water blessed by Pope Pius II, Colloidal Silver, Dieth, hydrochloric acid, and sulfuric acid. Hymn's truck came in spraying the mix in Auldicia's direction.

With little time to spare, Solis had to run amongst the frightened descendants to get to Nacio. The chant she called summoned an earthquake to shake the ground, making it difficult to get to the altar where he lay shackled and sick with silver poisoning. The wind made it difficult to see in front of her, but she caught a glimpse of Auldicia's glowing green eyes. She sank her extended fangs into the neck of Ellis Darbin. She bit him with speed faster than a striking cobra.

She drained him except for a few ounces, initiating the change turning him to a vampire. The first blow of the mix hit Auldicia in the face. The smell of a rotting corpse centuries old filled the vault of the cavern. The screams she made turned to sharp hisses, and the chemical mix eroded her skin away on contact. Solis continued her chant. Urgata joined in while the earth continued to shake.

Raising her sword high above her head, Solis sliced the air in the cavern as a supernatural portal opened up in mid air. The plane between the Realm of the Living and the Realm of the Condemned tore free, pouring light through the seam. Quickly, Solis called forth the voodoo gods to summon Vulkus to claim Auldicia.

"Gods of the dark, bring forth the one who claims this soul. Bring forth Vulkus." Solis drove her sword straight into the ground.

A hand in the form of black and red fire floated up from the ground and in through the ripped seam between the two realms. Auldicia instantly morphed into her true form of a demon. Crying out in defeat, she knew she would return to Hell as a prisoner forever. Once more a failure, she knew her destiny as a bedmate to Vulkus would cause her soul to burn each time he entered her womb. The liquid hand surrounded Auldicia, and then threaded strands of the fire through her body. She screamed her farewell to Nacio.

"Zuri, please…I can't leave without you."

Nacio lay on the altar near unconsciousness. Slowly, he turned his head in her direction and closed his eyes, smiling as the black fire singed her to a crisp. He encouraged Solis to continue her task.

"Keep chanting Solis. Send her back to Hell." Solis ran towards her husband to free him from bondage.

Growling that led to a demonic shriek brought the last few stalactites crashing to the ground. A large crack split the altar Nacio laid upon, stretching his body in quarters until the altar separated from the platform, crumbling into oblivion, swallowing him up. Solis cried out as she watched the altar fall into nothingness.

"Nacio, oh God, Nacio! Armando, help me, please!" Armando and Basrick continued spraying the mix on a few of the descendants in hopes of stopping those turning into vampires. She lunged forward trying to get to Nacio, only to watch her husband fall into oblivion.

"Basrick, please, please ripple the moment, so we can get Nacio!" Solis pleaded with Basrick to hold time in place to rescue her husband. Basrick teleported to where Solis stood. He began focusing on his abilities to freeze the moment. Unsuccessful, his efforts fell short as a cyclone gust of dirt blew them back against the cavern wall. The liquid black fire turned into a hideous face. Vulkus peered through the seam of the realm, swallowing Auldicia and Nacio into the bowels of the earth.

"No, no, no, God no! Nacio! Armando do something please!" Armando joined his son. They both took Solis by her arms. Hymn continued to empty the truck of its contents to stop the descendants.

"We have to leave now!" The two rushed her to the cavern entrance, prompting Menlo and Urgata to follow. The sisters started their trek and took note their sinister cousins had escaped. Childress, Klein, and Erland had vanished.

"Where did they go?" Menlo pushed her sister toward the opening of the cavern.

"Don't know, but we have to leave now." Urgata stumbled as she tried to keep up with her sister's pace.

Broken arms and mangled flesh littered the path toward the cavern entrance. The descendants remaining in the distance ran, attempting to escape falling into the black oblivion along with Nacio and Auldicia.

Solis wept openly. Armando and Basrick helped her into the truck, as they raced to escape the falling earth. Her heart wrenched at the thought of the last time she heard him speak to her. Nacio fell away into the netherworld along with his maker. Nothing made any sense about what happened. Emotional numbness set in, beginning from the bottom of her feet, and filling her chest cavity with woe. Soon she could no longer breathe. Her breaths became shorter and shorter, until the air disappeared and she blacked out.

✝

Cool air floated in over her face when she opened her eyes. The ceiling fan spun around slowly. Someone had put her in her bed. She slowly began to recall what occurred the night before. The descendants escaped into the night, leaving a trail of blood and flesh from the opening of the cavern to the trail leading to the open road. Sirens blared in the distance, possibly from some others feeling the seismic activity. Realizing how her future had changed caused her to shake uncontrollably. The earth had opened up and swallowed Nacio after the plane between the Realm of the Living and the Real of the Condemned split, causing Vulkus to break-through from Hell to reclaim Auldicia as his bedmate.

Their house held so much joy for her, but now only seemed like a mausoleum of grief. Feeling again like she couldn't breathe, she let go as the tears fell. She lay back down and closed her eyes. Regaining control of her breathing, she realized the door to her room opened up. Patience had cleaned her room again, and she probably wanted to bring some clean sheets. Everyone in the home knew she wanted privacy for a while, so visitors must only stay for a short while to check on her.

To her surprise, Hymn stood in the room at the foot of her bed. Solis jumped to her feet, ready to rush him off so she could return to her bereavement in private. From his stance and his gaze at her, she knew he would not move. His black button down shirt opened in the shape of a V all the way down to his navel. Abdominal muscles flexed and rippled, demonstrating his core strength and the control he had in his shoulders.

"I'm here to check on you. I needed to know you're okay." Moving forward, the heat that rolled off his body made her tremble even more.

"I'm fine, thanks for stopping by. Now if you'd excuse me, I'd like to return to my privacy. Besides, I thought you'd be gone by now?"

The distance between the two of them shortened, until Hymn pulled her into his arms. His tongue set her ablaze, sliding over her lips. The heat of desire raced up and down her spine. His shaft pressed against her abdomen, causing her to respond reflexively. Her negligee stretched as her nipples pressed against the satin, keeping them restrained. The tips of his fingers threaded through her hair while he palmed the nape of her neck. His swollen loins, pressed against his jeans, anticipating her touch. He broke their kiss, only for a moment to trace her lips with his finger, and then with his own moist lips. Holding her in an embrace, he licked down the side of her neck, calling forth soft murmurs from her.

Lost in the flirting, Solis gently pushed away from Hymn's

embrace. His desire for her burned so strongly, he began to unbutton his jeans. Anxious, he pulled her in for another kiss. Again, she gently pushed his chest away, when suddenly the mood shifted in the room. A pair of charred black hands picked Hymn up and flung him twelve feet in the air like a rag doll. His massive body imprinted the sheetrock on the wall. A fierce growl rumbled in the corner of the room.

"Stay the hell away from my wife, human, or I will gut you and hang you with your own intestine!"

Back from Hell, Nacio had returned.

...*Read on for a sneak peek at Prey for Blessing*

The next book of the

Embellish Saga by R. L. Sloan

1

Klein can tell

With nowhere to run, the Treemounts hauled the last of themselves to safety. Filth and dirt covered them all as they hid in some bushes off the road in Garden Ridge. They knew they would need to seek shelter soon just as the little baby boy Erland had swaddled in his shirt began a shrill hunger cry.

"What am I supposed to do? I don't have anything to give this boy?" Erland began to get a little irritated at the incessant crying. Childress limped while the pain from the gunshot wound to the shoulder radiated across her chest. Her nerve endings lit up like Christmas lights while Klein's deadened to nothingness. Solis had injected him with a special punishment that ended his virility forever. He could tell his body had changed, but he wasn't exactly sure to what degree.

Once too sexy for his own good, Klein's looks often got him into a lot of trouble. In his mind, his manhood made him the pimp he thought he was. He fathered twelve children he knew of, but several more had his paternity as well. These children are the last he will have fathered. Taking her revenge against him, Solis Burkes Puente finally punished her rapist by chemically castrating him. When the injection hit him, his physical characteristics changed drastically.

A once svelte abdomen, rippling with steel muscle, now had a ring of fat embedded around his waist, similar to a tire tube. In a short distance below his waist sat hips, and a basketball-sized butt. Unable to get the saddlebag hips and basketball butt to work in unison when he walked, Klein now wobbled with each step. Walking sent his fat in different directions, wobbling and shaking all over the place. When he stopped walking, and stood in place, his fat still moved until it reached a slow stop. A gelatinous mess, Klein no longer recognized himself. Underneath, his abdomen, nestled in a bulging fat pad, sat a nub that used to be the head of his penis. His appendage had completely shriveled and retro-graded into his abdomen, hiding from the world, while his plentiful bosoms shimmied across his chest.

Solis made certain Klein would never climb on top of a woman, never willingly give his seed to another woman, and never again would he rape and pillage a woman in his life. A life of taunting and misery lie ahead in his future…beginning with words coming from his own sister.

"Hurry up you fat bastard. I need to get to somewhere so I can get some thread to stitch myself up, and I don't have time to wait for your breathing hard ass, so let's go."

Erland looked at his new softly made brother, trying to understand the basis of his transformation, while pointing to his chest as it shimmied.

"Hey man, are those real?" Erland grinned. "If they're real let this baby nibble on one 'cause he's hungry?"

A squeaky protest left Klein's mouth. "Look man, you'd better...hey what's wrong with my voice?" The poison Klein received when Solis shot him with the Dieth stripped the testosterone from his body, causing multiple side effects.

Even though her shoulder throbbed with intense pain, Childress reached out for the baby boy to quiet him. She held her nipple to his little mouth, and allowed the baby to suckle. Her breasts still swelled with milk in hopes of feeding her own baby. Still wondering where Justice took her child too, Childress kept the absent child's whereabouts on her mind constantly. Even though mad as hell at her deceased brother Justice, she looked at the beautiful little tow headed, green-eyed baby boy and smiled. The child reminded her of her younger brother when he was a little baby. Too pissed off to cry about his death, Childress made a decision early on, "You are the newest one to the family, and your daddy is gone now. You are a Treemount, and that's how I am going to raise you. You are going to take over this town and punish the one who killed your daddy, Cher. Your name is Justice Treemount junior and I'm gonna call you...JJ."

CPSIA information can be obtained at www.ICGtesting.com
Printed in the USA
LVOW051315140712

290077LV00001B/53/P